DO OR DIE

The Apache sprang at Fletcher, a low growl escaping his throat. He feinted to his left; then the bright steel blurred as he swung the blade blindingly fast to the right, leading with the razor-sharp edge, a cut designed to disembowel.

Fletcher was unable to block the blow, but he stepped back and knocked the Indian's arm down, and the knife flashed past his belly, opening up a six-inch slash in the thick sheepskin of Fletcher's mackinaw but failing to reach the skin.

The two men circled each other warily, Fletcher holding his Colt up and ready. With the forearm of his knife hand, the Apache wiped away blood from his mouth that ran in a scarlet stream from his smashed nose. But his black eyes glittered with hate and he showed no fear of the gun. Fletcher realized the warrior understood that he dare not shoot, so he was right in assuming there were others close by.

Around the men the land lay silent and snow drifted softly between them from the black canopy of the sky. The rock towered above their heads, a stony, unfeeling witness to a desperate fight that must soon end in death for one man and perhaps two.

Ralph Compton

Doomsday Rider

A Ralph Compton Novel
by Joseph A. West

A SIGNET BOOK

SIGNET
Published by the Penguin Group
Penguin Group (USA) LLC, 375 Hudson Street,
New York, New York 10014

USA | Canada | UK | Ireland | Australia | New Zealand | India | South Africa | China
penguin.com
A Penguin Random House Company

First published by Signet, an imprint of New American Library,
a division of Penguin Group (USA) LLC

First Printing, December 2003

ISBN 978-0-451-21080-7

Printed in the United States of America
10 9 8 7 6 5 4

THE IMMORTAL COWBOY

This is respectfully dedicated to the "American Cowboy." His was the saga sparked by the turmoil that followed the Civil War, and the passing of more than a century has by no means diminished the flame.

True, the old days and the old ways are but treasured memories, and the old trails have grown dim with the ravages of time, but the spirit of the cowboy lives on.

In my travels—to Texas, Oklahoma, Kansas, Nebraska, Colorado, Wyoming, New Mexico, and Arizona—I always find something that reminds me of the Old West. While I am walking these plains and mountains for the first time, there is this feeling that a part of me is eternal, that I have known these old trails before. I believe it is the undying spirit of the frontier calling, allowing me, through the mind's eye, to step back into time. What is the appeal of the Old West of the American frontier?

It has been epitomized by some as the dark and bloody period in American history. Its heroes—Crockett, Bowie, Hickok, Earp—have been reviled and criticized. Yet the Old West lives on, larger than life.

It has become a symbol of freedom, where there was always another mountain to climb and another river to cross; when a dispute between two men was settled not with expensive lawyers, but with fists, knives or guns. Barbaric? Maybe. But some things never change. When the cowboy rode into the pages of American history, he left behind a legacy that lives within the hearts of us all.

—*Ralph Compton*

One

Swollen by an unseasonable snowmelt across the Great Plains that early December of 1872, the Big Muddy threw itself against an arrow-shaped sandbar three miles downstream of Lexington, Missouri. The river was turned aside, white water foaming in angry impotence around the northern bank of the promontory. Frustrated, the Missouri channeled a swift torrent of brown water and ice around the bar and hurled it venomously into the path of the 212-foot stern-wheeler *Rajah*.

Rajah was firing hard, preparing to skirt the sandbar. Capt. Amos Buell, commanding, anxious to reach the city and unload his two hundred tons of freight and twenty-six passengers.

Rajah's boilers were glowing cherry red, her exhausts hammering, but Buell called for more power to the boat's two engines.

The river was coming at him fast and furious, challenging the stern-wheeler to reach its goal, no sure thing for a craft that drew just twenty inches and had 80 percent of her ramshackle bulk above the waterline.

The paddle wheel had been rotating at twenty times a minute. Now the cast-iron-and-wood monster, twenty-five feet wide and eighteen feet in diameter, churned faster, increasing its revolutions to twenty-three a minute. Startled fountains of foam were thrown up as high as the boiler deck as the wheel's paddles dipped into the river 168 times every sixty seconds.

Captain Buell recklessly hurled his boat against the flood. Huge chunks of ice slammed into *Rajah*'s bow and banged against her iron sides, to be slowly washed astern. Her exhausts, located on the foam-lashed boiler deck, were pounding now, rattling the stabilizing hog chain that ran from the stern to the wheelhouse.

Time and time again *Rajah* made a few feet of headway, only to be driven back by the river, the powerful torrent twisting the boat's bow violently toward shore.

Buell called for more power, but the *Rajah* had given all she had. There was nothing left to give.

The boilers would not take a pound more pressure than they were carrying, and the engineer warned that the boat was in danger of being blown apart.

Buell decided against another attempt to round the sandbar where the river narrowed and thus concentrated its mighty strength. He'd smash right through the bar, trusting *Rajah*'s weight and momentum to carry her through.

The captain reversed engines and *Rajah* backed up, going with the current, shuddering as huge slabs of ice thudded into her, threatening to buckle her thin plates.

Standing on the boat's hurricane deck, Buck Fletcher watched all this with interest but little joy. He was familiar with the stately, floating palaces that plied the Mississippi, but this boat was smaller and slower. However, he knew enough of river navigation to piece together Amos Buell's strategy and the thoughts running through the man's head.

As *Rajah* continued to reverse, Fletcher guessed that the captain was going to let her pick up speed and meet the sandbar head-on.

He did not give much for their chances, especially if the boilers burst and blew them all to smithereens.

But then, a man shackled hand and foot, guarded by a

nine-man infantry detail, had little to lose, including his life. He faced twenty years' hard labor in the hell of the Wyoming Territorial Prison, and that was just another kind of death, slower certainly, but just as certain.

"What's he going to do, Major?"

Fletcher turned as 2d Lt. Elisha Simpson stepped closer to him, his round, freckled face anxious, revealing the infantry soldier's instinctive distrust of anything that floated on water. The boy was a West Pointer and looked to be about eighteen years old.

Fletcher's bleak smile lit up his long, lean, and hard face, still brown from the sun and untouched as yet by the gray pallor of prison, his wide, mobile mouth revealing teeth that were very white under a sweeping dragoon mustache.

"I guess the captain is going to climb right over that sandbar ahead," Fletcher said. "He knows he can't buck this current and that's the only way he can make Lexington this side of spring."

Fletcher shook his head. "And Lieutenant, don't call me Major. The War Between the States is long over."

"Yes, Major," Simpson said, only half listening as he studied the ice-studded river beyond the bow of the boat. The boy stood in silence for a few moments, his face screwed up in thought; then he turned his head and called out over his shoulder, "Corporal Burke!"

The corporal, a grizzled veteran in his early fifties, stepped smartly beside the young officer and saluted. "Yes, sorr."

"Strike those chains from the major," he said. "If we have to swim for it, I don't want him weighed down by thirty pounds of iron."

Burke's face was a study in confusion. "Sorr," he said, his Irish accent strong, "does the lieutenant think that's wise?"

Such was the reputation of Buck Fletcher as a skilled and ruthless gunfighter and convicted murderer that the corporal was completely taken aback, an understandable reaction not unmixed with a certain amount of fear.

"Yes, Corporal," Simpson said, "the lieutenant is sure."

The officer studied Fletcher closely, taking in the amused blue eyes in the hard hatchet blade of a face. "Major, will you give me your word as an officer and a gentlemen you won't try to escape if we have to swim?"

Fletcher smiled again. "Lieutenant, if this tub blows up, we'll all be dead and it won't matter a damn whether you have my word or not. If we have to swim, we'd last about two minutes in that freezing water, so it won't matter a damn that way either." As he saw doubt cloud the boy's eyes Fletcher's smile widened and he nodded. "Sure, Lieutenant, you have my word."

That was all it took. The young officer didn't question Fletcher any further. This man had once been a major of horse artillery in the army of the United States and he had given his word. That he might be lying did not, for even a single moment, enter into Simpson's thinking.

"Corporal Burke," the lieutenant said, "strike those chains."

Grumbling under his breath, Burke unlocked the padlock that held the chains together, releasing Fletcher's leg irons and then the manacles around his wrists.

The soldier gathered up the chains and laid them, clanking, on the deck. Burke gave Fletcher a sidelong glance, his black eyes ugly. "Sorr, permission to fix bayonets."

The young officer hesitated for a few moments, then nodded, saying nothing, his cheeks reddening a little as he refused to look Fletcher in the eye. Burke gave the order and the detail fixed twenty-inch-long, spiked bayonets to their newly issued Springfield rifles. The young soldiers stood alert and wary, mindful that they were guarding a dangerous prisoner, a gunfighter who was said to have killed a dozen men in shooting scrapes from Texas to Kansas and beyond. Such men were deadly, certain, and almighty sudden, and there was no taking even the slightest chance with them, especially now that Fletcher's chains had been removed.

Despite the cold, as he shivered in his prison-issue canvas pants and shirt, Fletcher was amused. He understood how the soldiers felt. Most of them were raw recruits, and he knew he'd feel the same way if he were in their shoes.

"She's slowing," Simpson said, looking back at the paddle wheel.

"Now the captain will order full speed ahead and challenge that sandbar," Fletcher said. He rubbed his wrists where the manacles had chafed them raw, a small motion nevertheless noticed by Simpson, who threw Fletcher an apologetic glance.

"Better brace yourself, Major," the young officer said. "When we hit, this boat could come to a mighty quick stop."

Fletcher grasped the rail in front of him and spread his feet wider.

Rajah's wheel was turning faster now, biting into the muddy water, propelling her forward. Thick black smoke and showers of sparks poured from her twin stacks, and her exhausts were thumping loud again.

Chunks of ice, some of them as big as river barges, slammed into *Rajah*'s bow and sides, and the little boat shuddered and recoiled under the impact. Up in the wheelhouse Buell blasted the whistle, defying the river to do its worst. The whistle's screams echoed along miles of the winding river valley, penetrating even the dank, crowded back alleys of Lexington. The ship's bell was pealing, adding its incessant clamor to that of the whistle.

It was said, Simpson yelled to Fletcher over the din, that

Buell had melted five hundred silver dollars into the metal from which the bell was cast to improve its tone.

"Sounds like six hundred to me," Fletcher said, but the lieutenant didn't hear.

Rajah charged ahead, her paddles churning, shouldering aside ice as she rammed through coffee-colored water, the sandbar getting closer with every revolution of the wheel. . . .

"Life is just one big wheel," Fletcher recalled warden Nathaniel K. Boswell saying to him just before he was taken under escort from the newly opened Wyoming Territorial Prison in Laramie two weeks before. "One day you're on top of the world; then the wheel turns and you're at the bottom again. That's where you are, Fletcher, at the bottom, and you can't get any lower."

The man had not gone into details about why Fletcher had served only a month of his twenty-year sentence before he was dragged from his cell and told he was being taken under army escort to Lexington, there to meet a man he didn't know.

"This man has a proposition for you, Fletcher," Boswell had said. "I'm told there could be a great deal of danger involved, but I think you'd be very wise to take it."

Boswell shrugged, scratched under his beard with the stem of his pipe, then waved an indifferent hand. Apparently bored, he added, "Take this man's proposition or stay here and rot with all the rest. The decision is yours, and I don't give a damn one way or the other."

It was a choice of a sort, but really no choice at all, and Fletcher had jumped at it.

"Who is this man?" he'd asked. "And why in Lexington?"

Again the warden shrugged. "I have no idea, but he has considerable power and influence. I know that." Boswell was a former United States deputy marshal and his eyes were cold and unforgiving. "If it was up to me, I'd pen you up forever, Fletcher, you and all your kind, paid killers and plunderers. But President Grant himself signed the order for your temporary release, and I can't ignore that kind of authority."

The warden nodded to the guards who flanked Fletcher. "Take him out of my sight until his army escort arrives." As Fletcher was shuffling from the man's office, his heavy leg irons clanking, Boswell had called out after him, "Do us all a favor, Fletcher. Get yourself killed."

"A man could get killed this way, Major," Lieutenant Simpson yelled to Fletcher above the roar of *Rajah*'s engines and her shrieking whistle, bringing him back to the present. "I've never had much love for boats."

Fletcher nodded and placed his mouth next to the young officer's ear. "Best you tell those boys of yours to find something to hold on to," he said. "When she hits the bar some of those men could end up going over the side."

Simpson half raised his arm in salute, then realized what he was doing and his face colored again. "Corporal Burke!" he yelled more loudly than necessary, covering up his mistake. "Get the men braced for a collision."

Thirty seconds later *Rajah* hit the sandbar hard. She rammed through half the bar's width and came to a jolting stop. Her wheel was still churning, throwing up high fountains of muddy water, black drops spattering Fletcher and the soldiers far forward on the hurricane deck.

Buell backed his boat off, readying *Rajah* for another try. It seemed that more ice was banging against her hull, driven by raging, ugly water, and now, adding to everyone's misery, sleet began to fall, driven by a rising wind from the north.

It had gotten progressively colder since the day began, and as the gray afternoon slowly shaded into night, the temperature plunged, surely ending any hope of residents along both banks of the Missouri that the recent snowmelt portended an extended Indian summer.

Rajah charged the sandbar again, backed off, charged a second time. Then a third, and a fourth.

Finally, her straining hull plates groaning, threatening any minute to tear away from their rivets, the boat rammed through the bar. *Rajah* brushed aside the white trunk of a dead dogwood tree that angled up from the sand, its branches spread wide like thin, surrendering arms, and, as she cleared the bar, fussily straightened her bow like an old dowager straightening her bonnet. Then, gathering around her what was left of her shabby, rickety dignity, she floated into calmer water.

Buell nosed his battered craft into a Lexington wharf, vented *Rajah*'s steam, and tied her up. As Buell ran out the gangplank for the passengers, mulatto dockworkers were already scrambling on board to unload her cargo, and the captain, somber, thin, and bearded, left the wheelhouse to oversee the operation.

Lieutenant Simpson turned to Fletcher, his eyes miserable. "Major, I must . . ." The young officer stumbled, trying to find the words, and Fletcher smiled. "You have a duty to do, Lieutenant. Best you do it."

Relieved, Simpson nodded and turned to Corporal Burke. "The shackles, Corporal."

"There's no need for that."

Every head swiveled toward the tall man who had just stepped onto the hurricane deck. He wore a black overcoat with an astrakhan collar, his eyes shaded by the brim of his top hat. The man took a step toward Simpson. "We must be discreet, Lieutenant," he said. "I don't want this man brought to my home in chains."

"I have my orders, sir," the young officer said, his face stiff. "I was instructed to conduct Major . . . uh . . . this prisoner by train and stage to Missouri, join the steamship *Rajah* in Jefferson City, and when we disembarked in Lexington remove him in chains to the home of Senator Falcon Stark."

"You've done well, Lieutenant," the man said. "I am Senator Stark, and I will take custody of the prisoner."

"Sir, I think I should provide an escort and remain with you until your business with the prisoner is concluded."

"I'll be quite safe, I assure you, Lieutenant," Stark said. His voice was as smooth as watered silk but it was edged by impatience and not a little anger.

This, Fletcher thought, *is a man grown well used to the arrogance of power, a man who cuts a wide path and expects lesser men to scramble out of his way.*

A sleet flurry scattered wet drops between Stark and Fletcher and the others. Through this shifting gray curtain a man as tall as Stark but dressed in a wide-brimmed hat and sheepskin mackinaw, a red woolen scarf wrapped around his neck, stepped to the senator's side.

The man's cold eyes swept the green young soldiers, dismissed them as unimportant and irrelevant, then came to rest on Fletcher.

"Been a long time, Buck," he said, without friendliness.

Fletcher nodded. "Wes Slaughter. You're a long way from El Paso."

The gunman shrugged. "You know how it is; in our line of work we go where somebody's doing the hiring."

"I don't know how it is," Fletcher said, his eyes changing from blue to a hard gunmetal gray. "In my line of work I meet my enemies face-to-face. What's your line of work, Wes?"

The gunman was stung and he let it show. "Damn you, Fletcher. Someday I'm going to take great pleasure in killing you."

Fletcher nodded, his smile thin and humorless. "You

told me that same thing in the Sideboard Saloon in Cheyenne not two months ago. But when we came right down to it and the talking was done, you wouldn't draw. I guess it will have to be in the back, a specialty of yours, I believe."

"Cheyenne wasn't the right time or the right place is all, Fletcher," Slaughter said, refusing to be baited further. "If we ever meet again when the talking is done and it's the Colts' turn to speak, it will be face-to-face, all right. I've seen you draw, Fletcher, and on your best day you couldn't come close to shading me."

"The day I can't shade a back-shooting polecat like you, Wes, is the day I hang up my guns for good," Fletcher said, his eyes holding a challenge he knew the other man could not ignore.

Angry, Slaughter opened his mouth to speak again, but Stark waved an irritable hand. "Mr. Slaughter, if you wish to remain an associate of mine, don't bandy words with a convicted criminal."

He turned to Simpson, who seemed baffled by this exchange. "Lieutenant, surely you understand that I don't want to attract the unwanted attention you and your men would cause by leading this prisoner to my home in chains. I have a carriage waiting, and I assure you Fletcher will be quite secure with me and Mr. Slaughter."

"I have my orders, sir," Simpson said, but this time he sounded uncertain.

"I'm countermanding them, Lieutenant," Stark snapped. "Or do I have to go over your head to your commanding officer?"

Fletcher smiled. "His commanding officer is in Wyoming, Stark. I'd say that's a fair piece from here."

Stark turned on Fletcher, his face black with anger. "You will address me as senator or not at all." Then to Simpson: "Captain Buell sails at first light tomorrow morning for Jefferson City. Make sure you and your men are on board." His voice softened a little. "I will personally inform President Grant how well you performed your duty. Ah, what is your name, Lieutenant?"

Defeated by this man's air of command, backed up by the real power and influence he wielded, the officer let his shoulders slump. "Well," he said, "my orders were to deliver the prisoner to you, Senator. I guess I've done that. And my name is Simpson."

"You've carried out your duty, Lieutenant Simpson, and again let me say most excellently."

The young officer turned to Fletcher. "Major," he said, "I've been meaning to tell you this before, but somehow I never quite got around to it. It was a long war and I guess you've no call to remember, but at Antietam your guns covered the retreat of a surrounded infantry brigade from the West Woods, despite the fact that you were under heavy fire yourself. You saved not only the brigade but also the reputation of the colonel in command." He stuck out his hand. "That colonel was my father. It's many years after the event, but on his behalf I wish to thank you."

Fletcher took Simpson's hand. "Lieutenant, there were a lot of woods and a lot of brigades in that war." He smiled, a wide, warm smile that relieved the hard severity of his features. "But now I study on it some, I do recollect supporting a retreating brigade at Antietam. I was going backward myself that day, in what's called a recoil retreat. I bet they didn't teach you that at the Point."

Simpson shook his head, and Fletcher continued: "You let your guns recoil and you reload and fire them from their new position. Then you do the same thing over and over again as long as you're able. The cannons dictate the pace of the retreat, but the main thing is you keep your face to the enemy and continue firing." Fletcher's smile grew wider. "When you come right down to it, I guess we've all had our duty to do at one time or another."

"This is all very interesting, I'm sure," Stark said, in fact shrugging a complete lack of interest. "But we have to be going."

The lieutenant ignored Stark. "Good luck, Major." He was silent for a few moments, then added, "It's been an honor."

Fletcher stood with Stark and Slaughter, watching Simpson and his detail walk down the gangplank to disappear into the sleet-lashed gloom.

"Mr. Slaughter," Stark said, nodding in Fletcher's direction.

The gunman's smile never reached his eyes as he opened his coat and drew a long-barreled .45 Colt from a cross-draw holster. He pointed the gun at Fletcher's belly. "You," he said, "git going."

"Remember, Mr. Slaughter," Stark said, "always discretion. Keep that weapon under cover until we get into the carriage."

Stark at his side, Slaughter following a few steps behind, his gun concealed under his mackinaw, Fletcher left the *Rajah* and walked onto the dock, where a closed carriage stood waiting, its twin lanterns glowing orange in the darkness. A coughing, red-nosed driver was up on the seat, his breath smoking in the cold air, and the horse stamped, its iron shoes clanking loud on wet cobblestones.

"Just a word of warning, Fletcher," Stark said as he ushered the gunfighter into the carriage. "One wrong move, even blink in a way I don't like, and I'll order Mr. Slaughter to shoot you." He climbed into the carriage and sat beside Fletcher. "Do you understand?"

"Perfectly," Fletcher said.

Wes Slaughter, his narrow, rodent face eager, sat opposite Fletcher, his Colt across his knees. "Do something the senator don't like, Fletcher," he said. "Give me the chance to kill you."

After the cold of the boat deck, the carriage was reasonably warm. Fletcher settled back against the leather cushions and smiled.

"Go to hell," he said to Slaughter.

Two

Stark's house lay on the outskirts of Lexington and the carriage clattered through streets almost empty of people, the cold and sleet driving everyone indoors.

Through a gap in the carriage curtains, Fletcher caught fleeting glimpses of candlelit, stately antebellum mansions that had somehow survived the ravages of war, including the battle that had been fought here in 1861.

The senator's home was a sprawling, redbrick building with a wood front porch, and when Stark entered, a high-nosed butler in a liveried uniform helped him remove his coat and hat. The man took in Fletcher's prison garb at a glance and sniffed disdainfully as he ushered him and Stark into a cozy drawing room where a log burned cheerfully in the fireplace.

Slaughter followed close behind Fletcher. The gunman had removed his mackinaw, and his Colt in its well-worn cross-draw holster was now in full view. Despite his reputation as a sure-thing hired gun who preferred to do his killing at a distance, Fletcher knew Slaughter was no bargain. The Texas gunman had faced his share of belted men in straight-up shooting scrapes, most recently in Wyoming, where he'd outdrawn and killed Noble Fagan, a gunfighter of reputation with six notches on the handle of his Colt.

That Slaughter had backed down from Fletcher in Cheyenne proved only that the man was a careful, hard-nosed professional. He would walk away from a fight if he didn't like the odds, knowing that there would be other, more favorable days when he could even the score, preferably with a rifle shot in the back from ambush.

Slaughter was a skinny, lantern-jawed man, his full yellow mustache sweeping over a thin, hard mouth. His eyes were gray and ice cold and they spiked into Fletcher with hostility and malice as Stark waved the gunfighter into a leather wing chair by the fire.

"Are you hungry, Fletcher?" Stark asked. There was no kindliness or concern in the man's voice. He asked that question as he would of a stray dog.

"I'm missing my last three meals, and the three before that were army biscuit and jerky and before that prison slop," Fletcher replied. "You could say I'm hungry."

Stark tugged on a sash beside the fireplace, and while the three men waited in silence, Fletcher had a chance to study the senator.

He looked to be about fifty years old and stood a good four inches over Fletcher's own six feet, but he probably weighed about the same, no more than one hundred and eighty pounds.

His predatory, aristocratic face revealed a careless, self-centered arrogance that could easily harden into cruelty, and his blue eyes were harsh, judgmental, and intolerant. He was clean shaven at a time when most men went bearded or sported the dragoon mustache then in fashion, and his iron-gray hair was cropped close to his head.

Stark stood upright, his back straight, and he looked like a soldier, though Fletcher guessed that he'd never served in uniform. His kind of stiff-necked, imperious pride was not the sort to bow to authority, especially the mindless, military kind.

There was a moneyed air about Falcon Stark, and it was not new money. The man looked like he'd been born to a life of wealth, privilege, and power and had greatly increased all three since.

He was a respected United States senator, a close confidant of President Grant and influential enough to get Fletcher sprung from the Wyoming Territorial Prison, a place where only the dead left before their sentence was complete. But what could such a man want in return?

The question perplexed Fletcher and he had no answer for it, not even an educated guess.

The butler bowed his way into the room and Stark waved a careless hand toward Fletcher. "Tell Cook to bring this man something. She needn't make a special effort; anything will do. Perhaps some cold beef."

The butler nodded again. "Yes, sir."

He gave Fletcher another of his disdainful looks and left, closing the door with practiced quietness behind him.

Stark sat in a chair opposite Fletcher and opened a silver box on the small table beside him. He selected a cigar, bit off the end, and spat it into the fire. Carefully, taking his time, he lit the cigar from the match Slaughter had hurried to hold for him.

The senator eased back in his chair and looked at Fletcher through a cloud of fragrant blue smoke. After a few moments he held up the cigar and studied it closely, not looking at Fletcher as he spoke.

"Mr. Fletcher," he said, "you are scum."

Slaughter giggled, and Fletcher, who'd been trying to ride out the tobacco hunger in him as Stark smoked, felt anger flare in him as the senator continued: "Oh, I'm not singling you out for that criticism. I'm talking about you and all your kind, hired gunfighters, men who will sell their services to the highest bidder."

Fletcher jerked his chin toward the grinning Slaughter. "What about him, your associate? Last I heard, he advertised that he'd shoot any man in the back or cut him in half with a shotgun for a hundred dollars."

Stark puffed on his cigar. He was relaxed, his voice unchanging. "Mr. Slaughter has reformed. He now works only for me, and I do assure you, I don't want him to shoot anyone in the back."

"Stark," Fletcher said, "what do you want from me?"

"Senator. I told you that already."

Stark waited for a few moments, then said, "Many of my business interests lie along the Missouri and Mississippi. That is why I maintain this house here in Lexington. The paddle steamer that brought you here is mine, and several others just like her. I also like to come here now and again to get away from the cares of Washington."

"What do you want from me?" Fletcher asked again, his dislike for this man making it hard for him to be civil.

If Stark noticed he didn't let it show. "President Grant has just begun his second term, which will be completed in 1877. I plan to step into his shoes and become the next president of the United States. I've been assured I will have the backing of both Grant and the Republican party."

Stark waved his cigar, tracing a circle of blue smoke. "I plan to run on a law and order platform, pledging to rid the nation, especially the West, of both Indian savages and the lawless element." He paused and smiled, a strained grimace that never reached his eyes. "Take men like you, Fletcher. I plan to hang your kind when I can, imprison them for life in the deepest, darkest dungeons when I can't."

"Is that why you brought me here, to tell me this?" Fletcher asked.

The senator shook his head. "No, that's not the reason. Let's just say, strange as it may seem, I suddenly find myself in need a man of your particular talents, a tough man who steps lightly and often over the line separating the lawful from the lawless.

"I'm told you're a man who won't back up for anybody, that fear doesn't even enter your thinking. You are also said to be the best with a gun west of the Mississippi."

"After me." Slaughter grinned.

"Perhaps so, Mr. Slaughter, but I wouldn't want to put the matter to the test," Stark said. "Besides, you are now a respectable businessman, remember?" He looked up as someone knocked on the door. "Ah, here is Mattie with your food." Then louder: "Enter!"

A plump, round-faced black woman stepped into the room, bearing a loaded tray.

She smiled at Fletcher and laid the tray on his lap. "You don't look like you've been eating too reg'lar," she said. "I declare, you're as skinny as a bed slat."

"Prison food doesn't put fat on a man." Fletcher smiled.

"Well," Mattie said, "this here will put meat on them poor bones. I brung you a thick roast beef sandwich, coffee, and a big wedge of my apple and raisin pie. You eat hearty now, you hear?"

"I surely plan to." Fletcher grinned. "And a special thanks for the pie."

"That will do now, Mattie," Stark said. "Leave us."

The woman gave Fletcher a last, warm smile and left the room.

Fletcher ate slowly, enjoying the taste of his food, as only a very hungry man will do.

Stark watched him eat for a while, then asked, "Ah, where were we?"

Fletcher swallowed and replied: "You were telling me why you want the help of the very kind of man you plan to hang."

"Ah, yes, that." Stark nodded. He sighed deep and long, then said, "As I told you, I plan to run for president, and for that reason I can't let the slightest breath of scandal taint my reputation. In fact, that's why I had you brought here and not to Washington." He hesitated, then said, "And that brings me to my daughter."

Fletcher finished his sandwich, which was good, and started in on the pie. He swallowed, laid his fork on the plate, and asked, "Your daughter?"

Stark crushed the stub of his cigar into the ashtray beside him. "I'm a widower, Fletcher. My dear wife died five years ago and I have but one child, my daughter, Estelle. She's almost eighteen and I plan to marry her well."

"Oh, I get it now. You want me to marry her," Fletcher said, smiling.

"Yes, very amusing, I'm sure," Stark returned. "No, I want you to go to the Arizona Territory, the Tonto Basin country to be exact, and bring her home to me. Here, to Lexington."

That made Fletcher sit up. "The Tonto Basin? Isn't George Crook fighting a full-scale Apache war down there?"

Stark nodded. "He is, and that's why I need a man with your gunfighting and tracking skills. Finding Estelle and getting her out of Arizona won't be easy. I first engaged the Pinkertons, but, efficient as they were, I came to believe that this was more in your line of work."

"Why is she in Arizona?" Fletcher asked, interested despite the alarm bells ringing in his head.

Stark exchanged a quick glance with Slaughter, then replied, "About a year ago, Estelle met a man in Washington. I never knew real his name, but he called himself the Chosen One."

"Looks like Jesus in one of them pictures you see in the Bible." Slaughter grinned.

"That will do, Mr. Slaughter," Stark chided. He turned to Fletcher. "Estelle is a child, an impressionable child.

She's had a sheltered life and maybe that's why she fell for this man's story hook, line, and sinker. She up and ran away with him and, from what I was told by the Pinkertons, is now with him in the Tonto Basin." He sighed. "She's said to be helping that lunatic and his followers convert the Apaches. Estelle calls it fulfilling her mission from God or some such nonsense."

Fletcher tried something then.

He moved in his chair, just a quick turn of the shoulders. But Slaughter caught it instantly and his Colt, which he'd held seemingly carelessly across his knees, came up fast, the muzzle pointing directly at Fletcher's head.

Fletcher eased back in the chair, smiling slightly. There could be no escape from this house, at least not at the moment, with Slaughter watching him like a hungry hawk. If he tried to rise, the gunman would put three or four bullets into him before he could even get to his feet.

"What is the Chosen One's story?" Fletcher asked Stark, accepting that he was pinned to his chair like a butterfly pinned to a card.

The senator had seen Fletcher's movement, recognized it for what it was, but seemed to dismiss it as a thing of no consequence, at least for the moment.

"The Chosen One, as only he calls himself, is the leader of a doomsday cult," Stark replied, his voice even. "He believes the world will end in a fiery holocaust nineteen hundred years after the death of the Savior, on March twenty-three, 1900, to be exact."

Stark leaned forward in his chair. "The Chosen One believes, or says he believes, that he was appointed by God to convert the Apache savages to Christianity before the world ends."

Fletcher smiled, his fingers straying from force of habit to the pocket of his rough canvas shirt. Disappointed, he dropped his hand and said, "I'd say he's got his work cut out for him. The Apaches don't take kindly to preachers, at least the ones I've known."

Slaughter, a perceptive man, had seen Fletcher's hand move to his shirt pocket. Like many Texans, Slaughter had picked up the cigarette smoking habit from Mexican vaqueros and, despite his intense dislike of Fletcher, he had the smoker's natural empathy for another in dire need of tobacco.

"Here," he said, tossing paper and tobacco sack to Fletcher.

Fletcher built a smoke and Slaughter threw him matches. The gunfighter drew deeply and gratefully, and said, "First one in many a week."

"Man shouldn't be without tobacco," Slaughter said. "Might put him on edge and maybe make him try something he could regret."

"A man might at that," Fletcher agreed. He turned to Stark. "If I find your daughter and get her out of Arizona, and that's a big if, what's in it for me?"

"For you?" Stark asked, his right eyebrow rising in surprise. "Why, nothing except a few more weeks of freedom before you continue your sentence."

Fletcher smoked in silence for a while, studying Stark, trying to determine whether the man really meant what he'd just said. He apparently did, because his face was set and determined and there was no give in his expression.

"That's way too thin," Fletcher said finally, stubbing out his cigarette butt in Stark's ashtray, immediately beginning to build another. "I might just head for Arizona and keep on riding, maybe all the way to Mexico."

"Try that, Fletcher, and I will do everything in my power to hunt you down wherever you are and see you hanged," Stark said, his voice level. "A man with your reputation and penchant for violence doesn't disappear easily, even in Mexico."

The senator thought for a few moments, then said, "Still, you make a valid point, and perhaps I should up the ante. I will concede this much: Bring my daughter home and then prove to my satisfaction that you've forsaken the gun to take up the plow and I'll see what I can do to have your sentence reduced." He hesitated. "Perhaps five years in the territorial prison. No more than that."

"The alternative?" Fletcher asked, lighting his cigarette.

"The alternative is that I send for the keen young Lieutenant Simpson right now and have you returned to Wyoming and your cell."

"Stark," Fletcher said, ignoring the man's sudden flush of anger, "I was railroaded into that murder charge. I never shot a man in the back in my life."

The senator shrugged. "A hick sheriff orders you out of his tumbledown Wyoming cow town. Later he's found dead in the livery stable, a bullet in his back, and you're standing over him, holding his own still-smoking gun in your hand." Stark's smile was cold. "I'd say it was an open-and-shut case, and so apparently did the jury."

"The sheriff was dead when I got there. Someone else killed him, knowing I was on my way to the livery stable and was sure to investigate the shot. That's why I picked up the gun."

Fletcher saw Slaughter's eyes flicker to Stark. The look was gone in an instant, but it spoke volumes. Did Slaughter know who the real killer was? And did Stark himself know?

At that moment Fletcher had no answers to those questions, and the very notion seemed wildly far-fetched, but it was something for a man to think about.

Stark was speaking again. "Whether you're guilty or not isn't my concern at the moment. Right now I need an answer, Fletcher. Will you bring back my daughter and

give me your word that you'll return here to Lexington
with her?"

Fletcher smiled. "You'd take the word of a hired gun
and plunderer?"

"I'm told that, despite your profession, you're said to be
a man of your word. Come now," Stark insisted, the man's
patience obviously wearing thin, "what's your answer?"

This time Fletcher did not hesitate. "I'll bring her
back," he said. "After that, well, we'll have to see how the
cards fall. I reckon even five years in prison can feel like a
lifetime."

Fletcher had expected Stark to raise some kind of objection, but to his surprise the senator nodded his accept-
ance. "Just get Estelle back here and then we'll talk. The
clothes you wore when you were arrested are here, and so
are your guns. I had them sent from the prison a few weeks
ago."

"A few weeks ago? You've been planning this meeting
for that long?"

"I'm a methodical man, Fletcher," the senator said.
"And the cost was not much."

Later, standing in Stark's bedroom, dressed in his own
hat, blue shirt, black pants and run-down boots, a red bandanna tied loosely around his neck, Fletcher began to feel
human again. Stark had provided him with a sheepskin
mackinaw and had replaced his Henry rifle with a new
Model of 1873 .44.40 Winchester.

Fletcher strapped on his gun belts, a short-barreled Colt
in a cross-draw holster, a second revolver with a seven-
and-a-half-inch barrel at his hip. He opened the loading
gate of this revolver and spun the cylinder. It was empty.

Stark smiled. "There will be plenty of time to load that
when you and your horse are on the Katy heading south."

"We ain't so stupid, Fletcher," Slaughter added, his gun leveled and unwavering.

"You have my horse?" Fletcher asked, surprised, ignoring the sneering gunman.

The senator shook his head. "No, not your horse, but one just as good. I have a big American stud in the stable out back. He'll serve you well."

The senator stepped to a dresser near his four-poster bed and reached into a drawer. He came up with a small canvas sack, pulled shut with a drawstring. "There's two hundred dollars in traveling expenses in this bag," he said, hefting the sack, letting the gold coins clink. "Use it wisely."

Stark laid the sack in Fletcher's palm and added, his cold, flat eyes suddenly animated, "Go to Arizona and bring back my daughter to me, Fletcher. She's all I've got in this world and I love her very much."

Fletcher stood and curled the brim of his hat, as was his habit when he had the Stetson in his hands and not on his head. "You sure believe in taking chances, Stark. I could take your money and your horse and just skedaddle."

"You could," the senator conceded. "But I don't believe you will. I was told by a very highly placed person that despite the wild, lawless life you've led since the end of the War Between the States, he still considers you as he did when you were an officer of horse artillery under his command. He calls you a man of great personal courage, integrity, and honor."

"Who told you that?" Fletcher asked, genuinely puzzled.

"Gen. Ulysses S. Grant," Stark replied.

Three

The boy beside him was dying. But he was dying too slowly, an arrowhead of strap iron embedded deep in his belly, shot from an elegant Apache bow of Osage orange wood.

The young trooper, who looked to be no more than seventeen, wore the blue of the Fifth Cavalry, and he was a boy making a man's attempt to bear a pain that would soon become too much to bear.

"How is he?"

Al Sieber, Brig. Gen. George Crook's chief of scouts, looked from the young soldier to Buck Fletcher, his eyes bleak.

Fletcher shook his head and Sieber nodded, saying nothing, knowing no words were needed.

Fletcher eased his position behind the rock, where he knelt and gazed out on a land held fast by January's cold, a wilderness of craggy mountains and mysterious valleys and infinite silences. It was a land pine-covered, the abode of the black-tailed deer, the cougar, the cinnamon and black bears, the fox, and the bobcat.

And the Apache.

But of the Apaches there was no trace, always a sure sign that they were there.

From down near the wagon the sergeant cursed again, a long, outraged string of profanity laced with the expressive

Gaelic of the old country. Then he screamed. He'd been alternately cursing and screaming for a long time now, at least an hour, but gradually the curses were growing less frequent as the screams grew longer and more shrill.

"Help him," the trooper said. "For God's sake, help Sergeant McDermott."

Sieber bit off a chew and wedged it into his left cheek. "You lie quiet, boy. There's no helping of McDermott now. He took his chances like the rest of us and he knew how it would be if he was caught." The scout chewed and spat a stream of brown tobacco juice over the rock where he crouched. "They got squaws with them down there. Apache squaws know how to cut a man."

The sergeant screamed and this time there were no more curses.

"And they're remembering Skull Cave," Sieber said, throwing the statement away as an afterthought.

Fletcher had learned from soldiers and settlers he'd met that just two weeks before, on December 28, 1872, seventy-six Indians, a few Apache and the rest Yavapai, were massacred at Skull Cave by three companies of the Fifth Cavalry. The victims were mostly women, children, and old men, and the Apache, eager for revenge, had set the whole Tonto Basin country aflame.

War bands roamed the basin and its bordering mountains, the Mazatzals, the Sierra Ancha, and the Superstitions, and raiders struck as far north as the Mogollon Rim.

Crook was out after the Apache with nine troop-strength detachments of the First and Fifth cavalries and their Pima and Maricopa scouts. The general's plan was to surround the Apache and Yavapai bands and drive them into the Tonto Basin, concentrating them there for the kill.

"The trail must be stuck to and never lost," Crook had ordered his officers. "No excuse will be accepted for leaving a trail. If your horses play out, the Apache must be followed on foot, and no sacrifice should be left untried to make the campaign short, sharp and decisive."

So far, the Apache had not obliged, fighting back with a ferocity born of desperation, fueled by an undying hate of the white man and all he represented. Army patrols had been ambushed and the cabins of isolated settlers south of the Mogollon Rim escarpment attacked, resulting in burned cabins and the scattered, violated bodies of men, women, and children.

The Apaches demanded an eye for an eye, a tooth for a tooth, and while there was still breath in their lean, sinewy bodies they'd fight on, defiant even as they saw their way of life and all that they held sacred being relentlessly and systematically destroyed.

And they were out there now, among the rocks, knowing they had three white men trapped. The Apaches were eager to finish this thing, but, patient and knowing as the stalking wolf, they were biding their time.

How many of them?

Fletcher studied the rocks behind the wagon. Had he seen one of them move? Just a moment ago he'd caught a sudden flash of red in the narrow vee between two gray boulders. And now he saw it again.

Fletcher sighted his rifle on the notch between the rocks and waited.

Above him the sun had climbed to its highest point and a vulture glided across the hazy green sky, slanting toward the towering, rugged bulk of Mazatzal Peak to the west.

There was little heat in the winter sun and it was cool here among the rocks. A stunted juniper spread twisted limbs over the small clearing amid the boulders where Fletcher, Sieber, and the dying trooper had taken refuge, casting crooked shadows on the sand.

Slowly, taking his time, Fletcher rested his rifle on the rock in front of him and built a smoke. He gestured with

the tobacco sack toward Sieber, but the scout produced a
chewing plug from his vest pocket, signaling his prefer-
ence.

Fletcher lit his cigarette and studied the notch between
the boulders again.

There it was!

The flash of red slowly grew into a headband around
the brow of an Apache. The Indian raised his head higher,
scanning Fletcher's position, his rifle coming up to his
shoulder.

Fletcher fired, and the Apache disappeared. But a fan of
bright blood spattered the rock close to where the man's
head had been.

"Get him?" Sieber asked, crawling beside Fletcher.

"Burned him, I think," Fletcher said.

Sieber nodded. "That will make them more careful. I
guess by now they figure we ain't a bunch of pilgrims up
here."

Another Apache, killed by Sieber, lay beside the wagon,
and Fletcher had shot a second during the Indians' first
wild charge at the wagon. But that warrior had been pulled
out of sight and Fletcher did not know if he was alive or
dead.

Fletcher had been in the Tonto Basin country for a week
now, chasing vague leads on Estelle Stark and the Chosen
One that had come to nothing. Mostly he'd heard confused
rumors of a white woman seen with Apaches, and in every
case the trail left by the girl had petered out.

Earlier that morning Fletcher had ridden south from the
Mogollon Rim, a long wind at his back, and had met up
with Sieber on the upper reaches of Cherry Creek.

Sieber was leading a supply wagon packed with hard-
tack and bacon to a detachment of the First Cavalry and
their Paiute scouts camped near the base of Mazatzal Peak.
Sieber, with only Sergeant McDermott driving the wagon

and the young trooper riding escort, had asked Fletcher to ride with them. Like many Western men of that time, Sieber had heard of Fletcher, and he was grateful for his gun skills and extra rifle.

Since he'd been following cold trails that led nowhere, Fletcher, at a loose end, had agreed.

An hour later the Apaches struck.

A dozen warriors had come scattering out of the rocks as the wagon neared Shake Ridge, and McDermott had gone down, wounded in their first volley. The young trooper—his name was McKinnon—had taken an arrow in the belly.

Fletcher and Sieber had each downed an Apache. Fletcher had grabbed the reins of the trooper's horse and galloped into an arroyo, then swung down when he reached a jumbled pile of boulders that marked the end of the canyon. He'd helped the trooper into the shade of the juniper, then, while Sieber fired at the oncoming Apaches, Fletcher had led the horses into the shelter of a rock overhang.

A few minutes later they'd heard the first agonized screams erupt from the sergeant's mouth.

"How long can they keep that up?" Fletcher asked Sieber.

The scout ran the back of his gun hand across his mustache, wiping away sweat. "If he's lucky, the rest of the day and maybe into the night. If he's unlucky, until tomorrow. And if he's real unlucky, the day after that. Like I said, I saw women with them, and they'll drag it out as long as they can."

Al Sieber was a handsome, wide-shouldered man of thirty. The hard life of an army scout had burned every ounce of fat from his lean frame, and his blue eyes were cool and unafraid. He was a fighting man to the core, and during the War Between the States had served valiantly at

Antietam, Fredericksburg, and Gettysburg, and had been wounded in action three times.

Now he spat a stream of tobacco juice, neatly nailing a basking lizard, and studied the arroyo before him.

"What you doing in the Arizona Territory, Buck?" Sieber asked without taking his eyes off the rocks where the Apaches lurked. "I seem to recall hearing you was up Wyoming way, selling your gun to a rancher in one of them grass and water wars everybody talks about."

"You heard right," Fletcher said. "But now I'm here."

He offered nothing more, and Sieber was quite willing to let it go, but then Fletcher said, "I'm searching for somebody. A girl. Her name's Estelle Stark." He turned and looked at the scout. "Ever hear of her?"

Sieber shook his head. "Name means nothing to me." He spat tobacco juice again. "Best you go talk to General Crook. He knows everything that's going on in this country."

"Where can I find him?" Fletcher asked.

"Last I heard he was at Fort Apache. That's about fifty miles due east of here, close to the big bend of the Salt River. It ain't much as forts go, just a collection of ramshackle log huts and tents, but then ol' George was never much of a one for fuss and feathers."

Sieber was silent for a few moments, then said, "Course, all that depends on us getting out of here alive, and right now I'd say that ain't looking too likely."

Down by the wagon, where one mule lay dead in its traces, the other stood patiently, waiting for whatever was to come. The Apache valued mule meat above all others, and, hungry as they were, would hope to fill their empty bellies after this fight was over.

Sergeant McDermott screamed, screamed a second time, and then fell silent, but his cries still echoed for long moments within the narrow canyon walls.

When McDermott shrieked again, Sieber, stone-faced, sang a ballad under his breath that was then highly popular in the barracks of the enlisted men.

> I'd like to be a packer,
> And pack with George F. Crook,
> And dressed up in my canvas suit,
> To be for him mistook.
> I'd braid my beard in two forked tails,
> And idle all the day
> In whittling sticks and wondering
> What the New York papers say.

Behind him, Fletcher heard the young trooper stifle a groan. Crouching, he stepped to the soldier's side. "Is it bad?" he asked.

The boy nodded, and said through clenched teeth, "It's real bad. I don't think I can bear it much longer. I want to go now." Trooper McKinnon, small and wiry like most of Crook's cavalrymen, looked down at the arrow, bright with colored turkey feathers, sticking out of his belly.

"Can you pull it free?" he asked. "I don't want to die with this inside me."

Fletcher shook his head. "All I'd do is cause you more pain. Best you lie real still and make your peace with God."

"I done that already," McKinnon said. "I figure I'm right with my creator." A slight smile touched the boy's white lips. "Know something? I ain't never sparked a girl. Not even once. Now that it's all up with me, I guess I never will."

"Aw, sparking a girl isn't what it's cracked up to be," Fletcher said, unable to relieve one kind of pain, trying to relieve another. "Why, I recall one time down El Paso way when I . . ."

His voice trailed off into silence. He was talking to a dead man.

Fletcher closed the boy's eyes, pulled the arrow from his body, and stepped back to his position behind the rock.

"Is he dead?" Sieber asked.

Fletcher nodded, suddenly feeling empty and old.

"He was a good soldier," Sieber said. "Done his duty." The scout nodded. "He'll make his ma proud."

"Well, he's no kind of soldier now," Fletcher said. "And I reckon I've already seen proud ma's enough that I don't ever care to see another."

Sieber opened his mouth to speak, but what he said was drowned out by another shrieking cry of pain from the sergeant.

"McDermott is a big, strong man and he's dying mighty hard," Sieber said. "He'll last a long time."

"Why do they do that?" Fletcher asked. "You know Apaches; why torture a man that way?"

The scout shrugged. "An Apache measures his own bravery against that of his enemy. The Apache believe a captive who lasts a long time under torture must be very brave, and that reflects much credit on the man who captured him. Better to conquer a mountain lion than a jackrabbit."

Fletcher glanced up at the sky and the yellow ball of the sun. "Pretty soon we're going to get mighty thirsty," he said. "Then we'll face our own torture."

Sieber nodded. "There's a canteen in the wagon. Maybe after dark I'll mosey on down there and see if I can grab it." He shook his head, his face grim. "That is, if we're still around."

"You won't make it," Fletcher said. "They'll be expecting us to try something like that."

"You got a better idea?"

"Maybe I have. At least, I've been studying on it some, though it's mighty thin."

"Well, thin or not, let's hear it, man," Sieber urged. "Seems to me the way our time is running out, beggars can't be choosers."

Quickly Fletcher outlined his plan, and Sieber's grin grew wider with each word. When Fletcher finished the scout slapped his thigh and said, "Hot damn, Buck, it might just work."

"It better work," the gunfighter said. "If the Apaches wait until almost dark and all rush us at once, we're dead."

Doubt clouded Sieber's eyes. "I ain't much good with a Colt's gun." He slapped the brass receiver of his Henry. "But I can use this here rifle pretty well."

Fletcher smiled. "You'll do, Al."

The two men waited. They needed Sergeant McDermott to scream again.

Four

The scream when it came was loud and piercing, a primitive cry of agony torn from the throat of a man who had long passed the limits of his endurance and was now bordering on madness.

Yet somehow, from somewhere deep inside him, McDermott found the strength to roar a string of Irish curses, each edged with the disbelief and outrage that what was unthinkable was actually happening and was happening to him.

The man finally fell silent again and the canyon walls no longer echoed to his raving, pain-driven shrieks.

"Right, Al," Fletcher said, his face set and grim. "Let's do it."

He set down his rifle and drew his Colt, and Sieber did the same.

Both men knelt and pointed their guns at the sand beneath them, and at Fletcher's nod each pulled the trigger. The guns went off simultaneously, bullets kicking up startled exclamation points of sand a few inches from their knees.

Quickly Fletcher shucked the empty shell from his Colt and reloaded the chamber.

He and Sieber scrambled back to the shelter of the rocks and waited.

The scout put his mouth close to Fletcher's ear and whispered, "Think it worked?"

Fletcher put his forefinger to his lips, signaling Sieber into silence. They waited.

Beside him, Fletcher saw Sieber run a nervous tongue over his top lip, and the man's knuckles were white on the stock of his Henry.

Was it going to work? They'd know soon enough.

Voices rose from the boulders where the Apaches were hidden, and Fletcher heard the slight scrape of a rifle butt against rock.

Another voice now, younger and louder than the rest, was saying something in a language Fletcher did not understand. He gave Sieber a sidelong glance, his eyes holding a question, and the scout moved closer.

"He says we're women, that we killed ourselves," Sieber whispered. "But some of the older bucks ain't so sure. They think maybe it's a trap."

"Damn," Fletcher swore, gritting out the word under his breath. "They're not falling for it."

The young man's voice was closer now, calling out to his companions.

Sieber replied to Fletcher's unspoken question: "He's saying the same thing again," he whispered, his voice hoarse and tense. "That we killed ourselves rather than risk being taken alive by the Apache."

More voices now and the slow, careful scuff of moccasined feet on sand.

The Apaches were getting closer. But how many?

Fletcher felt uncertainty spike at him. When he and Sieber rose up from behind the shelter of the rocks there had to be more than one Apache standing out there. If there wasn't, he and the big army scout would be quickly cut down by the others.

Sweat tricked into Fletcher's eyes, stinging, and his

mouth was bone dry. Above him the sun hung in the sky like a gold coin, and a few puffy white clouds drifted in winds too high to be felt in the arroyo. Under the overhang a horse snorted, bit jangling, and stamped a hoof.

An Apache war whoop rang out, echoing within the canyon walls, then another, and another.

It was now or never.

Fletcher gave Sieber a quick glance of warning and rose to his feet. There were seven Apaches in the clearing, moving warily, rifles at the port. It wasn't all of them. But it was enough.

The ability to draw a gun fast and the eye-to-hand coordination to hit a moving target are gifts given to very few men. One in a thousand, perhaps. Maybe one in ten thousand.

Buck Fletcher was one of those men.

He drew his Colt from its cross-draw holster, did a border shift, spinning the revolver to his left hand, and cleared the gun from his hip holster before the other Colt thudded into his palm.

Sieber saw all this out of the corner of his eye, and even as he fired and cranked his rifle he wondered at it.

Both Fletcher's guns were hammering now, the shots so close they sounded like a lethal drumroll.

The silver-plated railroad watch in Sieber's pocket ticked twice, and ere it ticked a third time the fight was over.

Seven Apaches lay on the ground, six of them dead and one dying, the warrior moaning softly, his collarless whiteman's shirt stained scarlet with blood. There was no answering fire from the rocks.

The surviving Apaches, mindful of the women with them, had gone. It was not fear that made them withdraw. The Apache had lost too many warriors in this fight and they didn't like how the odds were stacking up. Better to retreat now and fight another day, when the advantage would be on their side.

Brave and daring the Indian might be, but he was always a pragmatist, and there was no disgrace in running away when the battle turned against him.

Sieber looked around at the fallen Apaches and let his breath whistle slowly between his teeth.

"You did it all, Buck," he said, shaking his head in wonderment. "I never hit a single brave."

His face stiff, Fletcher was reloading his Colts, the acrid smell of burned black powder in his nostrils as thick gray smoke curled around his head. "You did your share, Al," he said. "I heard your rifle."

"But I didn't hit anybody," Sieber said again. "Every time I fired the man was already going down under your guns. Hell, man, you did it all." He nodded toward the Colts that Fletcher had just holstered. "You did it all with them. I ain't never seen the like in all my born days. A couple of years back, in Abilene it was, I saw Wild Bill Hickok shoot Colts, and I tell you right now, he ain't near a patch on you."

Wanting it over with, killing as it always did saddening and draining him, Fletcher said, "We were lucky, was all." He took off his hat and wiped sweat from the band with steady fingers. "Let's go see if there's anything left of Sergeant McDermott."

There wasn't much.

That the man had suffered a great deal was obvious, and before the Apaches left they'd cut his throat.

"I've seen that before," Sieber said, pointing with his rifle to the dead man. "It's always the young squaws who do that. Makes a man think about womenfolk in general and how they feel about things."

McDermott's entire scrotum, hacked and bloody, had

been stuffed into his mouth, and it was this that had finally stifled his screams.

"I guess it all depends on the woman," Fletcher said.

An eight-man cavalry patrol, attracted by the sound of gunfire, entered the arroyo an hour later. In time to bury the dead.

"You boys did well," Lt. Frank Michler told Fletcher and Sieber. "We counted nine dead Apaches." The officer pointed to an old man with thin, gray braids sitting with his back to a rock. "And my troopers rounded up another one." Michler called out over his shoulder. "Sergeant Wilson!"

The noncom, a huge man with a shaved bullet head and thick neck, stepped to the lieutenant's side and snapped to attention. "Bring that Indian over here. I want to talk to him," Michler said.

Since the start of the wars against the whites, old men were a rarity among the Apache, most warriors dying long before their thirtieth birthday. But this man looked to be around seventy years old, his black eyes filmed white by cataracts.

"Where are your people?" Michler asked.

The old man was silent.

"Maybe he doesn't speak English, Lieutenant," Fletcher said.

"You are the one with the barking Colt's guns," the old Apache said suddenly, his hazy eyes trying to focus on Fletcher. "Your medicine is strong." The Apache was silent for a few moments, then said, "But I see one whose medicine is also strong, and by and by you two will meet." The old man stretched out a skinny hand and laid it on Fletcher's arm. "Whose guns will bark loudest then? The answer to that is unknown to me."

"Where are your people, old man?" Michler asked, impatience edging his voice. "Will you lead us to them so we can talk and make peace?"

The old man shook his head, his lined face crumpling.

"How can there be peace when General Crook has too many *demasiadas cartuchos del cobre* and wishes to shoot all of them?" he asked.

Michler looked quizzically at Sieber and the scout said, "He means cartridges of copper."

The Apache nodded. "Too many cartridges of copper. My people were never afraid of fighting the Americans alone, but now our own people act as scouts and fight against us and we do not know what to do. We dare not go to sleep at night because we fear to be surrounded before daybreak. We dare not hunt because the noise of our guns brings the soldiers. We dare not cook mescal or anything else because flame and smoke will draw down soldiers. We dare not live in the valleys because of the soldiers, so we retreat to the mountaintops, thinking to hide in the snow until the soldiers go home. But the scouts find us and the soldiers follow. This is our land, but we have nowhere to go."

The old man's eyes sought Michler's face. "The young warriors are here. They are all dead. I do not know where the rest of my people have gone."

Lieutenant Michler waved away the Apache with an impatient hand. "Ah, he's hopeless. The old coot knows nothing. He's nuts."

The soldier stalked away, calling out orders to his troopers, and Fletcher stood looking at the old man. He built a smoke and took the Apache's hand, putting the cigarette between his fingers.

The old man, long exposed to Mexicans, knew what it was, and he put the cigarette between his lips and Fletcher thumbed a match into flame and lit it for him.

"You're blind, old man," Fletcher said, "but you see more than the rest of us, I think."

"No hard feelings Flet-cher," the old Apache said, in a strange, high, singsong voice. "You are a mighty warrior, Flet-cher. No hard feelings from me. You have your eyes open, Flet-cher, but you don't see. That is because nothing is as it seems. Everything is topsy-turvy, Flet-cher. There is evil for you here. It stalks you as the cougar stalks the deer. You don't know this thing because you can't see. But the evil is already here and it rides a gray horse. It is here, Flet-cher."

Sergeant Wilson stepped beside the old man and roughly grabbed his skinny arm. "Come on, you crazy old bastard," he said. "You're coming with us."

The Apache winced as Wilson's fingers dug deep, and Fletcher grabbed the soldier's wrist, his own strong fingers tightening like steel bands.

"Let him go, Sergeant," Fletcher said, voice soft as his eyes turned from blue to a cold gunmetal gray.

Sergeant Wilson grimaced in pain and quickly released his fingers from the old man's thin biceps. But Fletcher still held the soldier's wrist in a grip like a vise.

"It doesn't cost anything to be sociable, Sergeant," he whispered. "Now smile to the Indian and be downright sociable."

"Go to hell," Wilson gritted.

Fletcher's fingers tightened and color drained from the sergeant's face.

"All right, all right," he said. "I'll be sociable."

"Smile to the nice Indian," Fletcher said, a vague, undirected anger riding him.

The soldier's lips twisted into a grotesque approximation of a smile and Fletcher let his wrist go.

Fletcher stepped closer to Wilson as the man stood, rubbing his wrist. "I've took a notion to like this old man," he said. "If I hear that you've been abusing him I'll come looking for you."

Wilson glared at Fletcher, his eyes ugly. "You and me are going to meet again when there ain't an officer around, Fletcher; depend on it," he said. "And when we do I'll kill you."

"That's been tried before," Fletcher said. "Now take your prisoner and get the hell out of here."

"You sure have a habit of making enemies, don't you, Buck?"

Fletcher turned and found Al Sieber at his elbow.

"He didn't have to hurt the old man. There was no cause to do that," Fletcher said.

Sieber nodded. "Maybe so, but you watch that Andy Wilson. He fancies himself a pugilist and they say he once beat a man to death with his fists in a prizefight over to Dodge City way. He's four inches taller and maybe fifty pounds heavier than you, Buck, and that's something to bear in mind."

Fletcher's smile was thin. "I'm not hunting trouble. I'll stay out of his way."

"Unless you gun him, of course," Sieber said, grinning. "Then you don't have a damn thing to worry about."

Lieutenant Michler stepped beside Sieber and with little ceremony told the scout that he'd been ordered to report to General Crook at Fort Apache.

"That's why I was patrolling out this way," the soldier said. "I was instructed to relieve you of the wagon escort and give you your orders."

"Looks like we can ride up to the fort together, Buck," Sieber said.

Fletcher nodded. "Glad to have you along—and that Henry of yours."

Michler found them a battered coffeepot, salt pork, and flour and salt for pan bread and they rode out as the sun changed from yellow to bronze and the light of day began to die around them.

But as they were leaving Sergeant Wilson stepped out from behind a rock and laid a hand on the bridle of Fletcher's horse.

"I ain't forgetting what happened here," he said, his voice low and ominous. "Just so you remember."

Fletcher nodded. "Apparently there's something you don't know about me, Wilson."

"What's that?" the soldier asked, his hard, gray eyes belligerent.

"I don't scare worth a damn."

Sieber laughed and anger flared red in Wilson's face, but he dropped his hand from the bridle and stepped back. "I'll be seeing you," he said, no friendliness in his voice, only an unspoken menace.

"You're going to have to kill that man, Buck," Sieber said as he and Fletcher rode out, swinging their horses to the northeast.

"Or beat him to within an inch of his life," Fletcher said. "Seems to be the only language he understands."

Five

They camped that night near the dry wash of Deer Creek and staked their horses close to camp on a patch of black grama grass that grew as tall as a man's waist.

Around them the air crackled with frost, and cold nipped at their fingers and noses, and small creatures scuttled in the fallen needles among the surrounding pines.

Sieber made coffee and fried salt pork and pan bread on a hatful of fire, trusting to the bare branches of the sycamore spreading above their heads to scatter the thin ribbon of smoke.

A cold, waxing moon rode high in the sky, hiding its face now and then as dark clouds moved across its shining arc, their edges for a while rimmed with silver. The night smelled of sage and mesquite and of the piñon, cedar, and juniper that grew on the hillsides. A hunting mountain lion roared in the distance, perhaps angry at the twenty-dollar bounty the Territory had just placed on the heads of his kind, then fell silent.

On either side of Fletcher's camp stretched miles of rough, broken country. Gigantic boulders, hurled skyward from the sizzling mouths of ancient volcanoes, obstructed the streambeds that fed water to both grass and timber, and hemming in the basin on all sides were the towering, upflung peaks of the far mountains, vast arrowheads of snow on their red slopes pointing the way skyward.

After they ate, Sieber pulled his rifle close and lit his pipe, watching with careful, speculative eyes as Fletcher rolled a cigarette.

Fletcher lit his smoke and eased his back against the trunk of the sycamore. Without looking at the scout, he smiled and said, "Speak your mind, Al. Just sitting there studying me the way you are is spooking the hell out of me."

Sieber grinned around the pipe stem between his teeth. "Damn it, Buck, you don't miss much, do you?"

Fletcher let the question go and Sieber said, "I heard tell a while back, maybe it was when I was up Cheyenne way, that you took on a whole war party of Indians when you was just a younker. Them as told me called it Fletcher's Vengeance Ride, and they said after it was all over you'd taken twenty scalps." The scout took his pipe from his mouth and looked into the glowing bowl. "Did I hear the right of it?"

"Stories grow with the telling, Al," Fletcher said. He drew deep on his cigarette, thinking back, then said, "They were Sioux and there was four of them. My folks had a cabin up on Two-Bit Creek in the Dakota Territory, and the Sioux came down on them and killed them both. I was fifteen that year and near enough man-grown. I went after the Indians and killed them all, and I cut off the hands of the one that had scalped Ma."

"It was a reckoning," Sieber said, nodding his approval, a fighting man's recognition of another's courage and ability with weapons.

"That it was," Fletcher agreed. Then, lower and almost to himself: "It was a reckoning."

He threw the stub of his cigarette into the fire. "After that, with Ma and Pa gone, there was nothing for me any longer on the Two-Bit, so I headed east and joined the

war. I'd four long years of that and it made me grow up
fast."

Sieber nodded. "No matter how tall a man's daddy
was, he has to do his own growing, and that's a natural
fact."

Fletcher picked up his Winchester. "Better get some
sleep, Al. I'll take the first watch and wake you in four
hours."

Sieber nodded and put his cold pipe in his shirt pocket.
He lay back, his head on his saddle, and, with the fron-
tiersman's ability to drop off instantly, was soon sleeping
soundly.

The two men rode out at first light, heading north
across a timeless land untouched but for the passage of the
Apache, and before them the ancient Salado people who
had lived in cliff dwellings farther south but had probed
this far and farther in search of game. The hawk and the
eagle had crossed this land times without number, but had
touched it only with their shadows.

Cattlemen had not yet moved into the Tonto Basin in
numbers, and Fletcher and Sieber rode across flatlands between the hills and gorges, fertile, untilled land where
Blackfoot and Crowfoot grama grass grew so high the
seedy tips touched their stirrups.

Saguaro, cholla, prickly pear, agave, and jojoba grew
low on the hillsides and atop the mesas, and piñon and the
checker-barked juniper clung to the higher slopes.

To the north lay the colossal red and yellow rampart of
the Mogollon Rim, a mountain cliff with slopes that fell
away steeply to meet the dark green line of the timber.

Both men rode easily but alert, rifles ready to hand
across the horns of their saddles.

Of Apaches they saw no sign, though once they made
out talking smoke rising from a craggy spire of rock near

the southern bend of the Salt River. It was as yet too far away to be a signal of danger, but it was a thing to be aware of, and both men rode with their eyes restlessly scanning the hushed land around them.

Fort Apache lay among the foothills buttressing the escarpment of the Rim and was for Fletcher an opportunity to talk to General Crook and perhaps get a lead on Estelle Stark.

Even if it was a cold trail, it could be a starting point, and a sight better than wandering aimlessly around wild and broken country made dangerous by hostile Apaches.

The afternoon had not yet shaded into evening when Fletcher and Sieber crossed the Salt at the clear, pebble-bottomed shallows near the scorched ruin of Sean Costello's store and an hour later rode into Fort Apache. They saw a shabby collection of log huts and tents that was a fort only in name, occupied, at least temporarily, by three troops of the First Cavalry and their Paiute scouts.

A rising wind was blowing long and cold off the Mogollon Rim, smelling of mountain ice and pine, bringing with it flurries of snow, and the sky was heavy with gray clouds. Although it was not yet night, oil lamps cast yellow and orange shadows on the windows of the huts along officer's row, and the sentries on duty, muffled in greatcoats, fur hats, and scarves, stamped their feet against the cold, their breath smoking.

The few women who were in sight walked quickly, heads bent against the wind, shawls drawn tight around their shoulders.

Fletcher rode bundled in his sheepskin mackinaw, the collar up around his ears, as he followed Sieber to General Crook's headquarters, a log cabin with a shingle roof, twice as big as the rest, but just as badly built and equally shabby and unwelcoming.

Fletcher and Sieber dismounted, looped the reins of

their horses to the hitching rail, and walked inside, Fletcher's spurs chiming on the rough plank floor with every step.

A young corporal orderly sat at a desk, and in the far corner of the room a potbellied stove glowed cherry red, burning wood that smelled of mesquite. A coffeepot stood on top of the stove, and a few tin cups littered a small table close by.

"Coffee smells good, Lem," Sieber said to the corporal.

The man waved a hand toward the pot. "Help yourself, Al. Might as well, because if you're here to see the general he's tied up right now with the officers."

The soldier's eyes moved from Sieber to Fletcher, taking in his two guns and the relaxed but ready way he held himself, reading what was there to see and speculating on what was not. The corporal was familiar with weapons and their use, but this tall rider, quiet as he was, nevertheless spoke loudly of men, matters, and armed conflicts foreign to him.

Fletcher ignored the man's stare and poured himself a cup of coffee, then did the same for Sieber.

"How long will the general be?" the scout asked.

The corporal shrugged. "Who knows? They've been talking for an hour now, and you know how the general likes to talk once he gets going."

Sieber nodded. "I know. He's a right sociable man."

The door opened, letting in a blast of freezing air and a scattering of snow, and a tall man in buckskins and a shapeless black, broad-brimmed hat stepped quickly inside and slammed the door shut behind him.

"Cold as a mother-in-law's kiss out there," he said, striding quickly on moccasined feet toward the stove, hands already spread to its warmth.

The man, who looked to be in his late sixties, stopped and turned, recognizing Sieber.

"Hell, Al, I didn't notice it was you standing there," he said. "What you doing here? I thought you was down in the Gila Mountain country."

"Orders," Sieber replied, that one word saying it all. He waved a hand to Fletcher. "Charlie Moore, meet Buck Fletcher, a friend of mine."

Moore nodded at Fletcher and said "Howdy" with scant interest and continued his path to the stove.

Then he halted in midstride, recognition slowly dawning on him. He slapped the top of his thigh and said, "Hell, I knew that name seemed familiar to me, and now I recollect where I heard it afore." He turned to Fletcher, careful to make his movements slow and unthreatening. "It was when you was over to Abilene, runnin' with John Wesley Hardin and Gyp Clements and that hard crowd. I was in Kansas scouting for the Second Cavalry at the time. You boys was cutting a mighty wide path in them days, on either side of the law, and there were some as said Buck Fletcher was wilder and a sight more dangerous than any of them."

"Did some riding with Wes Hardin, but that was a spell back," Fletcher allowed. "A man changes. Gets older and maybe a little wiser." He smiled, remembering. "Wes is all right, but trouble naturally follows him wherever he goes."

"You could say that about a lot of men," Moore said, his old eyes shrewd and knowing.

The scout stood over seven feet tall in his Cheyenne moccasins. His buckskins bore Cheyenne beadwork, with its emphasis on red and white, and round-headed brass tacks were driven Indian-style into the stock of his Winchester Model of 1866 saddle ring carbine. His beard was gray, shot with black, and fell thick to his belt buckle, and hair of the same color spread over his wide shoulders.

Looking at him, sizing him up quickly, Fletcher decided that, despite his years, Charlie Moore was still a man to be reckoned with.

Fletcher didn't sense danger, just Moore's instinctive and carefully understated belligerence toward any man who sold his gun for a living. Killing was a thing Moore understood, and in the past he had done his share and would likely do so again, but killing for money was beyond his comprehension, as was the way of the gunfighter.

"Charlie, I ain't seen you in a right smart spell," Sieber said, dropping the words into the tense silence that hung chancy and expectant in the room. "Why are we standing here sipping coffee and jawin' when we could be over to the sutler's store a-drinking of Anderson's rye whiskey?"

"That sets fine by me, Al," Moore said, his shoulders relaxing, the tenseness draining out of him. "Been a long time since you bought anybody a drink."

"How about you, Buck?" Sieber gave Moore a sidelong glance. "I'm buying."

Fletcher nodded, his sudden smile unexpected and warm. "I'll drink any man's whiskey, so long as he's paying."

Sieber turned to the orderly, who had been listening intently to this exchange, and said, "Can you let us know when the general is free?"

"Sure thing." The man nodded. He hesitated, then added, "Only thing you should know is that Scarlet Hays is over to the sutler's store. He killed a man this morning, and he and his boys are celebrating another notch on ol' Scar's gun."

"Scarlet Hays," Fletcher said. "He's a long ways from Texas."

"I'd say he is," the corporal agreed. "Killed a muleskinner by the name of Long Tom Strider before sunup, and all over the last cup of coffee in the pot. Way I was told it, Long Tom drawed down on Hays. I don't know if Tom made many mistakes before, but that was sure as hell his last one."

"You know this Hays feller, Buck?" Sieber asked.

Fletcher nodded, his face hard and unsmiling. "Our trails crossed in the past. Scarlet's real good with a gun and he claims to have killed eight men, the last a couple of months ago, some hick sheriff down Laredo way with a tin star cut from a peach can pinned to his vest. Now I guess he's made it nine."

"Long Tom was no bargain his ownself," Moore said. Then he grinned, trying to take the offense out of what he was about to say. "You know, Fletcher, this isn't a criticism, mind," he began, "but it just don't come as no surprise to me that you and Scarlet Hays are acquainted."

Quickly Fletcher thought that through, decided to let it pass, and smiled. "In my line of work you meet all kinds of people," he said. "They come at you in a lot of different ways, wearing different faces, saying different things, but you learn to judge a man by what he does and how he is."

"And Hays?" Sieber asked, interested.

"He's a snake," Fletcher said. "And just like a snake he's fast and deadly and poison mean. He's a man best left alone."

"Well, there's three of us, so I'd guess he won't be inclined to cause trouble," Moore said. "Besides, looking around, I reckon that we ain't any of us pilgrims."

"Ain't that the damn truth." Sieber smiled. "So let's go belly up to the bar until the general gets through talking, and be damned to Scarlet Hays and his bunch."

The three men stepped outside into the cold evening, snow spiraling around them, driven by the keening wind.

They crossed the parade ground, leading their horses, and walked to the sutler's store, a low log cabin with a sagging roof, smoke belching black from an iron chimney sticking out of one wall. A faded sign hanging from rusty chains under the cabin's narrow porch said, *James Mulligan Prop., Liquor and Dry Goods,* and oil lamps glowed warm and welcoming behind its two front windows. But there was no welcome on the face of Scarlet Hays.

The gunman stood in the doorway of the store, watching Fletcher and the others come, his thumbs hooked into crossed gun belts, the walnut butts of his Colts worn from much handling.

As Fletcher tied his horse to the hitching rail, he studied Hays out of the corner of his eye.

The man stood straddle-legged and arrogant, the bellicose pose of a man-killer confident of his considerable gun skills.

Hays was about twenty-five years old that January, dressed in a black shirt and pants and scuffed, run-down boots. He wore a derby hat tipped forward over his eyes, and a muffler of bright yellow wool was looped carelessly around his neck. But the scarf was for show, not warmth. The cold did not make Scarlet Hays shiver, since his heart was icier than any winter wind. Nor did summer's heat make him sweat, because the angry furnace in his belly that drove him was hotter than any sun. If this man once had a soul it had died long before, leaving only an empty husk that knew nothing of love, compassion, or the slightest empathy for a fellow human being.

His skin was an unhealthy gray, marred by angry red eruptions across cheeks and forehead, and his flat blue eyes were set close together at the bridge of a narrow, pinched nose that whistled softly when he breathed.

Hays was around five-foot-five and probably weighed no more than one hundred and thirty pounds, but he had the coiled strength of a rattlesnake and the ability to strike fast and without warning.

In a gunfight Scarlet Hays was sudden and pitiless, and lesser men feared him, a fact known to him and from which he derived much pleasure. He stepped constantly along the ragged edge of insanity and it took very little to tip him over into the precipice.

Buck Fletcher, as he stepped up onto the porch of the sutler's cabin, spurs ringing, did not fear him, and this fact was also known to Hays, and from this he derived no pleasure.

Fletcher, Sieber and Moore crowding close behind him, stopped a couple of feet from Hays. The man did not budge, still blocking the door. Fletcher's coat was open, freeing his guns, and there was ice in his eyes.

"Scar," Fletcher said, "you can step aside and let me pass or I'll walk right through you. The choice is yours."

The gunman quickly thought this through, weighing his chances.

Fletcher watched him close, knowing Hays was frantically trying to remember how fast he'd seen the big man before him draw a gun. He remembered at last, drew no reassurance from that memory, and, his eyes ugly, tried a bluff.

"I step aside for no man, Fletcher," he said.

There was a time for talking and a time for doing, and Fletcher, tired from the trail and cold, was in no mood for more talk.

He reached out fast, grabbed the end of Hays's muffler, and jerked the gunman close to him. Fletcher backhanded Hays across the face, then did it again, blood spurting sudden and red from the man's mashed lips.

Hays tried for his guns, hands streaking toward the butts of his Colts, but Fletcher saw it coming. He turned the gunman around and slammed him hard into the cabin wall.

Hays's head hit with a sickening thud, and his Colts

dropped from suddenly nerveless fingers. Fletcher stepped aside and let the unconscious gunman fall to the muddy boards of the porch.

Al Sieber stepped to Fletcher's side and looked down at Hays's bloody face without sympathy. "I got to hand it to you, Buck," he said, shaking his head. "You sure have a way with folks."

"I asked him to step aside and he couldn't quite see his way clear to do it," Fletcher said. "I can't abide incivility in a man for its own sake, so I gave him his chance."

"How's about that drink?" Moore asked, his long legs stepping over the prostrate gunman. "Fletcher, I guess you're buying."

Three of Hays's cronies were at the bar when Fletcher and the others stepped inside. But they left quickly, and from the window Fletcher watched them carry the rubber-legged gunman to a nearby tent.

Fletcher rejoined the others at the bar, and Jim Mulligan, a big-bellied, red-faced man with pomaded hair parted in the middle and arranged in kiss curls on either side of his forehead, wiped off the rough pine plank in front of them.

"What will it be, gents?" he asked.

"Whatever you got that passes for rye and three o' them eight cent cigars," Moore said. He nodded to Fletcher. "He's buying."

Fletcher shot a quick glance around the store. It wasn't much, as sutler stores went.

Dry goods and burlap sacks littered the rough counter beyond the bar, and rough-cut shelves divided their length between canned goods—mostly beans, beef, and peaches—and empty space. There were stacked boxes of ammunition and a rack with rifles for sale that could shoot them. On a shelf at the base of the rack lay an assortment of revolvers, mostly army Colts, and a single nickel-plated .40-caliber derringer. Plug tobacco, as strong-smelling and black as Jamaica rum, lay on the counter in open cardboard boxes, along with a jar of pink-and-white peppermint candy canes. Newly ground coffee, as black and just about as pungent as the tobacco, was lined up in a dozen paper sacks, and a small basket of brown eggs, speckled with straw, lay nearby, bearing a hand-lettered sign that read, *Fresh*.

When the rye came it was surprisingly good for soldiers' whiskey, and Fletcher gratefully decided it hit the spot against the raw cold of the evening.

Fletcher drained his glass, refilled it from the bottle in front of him, and bit the end off his cigar. "Who were those three who left as we came in?" he asked the sutler, his eyes searching the man's face.

Mulligan shrugged. "They've been in here drinking all day with Scarlet Hays. I guess you heard he killed another man this morning." The sutler nodded toward the Franklin stove against the wall. "Right over there. Long Tom poured the last cup of coffee from the pot and Hays took exception to that."

"I heard," Fletcher said, lighting his cigar. "Hard thing, to die for a cup of coffee."

"Mulligan, I didn't recognize any of those boys," Sieber said. "Did they just get in?"

"A couple of days ago. They drifted into the fort with Hays, and General Crook signed up all four of them as muleskinners." Displaying the bartender's easy way with gossip, Mulligan continued: "The older of the three, the big fellow with the yellow hair, is Asa Clevinger. The small man in the sheepskin vest is Milt Gittings, and the youngest goes by the name of the Topeka Kid, I guess because he hails from up Topeka way. The Kid fancies himself as a fast gun, and he's said to have killed his share. Clevinger and Gittings are no bargain either, come to that."

Fletcher sipped his whiskey, enjoying the rough, warm taste. "Odd thing for Hays to do, signing up as a mule-skinner, I mean. It isn't his line of work, not that I've ever known him to work."

Mulligan shrugged. "Maybe he needs whiskey and women money. I know he visits the laundresses down on suds row from time to time. The general don't hold with smoking, drinking, and cussing, but he turns a blind eye to loose women. Or at least, he has until now."

It was possible that Scarlet Hays, absent gun work, might turn to honest labor for money and travel to where the army was hiring. But that wasn't like the man. It was a deal to think about and a worrisome thing.

Fletcher felt a tug at his pants leg and glanced down. A little girl about four years old with long dark hair and a pair of wide, earnest hazel eyes was looking at him. She held a doll in both hands, holding it up to him.

"Baby," the child said.

Fletcher smiled. "She's a real pretty baby," he said. The doll was probably from a traveling peddler and would be expensive, no small thing to buy for a child.

He had noticed the girl earlier with a woman who was arranging bolts of calico cloth and work boots at the back of the store and he guessed she was Mulligan's wife.

"Up," the little girl said, extending her arms even higher.

Without embarrassment, Fletcher picked up the child and held her in the crook of his left arm. "What's your name?" he asked.

The girl smiled, showing not a trace of shyness, being well used to men of all kinds. "Amy," she said. "Amy Mulligan." She held up the doll again. "And this is Rose."

"Pleased to meet you, Amy." Fletcher smiled. He shook the doll's tiny hand. "And you too, Rose."

"Seems like you made a friend there, Fletcher," Moore said. "Two of them, come to that."

Fletcher nodded. "I don't know why, but little kids just naturally cotton to me. And stray dogs and sick animals."

"That's on account of how younkers and animals don't pay much attention to how mean and downright homely a man looks on the outside," Moore said, a gleam of growing respect in his eyes. "They can see right through a man and know what lies beneath."

"Had an orphaned wolf cub follow me one time," Fletcher said, Moore's laconic and double-edged praise making him feel uneasy. "Finally gave him to a prospector who swore to me he'd treat him right."

Mrs. Mulligan, a thin, careworn woman with hands red and rough from broom, washboard, and lye soap, bustled up to Fletcher and said, "I'm so sorry. I've told Amy not to annoy gentlemen when they're at their whiskey and cigars."

Fletcher grinned. "She's not annoying me in the least. Been a long time since I held a child."

Mrs. Mulligan gave Fletcher a quick, appreciative smile, then took Amy from his arms and said to the girl, "Amy, we've still got a lot of work to do, so you'd best come and help."

The child waved good-bye, not with her whole hand as adults do, but only with her fingers, and Fletcher, feeling more than a little foolish, grinned wide and did the same.

He glanced at Sieber and Moore, but both men were studiously ignoring him, suddenly finding the amber whiskey in their glasses a thing of intense interest, though both were smiling.

"Like I said," Fletcher told them, "kids just naturally cotton to me."

"It's got to be your kind, generous, and downright peaceable nature, Buck," Sieber said, and Moore laughed.

Fletcher was saved from further embarrassment when the orderly corporal stuck his head through the door and told Sieber and Fletcher the general would see them now.

Six

The corporal conferred with Crook behind a closed door for several minutes, then reappeared, his eyes guarded, and ushered Sieber and Fletcher into the office.

Gen. George Crook was somewhere in his middle forties, a couple of inches over six feet, spare, athletic, and sinewy. His eyes were blue-gray and he wore his fair hair cropped close to his skull, his only vanity a full beard parted into two forks at the point of his chin.

He sat behind a rough-hewn desk made by a carpenter at the post and wore battered canvas pants, the suspenders pulled up over a faded red undershirt.

Crook showed no badges of rank and looked more like one of his own muleskinners than a brigadier general in the United States Army.

He didn't drink or smoke and preferred Apache, his big, rawboned Missouri mule, to any horse.

Unlike his contemporaries, this skilled Indian fighter respected the Apaches and other tribes as valiant enemies who deserved to be treated fairly and humanely in defeat.

The Lakota chief Red Cloud once said of him, "Crook never lied to us. His words gave the People hope."

But now Crook's words to Al Sieber were short, terse, and to the point. He ordered the scout to pull out at first light and join a column of the Fifth Cavalry at the Verde

River east of Turret Peak at the very western edge of the Mogollon Rim.

"Guide them well, Al," Crook told him before waving a dismissing hand. "The sooner this miserable campaign is finished the sooner the Apache can be left in peace to grow his crops and sanity returned to this land."

As Sieber turned to leave the office, Crook indicated to Fletcher that he should stay behind and waved him into a chair in front of his desk.

"Now, young man, what can I do for you?" he asked. "I take it you want something from me and that's why you asked my corporal if you could come in here with Sieber."

Fletcher nodded. "General, I'm looking for someone, a girl."

Crook frowned his annoyance and his voice was curt. "Why come to me with that? I'm not in the habit of procuring girls, for you or anyone else."

"No, it's not that at all," Fletcher said quickly. "The girl's name is Estelle Stark, the daughter of Senator Falcon Stark, and he wants me to bring her home." Fletcher moved in his chair, and added above its protesting squeak, "She ran away from Washington with a man who calls himself the Chosen One. He's some kind of crazed prophet who told her he's on a mission from God to convert the Apaches to Christianity before the world ends. Estelle fell for it—and him."

Fletcher leaned forward in his chair. "Al Sieber told me you might know of Estelle's whereabouts."

Crook studied the gunfighter over steepled fingers. "Falcon Stark, eh? Young man, you move in exalted circles. I'm told that distinguished gentleman harbors dreams of the presidency."

"He does, after Grant ends his term. That's why he so badly wants Estelle returned. The slightest breath of scandal, even a runaway daughter with the best intentions, could adversely affect his campaign."

"And what's in all this for you, Mr., ah . . . "

"Fletcher, Buck Fletcher."

"Ah, yes, Mr. Fletcher. As I said, what's in it for you? Are you a private detective?"

"You could say that," Fletcher replied, unwilling to tell Crook the whole story lest the soldier be too quick to judge him.

"You don't look like a private detective, Mr. Fletcher." Crook spread his hands wide. "Detectives are gray men who melt into the background. You don't. In fact, I'd say with your guns and your considerable physical presence, almost arrogance, you very much stand out from the crowd."

That touched a nerve in Fletcher. Crook was being deliberately insulting—but why?

Crook leaned over in his chair and opened a drawer on his desk. He came up with a long-barreled Colt and a cream-colored envelope. Crook laid the gun on his desktop, close to hand, and passed the envelope to Fletcher.

"I wanted to hear your story from your own lips, and I believe, thanks to my little charade, I've given you more than a fair hearing. Now, Mr. Fletcher, you'd better read this letter."

Fletcher opened the envelope and took out the single sheet of thick, expensive notepaper. As he read, Crook's big hand closed around the handle of the Colt.

December 23, 1872
United States Senate
Washington, D.C.

General Crook,
    Sir, I have reason to believe a dangerous
escaped convict named Buck Fletcher could be

*heading into the Arizona territory for the express
purpose of murdering my daughter, Estelle, who is
currently in the area to study the flora and fauna of
the Tonto Basin. She is a willful child and has done
this contrary to my wishes, especially now that the
savages are intent on making war on our
government.*

*Fletcher plans to carry out this terrible deed
because of the hatred he harbors toward me. As
you may already know, I plan to run for president
after Grant's term is completed. I will campaign on
a law and order platform, and it was through my
direct involvement in the case that Fletcher was
sentenced to twenty years' hard labor for the
vicious murder of a sheriff in Wyoming.*

*Please do all in your power to protect my
daughter and apprehend Fletcher at the first
available opportunity.*

*General Crook, take no chances with this man.
He killed a prison guard during his breakout and is
ruthless and deadly. Take him alive if you can, dead
if you must. But take him.*

*If he is taken alive, I will arrange an escort to
return Fletcher to Wyoming, where he will again
stand trial for murder, and this time I guarantee he
will not escape the hangman's noose.*

*I remain, sir,
Your obedient servant,
Falcon Stark (Senator)*

Fletcher laid the letter carefully on Crook's desk, aware
that the general had almost casually pointed the Colt at his
chest.

"General, this is a pack of lies," Fletcher protested.

"Look at the date on the letter; it was written a day before Stark asked me to find his daughter."

"Were you sentenced to twenty years in prison for killing a sheriff?" Crook asked, his eyes cold.

"Yes, but I was set up. I didn't kill that man."

"Did you kill a prison guard during your escape?"

"General, I didn't escape. Believe me, nobody escapes from the Wyoming Territorial Prison. I was taken to Lexington by the army, an escort of an infantry lieutenant and eight men. Find that young officer—his name was Simpson—or any of his men and they'll confirm that I didn't escape. Hell, General, get in touch with the warden."

Crook shook his head. "Fletcher, I'm in the middle of a campaign here. I have no time to carry out a murder investigation."

The general held the Colt less negligently now, and it was clear by the way he handled the gun that he knew how to use it. "I'll keep you here until your escort arrives to take you back to Wyoming." Crook made a weak attempt at a smile. "Chin up, Fletcher; I'm sure Senator Stark will seek out the testimony of the warden and your alleged soldiers and see you get a fair trial."

"That's not going to happen, General. For some reason that I can't even guess at, Falcon Stark will never let me reach Wyoming alive." Fletcher's face was bleak and drawn as he struggled to make some sense of what was happening to him.

Why had the senator asked him to urgently find his daughter—only to stab him in the back before the job was done?

Fletcher desperately turned the thing over in his mind, trying to find the handle to the mystery. But there was none to be found, and his shoulders slumped, defeat tasting bitter in his mouth.

"Corporal!" Crook yelled, no longer quiet-spoken, using the authoritative bellow of the parade ground.

The door crashed open and the corporal, a grizzled sergeant, and six troopers in tow barged inside, rifles hammer-back and ready.

Fletcher stood slowly, warily moving his hands away from his guns so there would be no misunderstandings.

The sergeant removed the Colts from their holsters and said, "Buck Fletcher, you are under arrest for murder."

Fletcher felt a rifle muzzle in his back, and when he looked at General Crook the soldier's eyes held only contempt and anger.

"Fletcher," he said, "I don't hold with killing women. In my opinion, any man who would plan such a thing as an act of revenge is low-down, lower than a snake's belly in an army wagon track." He turned to the sergeant. "Take this man out of my sight."

Seven

The log cabin was about twelve feet long by six wide, lit by a single oil lamp that hung from a hook on a beam supporting the shingle roof. There was an iron army cot with a thin mattress and a folded blanket pushed against the wall and nothing else.

The door was of heavy oak and barred from the outside, and set high on the wall opposite was a tiny window with thick wooden bars. The floor was tamped-down earth, frozen hard as iron, so hard only a powder charge could blast a hole in it.

Inside the cabin it was insufferably cold, and Fletcher sat on the edge of the cot and pulled his mackinaw close around his ears, his breath smoking in the damp chill.

A few flakes of snow drifted through the unglazed window and fell, unmelted, on his shoulders, and Fletcher let them stay.

Outside he heard one of the two soldiers who guarded the cabin cough, and the other trooper stamped his feet and cursed softly and with great dedication. "Hey, Bill, why didn't ol' George string this killer up instead of holding him here?" this soldier asked of his companion after a while.

After a fit of coughing, the other man replied, "Hell if I know. But I do know this: If officers had to stand guard duty he'd have been hung right quick."

"Damn right," the first soldier agreed. "Damn officers."

The oil lamp, flickering in a draft from a chink between the logs, cast a dancing circle of yellow light around the cabin, and Fletcher smelled the smoke of burning cedar in the cold air that blew through the tiny window.

Fletcher's numb fingers fumbled in his shirt pocket and found tobacco and papers. He tried to roll a cigarette, failed, spilled tobacco over his coat, and tried again. This time he managed to build a crooked approximation of a cigarette and he thumbed a match into flame and lit it gratefully.

"Fletcher, that smoking habit of yours is going to stunt your growth, you know."

It was Charlie Moore's voice, just a low whisper, and it came from the window.

Fletcher stepped away from the cot, back toward the front wall of the cabin, where he could look up and see the window.

Because of his great height, the top of Moore's hat was just visible, and Fletcher stepped closer again.

"Nice of you to visit, Charlie," he said.

"Visit, hell, I'm getting you out of here."

"You don't owe me anything," Fletcher said. "There's no need to stick your neck out like this."

"You're a friend of Al Sieber's, and any friend of Al's is a friend of mine," Charlie said. He chuckled softly. "Besides, it would be mighty quiet around here with you locked up . . . and there's one thing else."

"What's that?"

"I don't like to see any man railroaded and, gunfighter, I think you was railroaded."

"Charlie, don't—" Fletcher began, but the big mountain man was gone.

A few moments later Fletcher heard a dull thud, then very quickly another, and then the bar slid open on the door. Moore pushed his way inside and said urgently, "Let's go. I got your hoss outside."

"The soldiers?"

"Sleeping like two little babies." Moore read Fletcher's face and added, "Aw, don't worry; they'll be all right. I just banged their heads together a couple of times, and not too hard at that."

Fletcher quickly walked outside, stepped over the recumbent form of one of the soldiers, and swung into the saddle, Moore doing the same thing beside him.

"They overlooked your Winchester on account of how it was still in your saddle boot," Moore said, his breath steaming, eyes tearing from the cold as the snow stung his face. He handed Fletcher two Colts. "And I brung you these. Got them off them two soldier boys."

Fletcher shoved a gun into both pockets of his mackinaw and Moore nodded his approval. "Now we just ease on out of here real slow and easy, like we owned the place. If we ride out fast we'll attract the attention of the pickets, at least them who haven't as yet froze to death."

Fletcher and Moore rode out of Fort Apache without a single head turning in their direction.

An hour later they were riding among the hills and canyons along the northern bank of the Salt River, the craggy slopes of the Mogollon Rim to their right lost in darkness and swirling snow.

The riders crossed the partially frozen Dead Coyote Creek, then climbed a low hill crested by manzanita, mesquite and scrub oak, some of the mesquite topping thirty feet in height.

Moore reined up among the trees and tilted his head toward a sky he could not see, the low, black clouds lost in the darkness.

"Fletcher, we got to take shelter," he said, taking off the fur glove on his right hand, blowing into numb, curved fingers. "It's getting colder, and a man could freeze out here afore morning."

Fletcher nodded, his face troubled. "What about Crook? Won't he have discovered we're gone by now?"

Moore peered at Fletcher through the gloom and fluttering snow and shook his head. "Fletcher, I never took ye for a pilgrim. Listen, Crook's here to fight Apaches, and about now he's saying to himself, 'Well, the hell with him.' Trust me: He don't care a hill of beans about recapturing you so long as he's got a war on his hands. And secondly, ain't nobody in their right minds will be riding out on a night like this except poor, fugitive creatures like us."

"Moore, I'm real sorry I got you into this," Fletcher said, meaning it sincerely.

"You didn't get me into anything. I done it my ownself and I'd do it again."

The old mountain man pulled on his glove and inclined his head to the north. "We come down off this hill and head thataway for maybe three miles. We'll reach another hill, kinda like this one, but there's a cave among a stand of sycamore and ash where we can shelter and build a fire."

Moore kneed his horse forward, then turned his head in Fletcher's direction. "I told you wrong. It ain't exactly a cave, but I reckon it will have to do."

They rode off the hill and back onto the flat, their horses' hooves crunching on snow covered by a brittle frosting of ice. Above them the crescent moon horned the clouds aside for a few moments, revealing a patch of purple sky. But this was soon lost as darkness again covered the moon and the sky was as black as before. Falling snow was slanting into Fletcher and Moore, whitening the mountain man's beard and eyebrows, adding winter's aging to Fletcher's mustache.

Moore reined up his horse. "Not far," he said, his breath

forming a drifting gray haze around his face. "The hill is right ahead."

Fletcher peered into the gloom and made out a steep-sided butte. Trees covered its slope, and shadows rising from the plain shaded the narrow arroyo on its southern flank into an inverted vee of blackness. The rise looked cold, stark, and unwelcoming in the distance, just another hill to climb in a harsh and unforgiving land where there were many such.

Moore led the way and Fletcher followed, the collar of his sheepskin pulled up around his frozen face. His horse was tired, drained by cold and distance and badly in need of rest. Yet when he and Moore reached the base of the hill and began to climb, the big stud suddenly found the energy to rear, head twisting violently this way and that as he fought the jangling bit.

Taken by surprise and only half-awake, Fletcher tumbled backward out of the saddle and landed in the snow on his back, the reins still in his hand.

He lay stunned for a few moments, then jumped to his feet and fought the frightened horse as it tried to turn and run. Finally the stud quietened down, though it was trembling hard, its eyes rolling white, and Fletcher looked up to see Moore, still mounted, looming above him.

"Cougar," the old mountain man whispered. He put a gloved finger to his lips, hushing Fletcher into silence. "Just up ahead."

Moore rode a mustang, mountain bred and well used to the smell of cougar, and its calm presence seemed to steady Fletcher's stud.

The mountain man nodded in the direction of their back trail, silently indicating that they should go back the way they'd come.

Fletcher led his horse to an outcropping of granite about a hundred yards from the base of the hill and looped the reins around a dead, stunted spruce gnarling out of a cleft in the rock.

Moore swung out of the saddle and left his mustang, reins trailing, close to the stud. He pulled his Winchester from the boot, and Fletcher did the same.

"We don't have time to ride around that cat if he's got a mind to stay on the hill," he said. "Let's go see if we can scare him off."

The two men walked across the flat, rifles at a high port and ready, and again found themselves at the base of the hill.

"Damn, it's as dark as the inside of a buffalo," Moore said into Fletcher's ear as they slowly climbed the slope. "Step easy. I've never known a cougar to attack a human afore, but there's always a first time." The old man pointed to the distant Mogollon Rim with the muzzle of his rifle. "The deer are climbing higher on account of the snow and too many sodjers and Apaches down here shooting at them. That cat could be almighty hungry, an' if he's hungry he'll be testy."

The men climbed, doing their best to keep their footfalls quiet, red-rimmed eyes trying to penetrate the snow-flecked gloom around them. Above lay the stand of sycamores, dark spruce growing among them, and a few scant and scraggy cedars struggling to live on the thin soil.

Fletcher misjudged his step over a fallen tree limb, slipped on a patch of ice, and fell flat on his face. He lay there still, the breath knocked out of him, the rowel of his right spur spinning and squeaking.

Stepping beside him, Moore extended a hand and Fletcher took it, and the big mountain man hauled him effortlessly to his feet. Fletcher, breathing hard and cussing a blue streak, rubbed snow from his mustache as Moore raised a disapproving eyebrow.

"Them Texas boots and jinglebobs ain't exactly what a

man should be wearing when he's hunting lion," he said. "No offense, mind, but I just thought you should know."

A sharp reply didn't immediately spring into Fletcher's head, and he contented himself with picking up his rifle and cussing some more, especially at the snow that had somehow worked its way deep inside the waistband of his pants.

"Well," Moore said, "if that cat was hanging around, he's sure enough to hell and gone by this time. Fletcher, you made more noise than a Missouri mule in a tin barn."

"Sorry," Fletcher said, knowing how inadequate it sounded, but, annoyed with himself as he was, deciding to try no better.

Moore shrugged, his long hair blowing in the wind. "No harm done. But let's just go make sure all that cussin' and fussin' really did drive the lion away."

They found the cat higher up the hill, lying beside a deer trail. He'd been dead for hours.

The cougar's jaws were drawn back in a defiant snarl as he'd fought the inevitable destiny of his dying to the bitter end. He'd been very old and his teeth were worn almost to the gum and he'd starved to death. But his eyes still blazed with fire, and soon he'd fade away and become one with the land and give it strength.

Fletcher and Moore stood for a few moments, looking down at the cat, wondering at his great size and his determination to live. Then they dragged him away from the trail into a clump of mescal, and there they left him, returning a few minutes later for their horses.

The cave Moore had talked about was just a shallow depression at the base of a rocky outcropping jutting like the prow of a ship from the side of the hill. No more than six feet deep and twice that wide, the cave nevertheless provided shelter from the snow and the worst of the wind, and with a fire it could become fairly snug.

After Moore stripped the saddles and blanket rolls from the horses, Fletcher staked them out on a patch of grass that grew in a small clearing among the trees and was relatively free of snow.

By the time he returned, Moore, with a mountain man's expertise, had coaxed a small pile of dead leaves and twigs into flame and was already cramming snow into a battered pot for coffee.

The old man, who seemed to be prepared for any eventuality, produced a small slab of salt pork and cut some thick slices, ready for broiling.

After they'd eaten and passed their only coffee cup back and forth, Fletcher built a smoke, enjoying his blankets, the taste of tobacco, and the closeness and warmth of the guttering fire.

It was still snowing, wide flakes swirling in the wind, and the air smelled of sage and pine and of the thin pane ice along the creekbanks. And it smelled of winter and of mountains and of high, secret places and of bears and wolves and the cry of the hawk.

Moore lit his pipe and studied Fletcher in silence for a few moments, then he said, "Man feels like talking, he should talk. Good for a man to tell his story, get things off his chest." He shrugged, giving Fletcher a way out. "Maybe it is."

It was a way of asking without asking, and Fletcher recognized it as such.

"How do I tell the story, Charlie?" Fletcher asked. "Some of it I understand; much of it I don't."

"Seems to me," Moore said, his pipe clenched in teeth that were still white and strong despite his years, "a man starts at the beginning and takes it from there. That is, if he feels so inclined and ain't being pushed to it none."

"You're not pushing me, Charlie," Fletcher said, smiling. "Well, not hardly."

And he told his story.

Fletcher began with his arrest for the murder of the Wyoming sheriff, his meeting with Falcon Stark, and the senator's plea to find his daughter. He described his journey from Lexington to Arizona by steamship, train, and horse, his brush with Apaches, and finally his arrest by General Crook.

"And the rest you know," Fletcher wound it up, "and I haven't jawed so much since the time I talked the loincloth off a wooden Indian."

"Like I said, sometimes it's good for a man to talk," Moore said, thumbing a match into flame, relighting the pipe that had gone cold during Fletcher's story.

"Well, what do you think?" Fletcher asked after a few minutes of silence had passed and Moore showed no inclination to speak.

"About what?"

"Hell, Charlie, about what I just told you."

"Oh, that."

"Yeah, that."

"Well, for one thing, I wish you'd spoke to me about Estelle Stark afore you went barging in to see ol' Georgie Crook."

"How come?"

"Because I know where she's at."

Eight

Fletcher sat up in surprise. "You know where she is?"

Moore nodded. "I surely reckon I do."

The old mountain man moved in his blankets, easing his hips into a more comfortable position. "About a week ago I was down on t'other side of the Salt a fair piece south of here and I got to talking to a feller by the name of Indian Jake Hooper. Jake trades with the Apache out of a horse and wagon and he's got hisself a Tonto wife, a passel of breed kids, and a bad case of the piles. On account of that particular misery, he does a lot of standin', you understand."

"What did he tell you, Charlie?" Fletcher asked, prodding, impatience riding him.

"I'm getting to that. Well, anyhoo, Jake says the Apaches have been telling him about a white woman with yeller hair who's been seen at the old Indian cliff ruins in the black basin timber country south of here. They say she's got a man with her, a young feller with a beard and long hair like mine and he dresses in a white robe most of the time."

"That sounds like Estelle," Fletcher said. "The man in the white robe calls himself the Chosen One, and he claims he's on a mission from God to convert the Apache."

"So I heard tell," Charlie said. "Only the Apache, riled up the way they are, don't much feel like being converted right now, so this Chosen One feller could find himself staked out on an anthill, maybe a piece sooner than later. I reckon the only reason the young bucks haven't done it so far is because they think he's plumb *loco*, and Apaches tend to steer clear of crazy folks."

Moore laid his cold pipe on the ground beside him, close to hand. "I was told by Indian Jake that, crazy or no, the Chosen One is attracting a lot of people to them ruins, men and women and a passel of young 'uns. And there's one thing more."

"What's that?"

"The yeller-haired woman, if she is Estelle Stark, is out to here," Charlie said, sticking his cupped hand in front of his belly.

"You mean she's pregnant?"

Moore nodded. "Either that or she's eatin' too many of them Mexican beans."

"Listen, Charlie, this is important," Fletcher said, ignoring Moore's grin. "How pregnant would a gal have to be to get that size?"

"Buck, a woman can't be a little bit pregnant. I mean, she either is or she ain't."

"I know that, but how many months?"

Moore thought for a while, then said, "Well, I've been married maybe seven times to Indian women, and thinking back on it now, for a woman to be out to here"—he put his hand in front of his belly—"maybe five, six months."

"Then she was already expecting the Chosen One's baby when she fled Washington," Fletcher said. "That's the scandal Falcon Stark is afraid of! He's terrified the voters and his own party will discover that his daughter has a bastard child—to a crazy, doomsday prophet, of all people."

"Could be," Moore allowed. "But why would Stark send you down here to find her?"

Fletcher shook his head. "He never wanted me to find Estelle. Charlie, I think he aims to kill her and then have the murder pinned on me. It would be real convenient to have a dangerous escaped convict like Buck Fletcher take the blame."

"You mean you was set up all down the line?"

"I mean just that, and getting railroaded into prison for the killing of that Wyoming sheriff was only the first of it."

Moore whistled between his teeth. "That Falcon Stark feller leaves nothing to chance, does he?"

Fletcher rolled another smoke, taking his time to collect his thoughts. He lit his cigarette with a brand from the fire, then said, "That could explain why Scarlet Hays and his boys are in the Territory. Maybe Stark has paid Hays to kill Estelle and then pin it on me, or better still from his point of view, kill me as well."

Moore thought this over, then said, "I'd say Senator Stark cuts a mighty wide path in Washington and he has a lot of power and influence. Do you think maybe George Crook is in on it?"

"Could be, Charlie," Fletcher replied. "He was pretty quick to believe Stark's story and dismiss mine."

"Well, the way I see it, his plan could still unravel. All you have to do is get the warden to speak up for you and them sodjer boys that escorted you to Lexington."

Fletcher shook his head. "The warden is a political animal and he'll do or say whatever Stark tells him. As for Lieutenant Simpson and his men, they're either dead by this time or buried alive in some forgotten outpost in the middle of Sioux country. Besides, Simpson is a professional soldier, a West Pointer, and if it ever came right down to it he'd obey orders and do as he was told. It would be either that or throw away his entire military career. He told me he's beholden to me for saving his father's reputation at Antietam, but even so, I don't think he'd be willing to sacrifice his future for me."

"Seems like this Senator Stark went to a heap of all-fired trouble with all his planning," the old mountain man said. "Why would he do that?"

"Because he can," Fletcher said.

Moore put his cold pipe in his mouth and gazed out at the spiraling snow driven by a sighing north wind. After a few moments' silence, he said, "Here's what you do, Buck. You fork that big stud of yours, head him north, and get the hell out of Arizona."

Fletcher shook his head. "I can't do that, Charlie, not now."

"Hell, boy, if it's money you need—"

"I've got money." Fletcher slapped the money belt under his shirt. "Right here."

He sat quiet for a while and said, "My parents built a cabin on Two-Bit Creek up in the high country of the Dakota Territory. Even if I went there, I'd constantly have that twenty-year prison sentence hanging over my head, and the shadow of Falcon Stark would always be nipping at my heels."

Fletcher tossed his cigarette butt into the fire. "It wouldn't work. I'm not a man who borrows trouble, but it seems to just naturally follow me. I couldn't stay hidden for long."

"Then what are you planning to do?"

"Find Estelle Stark and the man who's been paid to kill her. I'll beat a confession out of him if I have to, and in front of witnesses."

"It's thin, Buck," Charlie said. "Mighty thin."

"I know it's thin, but right now it's all I got."

Charlie lay back on his blankets, his head on his saddle. "Well, it's time for this old man to get some shut-eye, an'

I suggest you do the same, Buck. We got a long ride ahead of us tomorrow."

"We?"

"Sure, if you don't mind me tagging along." Charlie rose on one elbow, studying Fletcher in the weak glow of the firelight. "Buck, I'm a man who pretty much has lived his life alone. Oh, I've spent some time with Indians, and like I told you, I settled down to married life for a spell at various times, but mostly I lived my years in the high country, up in the mountains among the beaver and the tall pines." He smiled. "I'm getting stiff, Buck, and old, and recently I've begun to figure all my adventures were behind me. Then I ran into you."

Fletcher laughed. It was from genuine amusement and it made him feel good. "Charlie, it seems I've caused you nothing but trouble and now you're in it as deep as I am."

The old mountain man nodded. "That's my whole point. Like you said already, trouble just naturally follows you, Buck, and I want to be in on it. Hell, man, I don't want to stiffen up and grow old and someday crawl into a cave like this one and just die." Charlie's eyes were faded in the firelight and the shadows crawled into the wrinkles around his eyes. "You saw that old mountain lion down there on the trail. I don't want to end up like him. When death comes for me, I want it to be mighty sudden and with a rifle in my hands and my belly full of fire and the sheer joy of having lived."

Charlie lay back on his blankets. "Maybe you don't understand and maybe I'm just an old man who talks too much."

Fletcher smiled. "Charlie I'd be right proud to have you ride with me, and I couldn't think of a better man to have at my side in a fight." He stretched out his arm toward the old man. "Will you give me your hand on it?"

Charlie took Fletcher's hand and shook it. "We're going to have some fun, ain't we, Buck?"

Knowing what the old man wanted to hear, Fletcher nodded. "I'd say we are."

"Only one thing," Charlie said, lying back on his blankets, staring at the roof of the cave. "If I fall, don't bury me in the ground."

"You aren't going to fall, Charlie. You're too mean an old coot for that."

"But still, Buck, if I do, promise you'll haul my carcass up a tree or some other high place and leave me there. That's the Indian way and it's a good way. I don't want to be buried under dirt. It will lay heavy on me." He raised up on an elbow again. "Promise me that, Buck."

Fletcher realized there was no room for or point in further argument. "I'll do that for you, Charlie; I promise."

"You'd better; otherwise I'll come back and haunt you." Charlie sighed deep and long. "Yup, it's the Indian way, and it's a good way because a man can lie quiet with the sun on his face and at night see the stars. Now get some shut-eye. Damn it, boy, I'm all talked out."

Fletcher closed his eyes and, the long day catching up to him, was asleep within moments.

The fire burned lower, shading the glow in the cave from yellow to a pale orange.

Outside, the snow continued to fall, covering the entire basin, the grassy flats, the red, saw-toothed ridges, the rocky slopes, and the deep, shadowed canyons. The spruce on the rim escarpment turned to silver, and around them the snow hushed the land into silence, and even the owls standing midnight sentinel in the scrub oak and sycamore around the cave ceased questioning the night, as though unwilling to draw a screeching chalk line of sound across the sweet face of the darkness.

A coyote, hungry, slat-sided, and miserable, walked on

cat feet through the snow and stopped near the cave, nose tilted, reading the wind. Not liking the man smell, he trotted away, head bent against the night, snow frosting his muzzle with white.

Fletcher and Charlie Moore slept on until the long dark slowly shaded into day and fingers of gray light explored the roof of the cave.

Fletcher woke, put on his hat, and pulled on his boots, then added sticks to the weak fire. After satisfying himself that the fire would blaze for a while, he stood, buckled on his guns, and shrugged into his mackinaw.

He stepped out of the cave, shivering in the morning cold, and checked on the horses. They'd fared well in the night, sheltered as they were by the surrounding trees, and even Fletcher's grain-fed stud had managed to forage under the snow for grass.

Fletcher did what he could to clear away more snow with his boots, then walked back to the cave. He got the coffeepot and filled it with snow and placed it on the fire and began to slice up the dwindling slab of salt pork.

Charlie woke and rose stiffly to his feet. He coughed, then stepped to the mouth of the cave and glanced up at the gray sky.

"Snow's still coming down," he said. "I'd say it's getting heavier."

Fletcher looked past Charlie and out into the gathering day. The snowflakes were falling thick, driven by an unceasing wind off the rim, and the bare limbs of the sycamores looked like they were made of frosted glass.

"This ain't a day to be riding out," Charlie said. "I reckon we'd better stay right here until it clears."

Fletcher added a handful of coffee to the pot. "We don't have time to waste, Charlie. I've got to get to Estelle Stark before someone else does."

Charlie turned and nodded. "There's truth in what you

say, Buck, but a couple of men frozen to death on the trail ain't gonna be of much use to anybody. Besides, if we can't move, nobody else can either. This whole country is locked in tight as Dick's hatband."

Fletcher looked at that statement every way he could and reluctantly came up with the conclusion that Charlie was correct. The old mountain man was weather wise, and if he said they could freeze to death out there in the blizzard, then he was right and there was no questioning him.

"When do you think it will blow over?" Fletcher asked, seeking even a slight gleam of hope.

"Tomorrow, maybe, or the day after," Charlie said. "That is, if the horses can last that long out there."

Fletcher shook his head, saying nothing. If the blizzard lasted longer than Charlie predicted, they were in a heap of trouble—and so was Estelle Stark.

Two days later the snow stopped.

As the night died around them, making way for a bright morning, Fletcher and Charlie Moore breakfasted on a single strip of salt pork and a cup of twice-boiled coffee, then left the cave and saddled their horses.

The animals were lean and had begun to grow a ragged, shaggy winter coat, but they stepped out willingly enough and seemed anxious to be back on the trail and away from the thin graze of the forest clearing.

The two riders once again descended into the basin, making their way down the slope and then across benched ridges made treacherous by deep snowdrifts. They left behind the stands of cedar and juniper on the heights and rode onto flat grass country surrounded by tall, rugged hills crowned by pine. Behind them, the Mogollon Rim showed as a vast, snow-plastered wall, traces of red rock showing here and there across its width.

Here the land was not completely flat but rose now and

then into rolling, undulating hills, most of them shallow and thick with manzanita and cactus, scrub live oak growing on their southern slopes.

The two men got their first glimpse of the sun rising over the Mazatzals near Fortunate Creek, and Fletcher saw the tracks of deer on the frosted crust of the snow and once the narrow, short-coupled prints of a hunting coyote. But nothing moved across the entire breadth of that seemingly limitless wilderness. It was as though the land was holding its breath, waiting for something to happen.

Fletcher and Charlie reined up in a stand of manzanita to rest the horses for a few minutes and let them nose under the snow for whatever sparse grass was growing there.

With numb fingers, Fletcher built a smoke and Charlie fumbled to get his pipe lit.

"We'll reach Costello's store, or what's left of it, and cross the Salt at the shallows," Charlie said, drawing hard on the pipe to get the fire going.

"Mighty close to the fort," Fletcher pointed out.

Charlie nodded. "I know, but it can't be helped. There isn't another decent place to cross this side of the Mazatzals, unless these horses can climb down gorge walls." The mountain man got the pipe going to his satisfaction and puffed contentedly, his face and beard wreathed in blue smoke. "Besides, we can see sodjers coming from a long ways off from the Costello crossing, and Apaches too, come to that."

Fletcher finished his cigarette and threw the butt into the snow. He kneed his horse out of the manzanitas and Charlie followed.

Now that he was seeing it in the daylight, Fletcher realized Costello's store had burned down very recently, charred straight and angular wooden beams sticking out of the ash at odd angles.

Following Fletcher's eyes, Charlie said, "Sean Costello

wasn't much. He was a fat man but not one of them jolly kind. A while back, when some starving Apache women came begging to him for food for their children, he laughed and told them to feed them their own dung."

Fletcher's smile was thin. "Nice feller."

Charlie nodded. "He were that. Anyhoo, when the Apaches under ol' Delshay raided this place, they crucified Costello to his own door with iron nails, then burned the store around him. From what I was told by Indian Jake, Costello did his share of screaming, even though they'd filled his mouth with horse dung."

The old man nodded, as though to himself. "Like I said, Sean Costello wasn't much, and after all was said and done he died like a dog."

The two riders crossed the Salt, then swung south, toward the black basin country and the ancient Indian cliff ruins.

After an hour's riding across a rough and broken landscape, they reached a place where a gradual slope merged onto a sunken road that showed signs of recent travel.

At least one wagon had passed this way, and several riders, and quite recently, since their tracks had not been filled in by snow.

The road led down a slight grade and was bordered for a stretch by jackpine, manzanita, and mescal. The track angled in the direction of the Mazatzals and Fort McDowell and once beyond the surrounding trees crossed a rolling area of wide meadows fringed by dark green forest, all of it covered in several feet of snow.

"This is an army road cleared by Col. Kit Carson back in 'sixty-three," Charlie said. "Now it's Crook's main supply route to Fort McDowell, an' then there's another hundred miles of it all the way to Fort Whipple."

Charlie swung out of the saddle and searched the road along the wagon tracks. He found what he was looking for, a pile of horse droppings. The old man looked up at Fletcher and said, "These are pretty fresh. I'd say no more than an hour old."

"You thinking what I'm thinking, Charlie?" Fletcher grinned. "Maybe we could convince those soldiers to part with some of their supplies."

"At gunpoint, you mean?" Charlie asked, grinning, one shaggy eyebrow rising.

Fletcher shrugged. "I'm not too popular with the army right now, so I don't really suppose there's any other way."

Charlie slapped his thigh and roared. "Damn it all, boy, I knowed I was gonna have some fun riding along with you."

The old man swung into the saddle, and he and Fletcher followed the tracks into the rolling meadow country.

They'd been riding for ten minutes when they found the dead soldiers.

The men lay close to the road, their blood spreading in a wide circle of scarlet around them.

Fletcher and Charlie dismounted and walked to the fallen men. One was a young cavalry trooper, the other an older, white-haired man, a major's shoulder straps showing where his bearskin coat had pulled away from his upper body.

The trooper had been shot in the back, the officer neatly between the eyes.

"I know this man," Charlie said. "That's Major Kenniston. He acted as General Crook's paymaster on account of how he was nearing retirement and too old for a fighting command."

"Apaches?" Fletcher asked.

Charlie shook his head. "Apaches would have cut them up some." He pointed at a scattering of footprints around the bodies. "Those were made by boots, Buck, the kind you wear. No Apache wears high-heeled, cattle-country boots." The old man frowned and pointed at a set of prints with his rifle. "All except these. They lead from here back to the wagon tracks."

"What makes them different?" Fletcher asked.

"The man who made those prints wore regulation cavalry boots. That's pretty strange. Why wasn't he killed with the others?"

"A hostage, maybe?" Fletcher suggested.

"Maybe. But his prints are alone. I mean there are no others around them. A prisoner would have men on either side of him, or at least following him close with a gun in his back. This man walked away from here and back to the wagon by his ownself."

The mystery of the army boot prints only added to a disturbing thought beginning to form in Fletcher's head.

"Does Crook send out a pay wagon regularly, Charlie?" he asked, frowning.

"He tries to," Charlie replied. "The men don't have much to spend their money on, except at the sutler's store, but the general says it improves morale to pay the troops reg'lar."

Deep in thought, Fletcher built a smoke, thumbed a match, and lit the cigarette before he spoke again, and when he did it was a question. "Does a civilian muleskinner ever drive the pay wagon?"

Charlie opened his mouth to reply, then, as a thought struck him fast, changed his mind about what he was going to say. Finally he asked a question of his own. "You're thinking about Scarlet Hays, ain't you?"

Fletcher nodded at the dead soldiers. "This sure is Scar's style."

"Civilians usually don't drive pay wagons, but right now Crook needs every man he can get. It's possible he ordered Hays to drive to free up a trooper."

"Or Scar talked him into it," Fletcher said.

Charlie nodded. "Crook knows how good Hays is with a gun. He maybe figured the wagon was a heap safer from the Apaches with ol' Scar's Colts around."

"Only he didn't know he was setting a wolf to guard the chickens," Fletcher said, his mouth a hard, bitter line under his mustache. "Scarlet Hays is an opportunist, Charlie. He saw his chance with the pay wagon and he damn sure took it."

The old man shrugged. "Well, it ain't any of our concern. It's the army's money and their dead. Let ol' Georgie Crook settle with Hays."

"But what if I'm right and Hays was sent here to murder Estelle Stark?" Fletcher asked. "If I can get the wagon back and get Scar to confess, Crook's got to listen to me."

"Too many ifs there, boy. You know Hays, and he ain't the kind to fess up real easy. You'll have to take him alive, and that won't be easy either. Scarlet is hell on wheels with a gun, maybe the fastest there's ever been. He's no bargain, boy, even for you."

Fletcher's face looked like it was carved out of stone. "Charlie, I've got to save Estelle Stark and clear my name. If we ride to the cliff ruins, maybe we can save Estelle's life, maybe not. But if we go after Scarlet Hays right now we can head him off and he'll miss his chance to murder the girl. With Hays and the pay wagon in tow it could be General Crook will be more willing to listen to me."

"Yeah, but suppose ol' Georgie is in on it?" Charlie said. "What then?"

Fletcher shook his head. "I don't know, Charlie. But that's a chance I'm going to have to take." He looked at the old man, his eyes softening. "Charlie, you don't have to—"

"Don't say that to me, boy," Charlie interrupted quickly. "I'm with you to the end, no matter what happens." He smiled slightly. "Just remember what I tole you. If the time comes, bury this old man in a tree."

Despite the worry gnawing at him, Fletcher laughed. "Charlie, you'll outlive us all. You're just too plumb ornery to die." He swung his horse around in the direction taken by the wagon. "Now let's find Scar Hays and make some war talk."

Nine

Fletcher and Charlie Moore rode side by side along the road, following the wagon tracks.

Around them, sweeping gracefully up from the flat, snow-covered foothills sparkled in the morning sunlight and rose up to meet craggy red rock peaks, most of them showing their own white crest. The land was quiet, serene, hushed, long miles stretching to the distant mountains.

Fletcher loved the mountains and the way they called out to him, the language they used written in the wind, telling him of silent places among the pines and rocky gorges deep with darkness and mystery, urging him to seek, explore, and find.

In his wild days, not long past, in the empty aftermath of hell-firing gun battles when men died, Colts roaring, on the filthy sawdust floor of saloons or in the dust of cow-town streets, he had many times sought out the mountains to restore his troubled soul.

The mountains did not judge, nor did they console; they were just there, unmovable, unchanging, defying the rains and the snows that would take a million times a million years to erode their hard blue rock to the depth of a man's fingernail.

Fletcher would spend a month, two months, riding among the pine-covered peaks, then, shaggy and uncurried, more wolf than man, descend once more to the flat to pick up his life and again become the person he had been, a man born to the gun with no other way to make a living than from his practiced skills, trusting to nothing but the Colt and the Winchester rifle.

It was a hard, unbending life, long on pain and fear and short on joy, but it was the life he had chosen for himself and there was no going back from it. Not now. Not ever.

As he looked at the mountains rising from the silent land far ahead of him, these thoughts filled Buck Fletcher's mind, and he found no comfort in them.

He rode on with a caution born of the years, his blue eyes never still, searching the land around him.

The shots racketed through the morning quiet, shattering the stillness into a thousand separate shards of sound.

More shots rang out, then more.

"What the hell!" Charlie yelled.

"Sounds like a battle up ahead," Fletcher said. He leaned down and pulled his Winchester from the boot under his left knee. "Let's go take a look-see."

A man doesn't ride headlong into gun trouble. Fletcher and Charlie walked their horses toward the noise of the shooting, their eyes constantly scanning the land around and ahead of them.

The road rose to meet them, then took a sudden dip down the other slope of the hill, leveling out about half a mile ahead. To the left of the track rose another hill, crested by a jumbled pile of huge boulders, here and there a stunted spruce growing among them. Angry gray puffs of smoke rising up from the rocks showed where men were holed up and shooting.

But at what?

The answer to that question became clear to Fletcher a moment later when he saw an Apache crawl forward on the snow in front of the rock, taking advantage of every scrap of cover he could find. The Indian put his rifle to his shoulder, fired, cranked the rifle, and fired again.

Another shot, this time from the rocks. The Apache threw up his hands, his rifle spinning away from him, and rolled down the slope, and landed spread-eagled at the base of a spiky mescal.

But that warrior was only one of a dozen who were converging on the rocks from all sides.

"Is it sodjers up there?" Charlie asked, his far-seeing eyes trying to penetrate the distance.

"Maybe," Fletcher replied. "Or Scarlet Hays."

"Hah, then let him die."

"Can't, Charlie. He's no good and I'd surely like to leave him to the Apaches, but I need him."

Fletcher turned to the old man, a fierce, laughing recklessness in his eyes that Charlie saw and noted, seeing it as an echo of other, wilder, times. "You ready?"

"Hell, boy, as ever was."

"Then let's go save Scar Hays's mangy hide."

Fletcher let out with a wild war whoop and spurred his horse. He threw his rifle to his shoulder, cranking and firing so rapidly the movement of his hand was a blur.

An Apache, startled, turned and ran toward Fletcher, his rifle coming up fast. Fletcher fired and the man screamed and went down. Another Apache appeared from a stand of mescal, and Charlie's shot took him in the middle of the chest.

Up on the rocks, two men appeared, both of them firing. An Apache went down, then another.

Now Fletcher and Charlie were among them. Holding his rifle like a pistol, Fletcher fired at an onrushing Indian and the man fell, blood staining the snow around him.

One of the men atop the boulders threw up his arms and toppled backward. But the other man, a towheaded youngster, was still shooting, handling his rifle well.

It was too much for the Apaches. They broke for their horses, leaving at least six of their number dead on the ground.

Charlie fired a parting shot at the Indians before they disappeared over the crest of a hill. He brandished his rifle above his head and yelled a wild, ululating war whoop, his old eyes shining with excitement.

"Damn it, Buck," he said, "we done it."

"Looks like," Fletcher allowed. "Now let's go see if Scarlet Hays is among the living."

There had been three men holed up in the rocks, and when Fletcher and Charlie dismounted and climbed among the boulders two of them were already dead. The top of Asa Clevinger's head had been just about blown off by a bullet, and Milt Gittings, who had been one of the men who climbed on top of the boulders to fire at the Apaches, lay on his back, his staring eyes unseeing, the blue shadow of death already on his face.

Only the Topeka Kid was still alive and unhurt, and right now his lips were curled into an insolent grin. "I guess I've got to thank you for coming to our rescue, Fletcher," he said.

"You don't owe me a thing, boy," Fletcher replied, his eyes as cold and level as his voice.

"Wasn't aiming to anyhow," the Kid said, his grin growing wider.

"Where's Scar?" Fletcher asked.

The Kid shrugged. "Who knows?"

"You were guarding Hays's back trail and seen us coming," Charlie said. "Were you and them other two laying fer us when the Apaches attacked, Kid?"

"Go to hell," the Kid said. "I don't have to answer questions from you."

"Boy, I ought to whup your ass," Charlie said, his face flushing red above his beard.

"Anytime you want to try it, old man, have at it," the Kid said, his hands moving to his holstered Colts.

Charlie moved toward the youngster, but Fletcher stepped between them. He looked at the Kid, fighting to keep his own rising anger in check. "Now, I don't much care for your manners, boy, especially toward your elders," Fletcher said. "But right now that's neither here nor there. What I want to know is where I can find Scar."

"You go to hell," the Kid said. "Anyhow, Scar ain't skeered of you, and come to that, neither am I."

The Topeka Kid was not much above medium height, but muscular and wiry. His eyes were an icy blue, and a fine, incipient mustache smeared his top lip, a vanity that every Western man with even the slightest claim to manhood sported in those days.

He wore dust-colored range clothes and a canvas mackinaw, but the guns in his belts were expensive and flashy, nickel-plated with grips of yellow ivory.

The Topeka Kid was said to have killed more than his share of men, and looking at him now, that arrogant, insolent grin on his face, Fletcher was willing to believe it.

He'd seen youngsters like this one before, back along a thousand half-forgotten trails. Young as he was, the Kid would be as dangerous as a striking rattler, and he'd be almighty sudden, deadly, and certain.

"Buck," Charlie said, the anger in him subsiding, "seems to me ol' Scar can't be too far ahead if'n he left these boys to finish us and then catch up with him."

Fletcher nodded. "Let's mount up and ride."

He turned to clamber back down the boulder-strewn slope, but the Kid's voice, icy cold and slightly mocking, stopped him.

"Hey, Fletcher," he said, "Scar told me he seen you draw one time and he says I'm beaucoup faster than you."

Fletcher turned, his eyes shading from blue to gunmetal gray. "He lied to you, Kid."

The Topeka Kid shook his head. "Nah, it don't work that way. See, ol' Scar, he never lied to me before."

"Well, he lied to you this time."

"I surely don't think so. I reckon maybe you're the damn liar."

At that moment, Fletcher knew the Kid was going to try it. The youngster wanted to go back to Scarlet Hays and tell him he'd outdrawn and killed the great Buck Fletcher. And after that he'd recount the same thing to every two-bit gunman he met, increasing his reputation so that armed and belted men would step wide around him, and talk soft and low in his presence.

Charlie, a perceptive man, knew it too. Now he tried to step in and make the whole thing go away.

"Kid," he said, "maybe you best mount up and ride on out of this territory. We saved your hide today; be content with that."

"You shut your trap, you old goat," the Kid said, never taking his cold snake eyes off Fletcher. "Well, Fletcher," he said, "I called you a damn liar. Are you going to take it and back down?"

Smiling slightly, Fletcher shook his head. "Boy, I've been doing this kind of thing for longer than you. Your gun won't even clear the leather. Now do as Charlie says and ride on out of here and no hard feelings."

The Kid thought that through, and Fletcher saw a slight doubt creep into his eyes. But there was no turning back from this and the Kid knew it, and so did Fletcher.

"Fletcher," the youngster said, "do I have to slap you into drawing?"

And the Topeka Kid drew.

He was fast, very fast.

But his fancy Colt was still clearing leather when Fletcher's bullet took him in the middle of the chest.

The Kid staggered back a step, his Colt coming up fast, and Fletcher fired again and again. Three bullet holes appeared in the center of the Kid's mackinaw, so close together they could have been covered by the palm of a woman's hand.

Slowly the Topeka Kid sank to his knees, his gun falling from his suddenly unfeeling fingers.

Fletcher stepped up to the boy, looking down at him.

"Hell, you ain't that fast," the Kid said, blood staining his lips. "I just seen you, and you ain't near as fast as Scar."

There was a well of kindliness in Buck Fletcher, buried deep but nonetheless there, that sometimes manifested itself at times like these. But this wasn't one of them.

"Kid," he said, "you weren't much."

The Topeka Kid, who would have been nineteen years old that spring, died with that realization, Fletcher's harsh words branding themselves into his brain before his eyes closed and he looked only into infinite darkness.

Charlie Moore stepped beside Fletcher, glanced down at the dead youth, and shook his head. "You didn't kill him, Buck. Scarlet Hays did."

"Maybe so, Charlie," Fletcher said, a cold emptiness in him, "but it sure don't make it any easier."

Ten

Fletcher and Charlie searched the trail ahead, but of the wagon and Scarlet Hays there was no sign. It was as though they'd vanished off the face of the earth.

Charlie had been kneeling, studying the tracks, and now he rose to his feet and stepped beside Fletcher. "They swung the wagon off the road here," he said. "By this time they could be anywhere among these hills. It would take a dozen Apache scouts a week to find them."

"Them? Who's with him?" Fletcher asked, not really expecting an answer.

But he got an answer of a sort.

"Don't know," Charlie said, shrugging. "But the man with Hays wears cavalry boots and rides an army hoss."

"How do you know? About the horse, I mean."

"Big, heavy animal with a long stride. I'd say he goes maybe seventeen hands and weighs almost twelve hundred pounds. Not too many of those around here except for army horses and that American stud you're forking."

"Maybe Hays stole the animal and he's got a new boy riding it."

"Maybe. But maybe there's a sodjer riding that horse and he tipped Scar off about the paymaster's wagon. Could be he was one of the escort."

Fletcher thought this through for a while, then said, "That would make more sense than Crook allowing a lowlife like Hays to drive a pay wagon. The general didn't strike me as being stupid, and, believe me, that's a rare commodity among generals."

With a groan, Charlie climbed stiffly into the saddle, and Fletcher realized the old man was growing bone-tired.

"What do we do now, Buck?" Charlie asked.

Fletcher jerked a thumb over his shoulder. "I saw some deer tracks back there. I think maybe it's time we did some hunting now we can't depend on getting grub from the army."

"Deer hunting." Charlie smiled. "Now, that's something I can teach you young 'uns."

"Teach away, Charlie." Fletcher grinned. "I sure am hungry."

An hour later a fat whitetail buck went down to their guns.

But it was Fletcher who made the killing shot.

They camped for the night in a stand of manzanitas beside a shallow creek with water running clear under a paper-thin sheet of pane ice.

The horses were staked nearby, and Fletcher and Charlie cleared away snow and gathered as much grass as they could, tearing it from the frozen earth by the roots.

It was hard, exhausting work, but Charlie, insisting that he make himself useful after having failed in the hunt, afterward skinned out the buck and cut some thick steaks. These they broiled over a small fire, both men wishful for coffee and salt, but having neither.

The old mountain man ate his steaks Indian style, holding the meat between his teeth, cutting a chunk off with a knife. It was a good way—if a man was careful of his nose, and Fletcher, the owner of a large, predatory beak, decided against trying it.

Some things were simply not worth the risk.

Earlier Fletcher had scouted a wide area around their camp, but the Apaches had gone. Crook's flying columns of cavalry had taught them the dangers of sticking around any one place for too long. It had been a bitter lesson and the Apache had begun to heed it well.

After they'd eaten and the day shaded into night, Fletcher lay in his blankets beside the fire, his rifle close to hand, and built a smoke. "Tomorrow at first light we'll head out for the old Indian ruins," he said, lighting his cigarette. "If I can get to Estelle Stark then I reckon the first half of my task is done."

"You think if Scar has been paid to kill the girl, he'll come after her?" Charlie asked.

Fletcher nodded. "I do, and that will make the rest so much easier."

"Not so easy, Buck," Charlie said, frowning. "Getting Hays to talk in front of witnesses will be no Sunday-school picnic. He'll come at you shooting."

"That," Fletcher said, "is a bridge I'll have to cross when I reach it."

Later Fletcher and Charlie talked of other things as men do while the long night swells around them, of guns and horses and of men and manners and places they'd seen and places they had not and of mountains and valleys they'd touched and of tall, white ships and the wild green seas that began where the land ended.

Slowly, as the campfire guttered and a coyote howled in the far distance, their talk slowed, then ended, sleep at last taking them.

Beyond the manzanitas, hidden by a stand of pine, a man sat his horse and studied the camp. After half an hour he swung his gray horse south, moving carefully among the pines, keeping to the base of the hills, silent and stealthy as a ghost.

*   *   *

Fletcher and Charlie ate a quick breakfast of venison steak, then saddled up and rode south, taking almost the same route as the man on the gray horse.

To the west, the towering spire of Mazatzal Peak touched low clouds heavy with snow, and the air was crisp and cold, like cracked ice on the tongue.

Shadows still lay dark in the ravines and canyons, and the game trail the two men followed wandered among low hills and thick stands of pine, always hiding what lay beyond.

At noon a light snow began to fall, dusting Fletcher's and Charlie's shoulders with white, and a rising wind stirred in the trees and set the pine needles to whispering.

They topped a rise and reined up in the shelter of some silver spruce. Charlie nodded to the south. "We should reach the ruins in an hour, maybe less." He looked at Fletcher. "Reckon she'll still be there?"

Fletcher rose in the stirrups, easing himself in the saddle as his stud tossed its head, the bit jangling. "I don't know, Charlie. I sure hope so. It will make what I have to do so much easier."

"Well, Indian Jake told me she's there," Charlie said, repeating what Fletcher already knew but seeking some reassurance.

Fletcher nodded, knowing how the old mountain man felt. "I reckon he did, Charlie."

"Jake, now, he ain't a man to make up stories," Charlie said, his eyes searching Fletcher's face, trying to read the other man's expression.

Again Fletcher nodded. "I don't suppose he is, but there's one way to find out. Let's ride on down there and see for ourselves."

As Fletcher and Charlie grew closer to the ruins, the land around them became wilder and more rugged. Brown hills, many of them sheared off into grooved, vertical cliffs, were covered in sagebrush, greasewood, and cholla. Cedar, pine, and spruce grew on their upper slopes, dark arrowheads of green against thick patches of snow.

The two men rode through a narrow valley hemmed in tight by the surrounding hills, then onto a flat open area, cut across by a creek with water that still ran fast and clear over a sandy bottom.

Fletcher and Charlie let their horses drink, then moved across the snow-covered flat. "Looks like another creek up ahead," Fletcher said.

Charlie rose in the stirrups, stretching to his great height, his eyes following Fletcher's nod. He shook his head. "Buck, that's no creek. It's tracks. A lot of tracks."

Charlie in the lead, Fletcher followed, and when he got closer he saw that what he'd thought was a depression in the snow made by the runoff from a creek was horse tracks. And Charlie had been right—there were a lot of them.

"Unshod ponies," Charlie said, leaning from the saddle as he studied the deep trail. "I'd say thirty riders, maybe more."

"Apaches?" Fletcher asked, already knowing the answer.

Charlie nodded. "Uh-huh, and only warriors. Apache women and children walk, and there are no footprints down there."

The pony tracks angled across the open ground and ended at the hills. Fletcher looked around him but saw no Indian sign.

"What you reckon they're doing this far south?" he asked Charlie.

"Dunno. But I think we'd better get to your Estelle Stark gal right quick. This many warriors could sure play hell with her and the rest of them pilgrims at the ruins."

Fletcher felt fear spike at him, not for himself but for

Estelle and the others. "Charlie, do you think they'll attack?"

"Apaches are mighty notional," the old man answered. "But this is a war party, probably all young bucks, and if that Chosen One feller has women with him . . . well, sure, they'll attack."

Charlie rubbed the back of his neck. "Got me an itch back there, Buck," he said. "Know what that means?"

Fletcher shook his head and grinned. "Way too late for mosquitoes."

The old mountain man's face was grim and unsmiling. "It ain't a critter bite. I only get that itch when somebody's watching me." He looked around at the hills. "And right now somebody's watching me."

Fletcher saw only the silent hills and the wind stirring the trees. But he trusted Charlie's instincts and he too felt something, something that made him feel exposed and extremely vulnerable.

"Let's ride," he said. "I don't want to get caught out in the open by those Indians."

"Amen to that, brother," Charlie said, and Fletcher caught an odd glint in the old man's eyes. It was just a flash that quickly came and went. But could it have been fear?

The two men crossed the flat and rode through a stand of pine just as the snow stopped and the parting clouds revealed a bright, cold sun. When they cleared the trees a wide basin hemmed in by hills opened up in front of them, sloping downward to end at an almost vertical cliff face.

In a shallow alcove in the cliff wall, about 350 feet above the floor of the basin, Fletcher made out the ruins of a sprawling pueblo, surrounded by a forest of giant saguaro cactus.

Higher than this by three hundred feet were more ruins, these with two stories, some of the ancient wooden ladders to reach the upper floor still in place.

Lower down the slope there was a smaller complex, a low, sprawling pueblo made up of a dozen rooms, and from several of these rose thin columns of smoke. A trail led up the slope to the higher pueblos, winding through a thick forest of saguaro, cholla, palo verde, ocotillo, and prickly pear.

Whoever had built these pueblos had chosen the site well. The spot was highly defensible with sweeping views of the entire basin and the hills beyond.

As Fletcher rode closer, he saw that the buildings on the lower slope ahead of him were made from quartzite blocks bound together by thick mud mortar, sturdy enough to turn aside any projectile except maybe a twelve-pound shell from a mountain howitzer.

Fletcher and Charlie rode toward the lower pueblo, and when they were a hundred yards away, a young woman stepped out of one of the rooms, shading her eyes against the sun as she watched them come. Another woman joined the first, then another, and several children appeared, shyly holding on to the women's skirts.

Was one of the women Estelle Stark?

Fletcher couldn't tell, but a couple of them appeared to be pregnant. But Estelle had just recently turned eighteen, and these women looked older.

As Fletcher and Charlie rode up to the women, a couple of men appeared from the ruins. They were young, with long hair and beards, and carried no weapons.

Fletcher touched his hat brim to the woman. "Howdy," he said, then introduced himself and Charlie.

One of the women, a pretty brunette with dark brown eyes, smiled up at him. "Brothers, have you come to join us?" she asked.

And from behind her the youngest of the men, his face eager, said, "Are you to help us in our great task?"

"Damn pilgrims," Charlie said under his breath.

Fletcher shot Charlie a look. "No," he said, "I'm looking for someone; her name is Estelle Stark." The women and the two men gazed at him blankly and Fletcher added, "I think she's in great danger."

"There's no danger here," another woman said. She was pregnant, her belly swelling big against her gray homespun dress. "Here we do the Lord's work as we await the day of doom that is soon to come."

"The hour of doomsday is close at hand," one of the men said, as though it were something he had learned by rote, and the other nodded and muttered agreement into his beard.

Fletcher tried another tack, fighting down his impatience. "If Estelle is here, please let me talk to her."

"Who wishes to talk with my wife?"

Fletcher turned and saw a man walking toward him. He was in his early fifties, very tall, almost as tall as Charlie, with a long beard to his waist, his hair falling in waves over his shoulders. The man wore a white robe to his ankles, tied with a piece of rope, and he had open-toed leather sandals on his feet. He carried a wooden staff surmounted by a large silver cross, and a similar cross hung around his neck, suspended from a rawhide string.

"Jesus," Charlie whispered.

Eleven

"No, not Jesus, but God's Chosen One," the man said. "Yes, chosen by Him to convert the Apache to the way of the Lord and prepare them for the doomsday to come."

More people had come out from the ruined pueblo, and now around thirty men, women, and children surrounded the Chosen One, hanging on his every word.

"I am a voice of one, crying in this wilderness; prepare ye the way of the Lord," the Chosen One said in a high, singsong voice. "March twenty-three of the year nineteen hundred is the appointed time of the doomsday. Prepare ye now for the terrible judgment to come. Amen and amen."

The people around him cheered and the Chosen One looked up at Fletcher and Charlie. "Now, brothers, will you join us?"

"Where is Estelle?" Fletcher asked, ignoring the man's question.

The Chosen One's eyes were bright with a strange, glowing fire, and Fletcher realized this man was far from sane.

"Why do you wish to see my wife? She is with child and she rests."

"Mister," Fletcher said, his patience rapidly wearing thin, "I believe Estelle is in terrible danger. There is a man in the basin right now who plans to kill her, and he will if we don't get her out of here fast."

The Chosen One shook his head, a faint smile playing around his lips. "Never fear; no harm can come to Estelle here. We are protected by the shield of the Lord."

Charlie kneed his horse forward. "Lookee here, Mr. Chosen," he said, "we came across the tracks of maybe thirty Apaches earlier today, all of them young warriors. You've got to get your people out of here before it's too late."

"The Apaches are our friends, our children. They leave us in peace."

"That's because they think you're nuts," Charlie said. "But I got a feeling them young bucks who made those tracks won't give a damn. They'll want your womenfolk and whatever else you have. Mister, you ever see what thirty Apaches can do to a woman?"

"If that time comes, I will talk to them and direct them to the path of righteousness," the Chosen One said, his strange blue eyes shining. "I have been appointed by God to show them the way, for the Apaches are as little children."

Realizing it was hopeless, Fletcher nonetheless tried. "The Apaches who will come here, maybe today, certainly tomorrow, are not children. They're warriors and they won't talk nice and they won't consider you their friend. They believe anyone who is not an Apache is an enemy, and that includes you, Estelle, and the rest of the people here."

"My disciples are with me," the Chosen One said. "And, like me, they do not fear the Apache. We are not their enemies and we will make them understand that."

Fletcher shook his head. "Mister, you can't make an Apache do anything he doesn't want to do. If you don't leave now, you'll all be dead by this time tomorrow, and then it won't make any difference."

One of the younger men, small and thin with quick

black eyes, stepped in front of the Chosen One. "You two ride on out of here," he said, his accent strongly Boston Yankee and accusing. "It's you who will get the Apaches all riled up and bring them down on us."

An angry murmur of agreement went through the rest of the disciples, and a dirty-cheeked youngster peeked out from behind her mother's skirt and stuck her tongue out at Fletcher.

"No! That is not our way," the Chosen One said, holding up his staff for quiet. "We will invite these men to break bread with us, and then they must leave us in peace."

Fletcher swung out of the saddle and walked to the Chosen One. "Know this: I'm not leaving here until I know Estelle is safe, even if I have to take her with me."

The man smiled. "I think that will be for my wife to decide."

Charlie and Fletcher led their mounts to the lower pueblo, but at a word from the Chosen One a pair of teenage boys took the horses. "We will stable them while you eat and we have grain," the man said.

The Chosen One waved a hand, taking in the surrounding hills. "The Lord has provided us with everything we need here. There are plenty of edible plants in the mountains and we grow corn and beans and squash. Next year we plan to plant cotton and weave it into our clothing."

"I don't suppose," Charlie said as they stopped at one of the doors to a room in the pueblo, "you have coffee?"

"That we cannot grow, though it is said it grows wild in the mountains."

"Just askin'," Charlie said, disappointment writ large on his face.

The Chosen One ushered them inside, and Fletcher and Charlie found themselves in a largish room warmed by a crude brazier in a corner that burned fragrant cedar logs. Woven mats covered the dirt floor, and a single shelf tacked to one of the walls held shards of brightly colored pottery.

"That was made by the old ones who lived here hundreds of years ago," the Chosen One said by way of explanation. "They were famous for their graceful water jars and cooking pots of red, black, and white, all decorated in scrolls and squares and triangles. These broken shards are all that is left. We collect them in the upper pueblos."

"What happened to them?" Charlie asked. "Seems to me they could hole up here forever if need be."

"No one knows," the Chosen one said. "Around four hundred years ago they just vanished."

Charlie nodded. "Apaches, probably."

"Perhaps," the Chosen One said. He waved a hand, directing Fletcher and Charlie to a mat. "We live very simply here. We use only mats for sitting and for sleeping."

A few moments later a young blond woman stepped into the room carrying a wooden platter of food and a jug. She was obviously pregnant, and she smiled at Fletcher as she laid the platter and the jug on the floor beside him.

"I will bring cups," she said, then turned and left.

"Is that Estelle Stark?" Fletcher asked when the girl had gone.

The Chosen One nodded. "She is my wife. Estelle is my right hand, my rod, and my staff."

Fletcher said nothing. The girl was in danger both from Scarlet Hays and the Apaches, and if he were to save her life he had to get her away from this madman.

Estelle returned with wooden cups, and into these she poured Fletcher and Charlie a clear liquid from the jar.

Fletcher tasted the drink hesitantly, while Charlie sat with the cup in his hand, waiting expectantly for his reaction. The drink had the strong, smoky taste of Irish whiskey and would probably get a man drunk just as fast, Fletcher decided.

"It's whiskey, Charlie," he said.

The old man's face lit up and he gulped from his cup. "Whiskey, hell, this is mescal."

The Chosen One shrugged. "It is a little luxury we allow ourselves, mescal and sometimes Apache tizwin, but only in the strictest moderation."

"I got to say, Buck," Charlie said, draining his cup, "things is sure starting to look up around here."

Estelle served them beans and roasted flat cakes made from the nutritious head of the mescal plant. The food was good, and Fletcher, being hungry, ate heartily.

Charlie wolfed down his food and then extended his cup to Estelle.

"It seems, wife, that our giant friend is in need of more drink," the Chosen One said, his voice tinged with faint disapproval.

If Charlie noticed, he ignored the man's comment, saying only that this was without doubt the best mescal he'd ever tasted, except maybe one time down Mexico way, but that was so long ago he could scarcely remember, so maybe he was wrong about that.

After Charlie had finished speaking, the Chosen One patted the mat beside him, indicating that Estelle should sit beside him.

When the girl did, he said, "Wife, Mr. Fletcher has something to say to you."

The girl was not particularly pretty, but she had a full, well-shaped mouth, and her eyes were very blue and full of vitality. It was hard to guess at her figure because of her pregnancy, but Fletcher decided she'd been slender and shapely and would be so again.

"What do you wish to say to me?" she asked.

Fletcher thought that through, forming in his mind how best to express it, but the girl stopped him cold.

"Is it about my father?"

"How did you know that?" Fletcher asked, surprised.

"A man travels this dangerous wilderness just to talk to me, so I can only assume he was sent here by my father."

Fletcher hesitated, deciding to take this one step at a time. "He wants me to bring you home."

The girl shook her head, a slight smile touching her lips. "My father hates me, and now"—she touched the back of the Chosen One's hand with her fingers—"more so than ever."

"Why would he hate you? Because you defied him and ran away from home with a man and got pregnant?" Fletcher shrugged, realization dawning on him. "I guess, now I've heard myself say it, for some men that's reason enough."

"It's more than that," Estelle said, her face suddenly pained. "When I was almost thirteen I caught scarlet fever. I almost died, but my mother nursed me through it and she made me well again. Maybe it was because she loved me so much and stayed so close to me that she caught the disease herself, and she wasn't so lucky. Despite the attentions of the best doctors my father's money could buy, she died. She was just thirty-three years old, and my father adored her."

Estelle leaned her head on the Chosen One's shoulder, an easy, intimate familiarity that surprised Fletcher.

"My father blamed me for my mother's death. He got so that he couldn't even bear to look at me any longer, and he packed me off to a boarding school in New York, as far away from him as possible. Then, when I was seventeen, he sent for me, intending to marry me off to the son of one of his political friends. But in Washington I met this one here, the one who has been chosen by God, and agreed to become his wife and share his ministry."

The girl smiled at Fletcher. "Doomsday will arrive in just twenty-seven short years. By that time my husband will be an old man, but I will be standing beside him when the trumpets of the Lord sound. And, Mr. Fletcher, we will be surrounded by Apache men, women, and children, all those we have guided onto the path to righteousness. Our work has just begun, and the journey will be long and difficult, but, oh, the harvest will be bountiful."

"Praise the Lord!" cried the Chosen One.

Charlie, caught up in the moment and more than a little drunk, yelled, "Hallelujah!"

Fletcher gave the old mountain man a hard look, then said, "Estelle, I believe your father has hired a gunman to kill you and plans to blame me for your murder. Senator Stark harbors dreams of the presidency, and right now you and your unborn child stand in his way. He can't let a breath of scandal affect his campaign, so he figures it's better if he can say you were murdered in the Arizona Territory as an act of mindless vengeance by the notorious gunfighter Buck Fletcher."

Estelle looked puzzled. "But why you?"

"Because I was accused of a murder I didn't commit, and I believe your father—don't ask me how—set up the whole thing, and all to get me down here to the Tonto Basin."

The girl shook her head vigorously to signal her lack of understanding, and it dawned on Fletcher that she was not too intelligent. His life hung by a thread and he'd hoped this dim girl could help clear his name. Now that hope looked more and more unlikely to happen, and Fletcher felt his spirits sink.

Charlie may have been half-drunk after liberally helping himself from the mescal jug, but he was shrewd and perceptive, and now he stepped into the conversation. "Tell her the whole story, Buck," he said. "From the beginning, and take it real slow and easy, just like you tole it to me."

Fletcher took a deep breath and told Estelle the story as

he'd recounted it to Charlie back in the cave, beginning with his arrest for murder in Wyoming and ending with his run-in with Scarlet Hays and his disastrous interview with General Crook.

When Fletcher stopped talking, a slow dawning of comprehension lit Estelle's face. "Yes, all that sounds like my father," she said. "He's not the kind of man who would leave anything to chance."

Fletcher nodded. "If your father's hired killer is Scarlet Hays, as I suspect, I'd thought to draw him here and get him to confess in front of you and other witnesses. But now there's an Apache war party out there and everything's changed."

"We have nothing to fear from the Apache," Estelle said, parroting the Chosen One's words.

"Right at this moment we have everything to fear from the Apaches," Fletcher said. He leaned toward the girl. "Estelle, come with me. We can leave here now and you'll be safe."

"But I am safe. I'm here with my husband."

The time for talking was over, and Fletcher knew it.

"Then me and Charlie are going to stick around here," he said. "You're the bait in my trap, Estelle, and I don't aim to lose you."

Fletcher and Charlie stood guard at the base of the hill as the day died around them. A light snow was falling again, and behind them the pueblo ruins in the higher reaches of the cliff stood stark and silent, their square windows blank eyes looking out on nothing.

Charlie was nursing a mescal hangover, surely the worst of all of them, and he was surly and uncommunicative, and Fletcher let him be.

Finally the old man said, "You know, Buck, there's maybe a dozen grown men back there and they don't have a single gun between them. They got hoes and spades and rakes, but not even a damn shotgun."

"Do you think the Apaches will come?" Fletcher asked.

Charlie nodded, an action he appeared to instantly regret. "They'll come, all right," he said, wincing. "I think they'll hit us at daybreak tomorrow."

"You're pretty sure, Charlie?"

"Sure as I'm standing here. Those tracks were made by a war party, and the only whites to make war on for maybe fifty miles around are right here."

Charlie rubbed the back of his neck. "Damn itch is still bothering me."

Fletcher saw that same strange look in the old mountain man's eyes and it troubled him enough that he had to say what he was thinking straight out. "Charlie, are you scared?"

The old man drew himself up to his full seven feet, his face stiff. "Buck, I ain't scared of anything I can see and I ain't scared of any living man. But when this itch starts on me, it's the not knowing that scares me."

"Is it the Apaches, maybe?" Fletcher asked, relieved that his worst suspicions were unfounded.

"Could be," Charlie said, "but I don't think so. Something or somebody is watching us, Buck, and I have no idea who or what it is."

"Keep your eyes skinned, Charlie," Fletcher said. "I reckon I got my own itch, and it's telling me we could soon be in a world of trouble."

By full dark, the Chosen One's disciples sought their mats in the pueblo as though they did not have a care in the world.

Fletcher and Charlie decided to stand watch in turns, and he let the older man sleep first, since his hangover took top priority.

A gentle snow was falling as Fletcher stepped out of the

room assigned to him and Charlie in the pueblo, his Winchester cradled in his arm.

He walked toward the slope, his eyes scanning the rise of the hill ahead of him. The breeze had dropped and the broad snowflakes fluttered slowly to earth, coating the branches of the pines with white. An owl glided past him on silent wings, a ghostly gray phantom that quickly faded from sight to become one with the darkness.

If the Apaches came this could be one avenue of attack, unless they skirted the hill and approached the pueblos from the narrow valley beyond.

The night had turned cold and frost hung in the air, and Fletcher's breath smoked as he walked along the base of the hill toward the valley.

On the western slope grew scattered spruce and cedar, and at its base rose an upthrust pinnacle of red, flat-topped rock about twice the height of a man, smaller boulders of the same color surrounding it on all sides.

Fletcher walked to the rock, stood in its meager shelter, and built a smoke. He thumbed a match into flame, trusting to the rock to shield him from the view of any sleepless Apaches who might be wandering around in the night.

In this, Fletcher's trust was badly misplaced.

Using cupped hands he raised the light to his cigarette—and the sky fell on him.

Twelve

The Apache jumped from the top of the rock and his moc-casined feet slammed into Fletcher's shoulders.

Fletcher crumpled under the warrior's weight and went to his knees. He saw a sudden gleam of steel and parried with his left arm. Too late. The knife raked across his ribs and Fletcher felt his side burn like fire.

The Apache closed on him quickly, holding his knife blade up for a fast, gutting slash. Still stunned by his fall, Fletcher grabbed the warrior's wrist and held on, twisting the Apache's arm hard to his left. The man yelped in pain, broke free, and sprang back, teeth bared, circling Fletcher warily.

Fletcher knew, isolated out here as he was, that he could not use his guns. A shot might bring a dozen warriors in this direction, and there would be no help from the pueblo except Charlie, and by the time he got here it would be too late. Like most men who lived by the gun, Fletcher carried no blade except for a sharp pocket folder, and that was lit-tle use against the Apache's broad-bladed fighting knife.

The warrior dived at Fletcher again, his muscular, wiry body taut as he sought to drive the knife home into Fletcher's belly. Fletcher turned at the last moment, drew his long-barreled Colt, and aimed a blow at the Apache's head. But the warrior was fast and saw the gun coming. He jerked his head away at the last moment and the barrel lost power as it slammed into the side of the Apache's cheek, staggering him but not knocking him down.

Fletcher stepped forward and the Indian jumped at him, his knife held high over his head. Fletcher let him come, then rolled onto his back, his booted feet coming up, catching the Apache in the belly. Fletcher's legs straightened, throwing the warrior up and over him, and the man somersaulted through the air.

The Apache let out a sudden, quick gasp of pain as his back crashed against the rock.

Fletcher scrambled quickly to his feet. The Apache, stunned, took a split second longer. He was on all fours beside the rock, and as he rose to his feet Fletcher kicked him hard in the face with the toe of his right boot. The warrior's nose was smashed by the impact and blood fountained around his head. But the man hardly slowed.

He sprang at Fletcher, a low growl escaping his throat. The Apache feinted to his left; then the bright steel blurred as he swung the blade blindingly fast to the right, leading with the razor-sharp edge, a cut designed to disembowel.

Fletcher was unable to block the blow, but he stepped back and knocked the Indian's arm down, and the knife flashed past his belly, opening up a six-inch slash in the thick sheepskin of Fletcher's mackinaw but failing to reach the skin.

The two men circled each other warily, Fletcher holding his Colt up and ready. With the forearm of his knife hand, the Apache wiped away from his mouth blood that ran in a scarlet stream from his smashed nose. But his black eyes glittered with hate and he showed no fear of the gun. Fletcher realized the warrior understood that he dare not shoot, so he was right in assuming there were others close by.

Around the men the land lay silent and snow drifted softly between them from the black canopy of the sky. The rock towered above their heads, a stony, unfeeling witness to a desperate fight that must soon end in death for one man and perhaps two.

Fletcher's mouth was dry and he watched the Apache's every move. He was not skilled at knife fighting like this warrior undoubtedly was, and he decided that if put to it, he'd use the Colt and to hell with the consequences.

But then he must turn the gun on himself. And quickly. Such a death would be quick and infinitely preferable to the one the Apaches would visit on him, full of pain and long drawn out. That was the Apache way, and there would be no mercy and no escaping it.

The warrior lunged again, a straight thrust to the belly. Fletcher danced aside, willing to take the cut that burned across his left hip just under his gun belt. He felt a hot gush of blood over his thigh as he hooked a vicious, short left to the Apache's chin. As the warrior's head snapped around under the impact of the blow, Fletcher slammed the barrel of his gun hard across the shattered bridge of the man's nose.

A shriek, quickly stifled, rose in the Apache's throat as he fell back against the side of the rock. But only for an instant. The warrior bounced off the rock and came at him again, his lips drawn back in a silent snarl.

Fletcher shook his head, not believing what he was seeing. God, this man was strong! And he was enduring, like all Apaches born to this harsh and relentlessly unforgiving land.

The warrior stood, watching Fletcher, eyes glittering and unblinking like those of a stalking cougar. He was taller than most Apaches, young, and thick with muscle in the chest and shoulders where it mattered. His shirt, woven by his womenfolk, and his buckskin breeches had been faded by many suns to the shade of dust, his only color the red band around his head and the gleam of copper cartridges in the belt across his chest.

Blood from his shattered nose stained the Apache's broad, flat face. But, trained from boyhood in the hard school of desert and mountains, where death beckoned daily and only the quick and the strong survived, this he ignored.

Fletcher knew with a growing certainty that there was no give in this man and there would be no surrender. He had to kill him and he had to do it soon.

He was losing blood from two knife wounds, both of them shallow to be sure, but nonetheless draining him. His breath came in short, hard gasps, and there was a dull fire in his chest.

But, despite all this, Buck Fletcher himself was no bargain.

Lean and big-boned, he bore on his body a dozen scars from bullet and saber wounds, and he was equally as strong and enduring as the Apache who faced him. He was stubborn in a fight, fearless, confident, and hard to kill. And he proved it now.

Fletcher did not wait for the Apache to attack again. He holstered his Colt and sprang at the man, his clawed right hand seeking the warrior's throat.

The Apache feinted with the knife, looking for an opening. But Fletcher grabbed the man's wrist and wrenched it upward, so that the warrior had to cut down with the blade, most of the power coming from his weaker triceps muscles.

Fletcher moved in closer and his fingers closed around the warrior's throat. His thumb sought the protruding Adam's apple and he ground hard, digging in deep with his wide, hard nail.

The warrior tried to twist away, but Fletcher's thumb dug deeper. The two men struggled close as entwined lovers amid the gently falling snow, muscles straining, each refusing to give up an inch of ground.

Fletcher looked into the Apache's eyes and saw only hate and defiance and the desire to kill. The warrior tried to hack downward with the knife, but Fletcher's grip on his wrist was like an iron vise, and though the man's arm trembled with the effort, the blade did not move.

His thumb dug deeper as Fletcher's fingers closed tighter around the Apache's throat, squeezing hard. He felt the man's right arm weaken as the warrior's breath was cut off, and Fletcher moved in even closer, his face only inches from that of the Apache as his fingers tightened like bands of steel around the man's throat and tightened more.

A low moan came from somewhere deep inside the Apache and the light left his eyes, no longer burning in the darkness like those of a wounded tiger. Fletcher felt the man go limp and he stepped away and let him drop to the ground.

The Apache lay unmoving, as dead as he was ever going to be, his face upturned to the sky and the falling snow.

Breathing hard, Fletcher looked down at the dead man for a few moments; then, his eyes wild and staring from the stress of combat and the nearness of death, he picked up his Winchester and began to walk back to the pueblo.

The flat, angry report of a rifle shot echoed through the still canyon of the night, and behind him Fletcher heard a muffled scream.

He spun around fast, cranking his Winchester, in time to see an Apache fall, the entire top of his skull blown apart.

Fletcher ran for the pueblo as a bullet, then another, split the air above his head. He stopped, turned on his heel, and saw a dozen Apaches swarming after him, a series of running, flickering shapes in the darkness.

Fletcher fired, cranked his rifle, and fired again. A bullet kicked up a fountain of snow at his left foot, and he turned and ran on.

Charlie's rifle spat orange flame from the pueblo, and Fletcher heard the old mountain man yell, "Run, boy!"

A bullet burned across Fletcher's shoulder and he stumbled and fell headlong into the snow. He looked up and saw Charlie step outside the pueblo, his rifle hammering, bright stars of flame from the muzzle flaring in the darkness.

Fletcher picked himself up and ran. He reached Charlie, turned, and threw his Winchester to his shoulder, seeking a target.

The Apaches were gone.

Charlie slapped Fletcher on the back. "Damn it all, boy, that was close. For a spell there I figured fer sure you was a goner."

Fletcher smiled. "That makes two of us." He shifted his rifle to his left hand and extended his right to the old man.

Charlie looked down at Fletcher's hand suspiciously. "What's that fer?"

Fletcher laughed. "Why, you old grizzly, for saving my life back there. That was one hell of a shot you made in the dark."

The old man's face was puzzled. "You can drop your hand, Buck, less'n you just want to shake for the sake of it. I didn't make that shot. Hell, boy, I'm good, but I'm not that good."

"Then who did?" Fletcher asked, now as perplexed as Charlie.

"Beats me, boy. But I'll tell you who it wasn't—it wasn't one of these here pilgrims, since they don't hold with guns an' shooting folks an' sich."

But someone had shot that Apache back at the slope, someone with considerable marksmanship skills who killed at a distance, and Fletcher, knowing in such matters, recognized him for what he was: a professional.

"Seems to me, Buck, you got a guardian angel looking out for you," Charlie said. "Maybe he accounts for the itch at the back of my neck."

Fletcher nodded. "Maybe he's an angel, Charlie. But could be he's something else entirely."

All the clustered rooms in the lowest level of the three pueblos were occupied, and now people were pouring out of them, looking first to Fletcher and then to Charlie.

"What happened here?" asked a tall, skinny man, his receding chin and the wattles under his neck giving him the look of an outraged turkey. "What was all the shooting about?"

"Apaches," Fletcher replied. He pointed with his rifle into the darkness. "Out there."

"You didn't hurt our friends, did you?" the man asked.

Fletcher felt anger flare in him. "Mister, your friends were doing their level best to hurt me. I got two knife wounds and a bullet burn across my shoulder. I wouldn't say that was right neighborly."

The Chosen One, Estelle behind him, appeared from the farthest door of the pueblo and walked rapidly to Fletcher, the huge cross on his breast swaying with each step.

"Apaches," Fletcher said again before the man could speak. "One attacked me over there by those standing rocks, and there's another dead one on the slope. That one wasn't killed by me, and I don't know who did it."

"Two?" The Chosen One gasped, his face shocked and unbelieving. "Two of our children dead?"

"There will be more," Fletcher said, his voice harsh and uncompromising. "I think the Apaches will attack this pueblo come first light. You'd best get ready."

"If that happens I will speak to them," the Chosen One said. "The power of the Lord is in me, and by his grace I will make the Apache see the light. They will forsake the rifle and the bow and take up the hoe and the plow."

"Mr. Chosen," Charlie said, "you'll be whistling at the wind. Those are wild young Apache bucks out there and they ain't about to listen to reason."

"They will, Mr. Moore; they will listen to me because the mighty voice of the Lord is in me and I speak with his tongue."

There was a scattered chorus of "Praise the Lord" from the disciples; then the turkey man stepped belligerently toward the Chosen One.

"We must send these men away," he said, waving a thick-veined hand toward Fletcher and Charlie. "They bring us only violence and death."

"Emmanuel is right, Chosen One," another man said. "They are killing our children and even now are planning to kill more."

An angry chorus of approval went up from the crowd, and the Chosen One bowed his head, his lips moving in silent prayer. After a few moments he looked up, his eyes shining, and said, "I have prayed for guidance and it has been given unto me. If our children come tomorrow as these men say they will, I will preach to the Apache of Christ crucified and prepare them for the day of doomsday and the terrible judgment to come. The Lord, in his infinite wisdom, has made the Apache his chosen people and I am but his instrument."

The Chosen One turned to the crowd behind him. "Bring these men their horses. They must depart from us now before the sun rises."

Desperately Fletcher made a last attempt to convince Estelle to leave with him.

"Come daybreak there will be few of these people left alive, and those who are will be cursing God for allowing them to live," he said. "Come with me now, Estelle. We can ride out of here together and I'll have General Crook protect you."

The girl smiled. "Oh, don't be a silly Billy. My place is with my husband."

Fletcher shook his head. "Then you will die here."

"That's silly," Estelle said, and, looking at her, a despairing Fletcher could see no depth of intelligence in her eyes.

"Your horses," the Chosen One said.

A man handed Fletcher the reins of his stud and he swung into the saddle, and alongside him, Charlie did the same.

The Chosen One stepped closer to Fletcher. "Go with the Lord, my friends."

Fletcher looked down at the man, the single-minded madness in the Chosen One's face a strange, unholy light.

"God help you," Fletcher said.

Thirteen

Fletcher and Charlie rode east, away from the Apaches and in the direction of the high Natanes Plateau country, then swung due north and splashed across a narrow tributary running off of Canyon Creek.

There was no wind to drive the snow, and it floated slowly to earth around them, settling thick on their hats and shoulders.

An hour passed and there was silence between the two men; then Fletcher reined up and pointed to a thick stand of juniper at the base of a hill.

"Charlie, let's hole up in there until daybreak."

Without waiting for the older man to reply, Fletcher swung his horse toward the juniper. When he reached the tree line he dismounted and led his horse among the checkered trunks of the pines. He tied the reins to a low-hanging branch and found a place clear of brush where he sat, his hat low over his eyes.

Charlie tied up his mustang, then dropped stiffly to the ground beside Fletcher.

"You hurt bad, Buck?" he asked. "You got blood all over your pants."

"I'm cut up some," Fletcher replied, "but none of it is real bad."

He opened his mackinaw, revealing a red stain on his

shirt where the Apache's knife had raked across his ribs. "This one is the worst, maybe."

"Let me see that," Charlie said. The old man studied the wound for a few moments, then said, "Stay here. I'll be right back."

When Charlie returned he was chewing something, his bearded cheeks bulging. He squatted beside Fletcher and spat out green pulp, then took a syrupy white wad from his mouth and said, "Pull up your shirt and let me take a look at that there cut."

Fletcher did as he was told, and Charlie quickly spread the chewed ooze over the wound before the younger man could object.

"What the hell is that?" Fletcher asked, looking down at the thick paste in considerable disgust.

"Maguey, mescal, century plant, whatever you want to call it." The old man grinned. "The pulp from the leaves will stop the bleeding and help you heal."

"Thanks," Fletcher said. He pulled down his shirt. "I think."

Fletcher rolled a smoke and lit the cigarette, aware that Charlie was watching him closely. "Say what's on your mind, Charlie," he said, his eyes shaded by his hat brim.

The old mountain man eased his back against the unyielding trunk of a juniper and brought out his pipe. "Only this, Buck—if Estelle Stark is killed by the Apaches come sunup, then her pa's work is done for him. Who's to know she was pregnant? It's no disgrace to have a dutiful daughter murdered by Indians while she was innocently studying plants and flowers and sich. In fact, it might help his campaign, get him the sympathy vote, if you know what I mean."

Fletcher nodded. "Then he only has to get rid of me."

"That's a natural fact," Charlie agreed.

Without looking up, Fletcher said, "Only it isn't going to happen that way, Charlie."

"What do you mean, it ain't gonna happen that way?"

"I mean, we're heading back to the pueblos before sunup."

"What fer?"

"To save Estelle Stark, if I can. She's not too smart, but I need her if I ever hope to clear my name."

"Buck, maybe you haven't noticed afore, but there's only two of us."

"I know, but it seems to me that's an army." Now Fletcher raised his head and he was grinning. "Or haven't you ever noticed that afore?"

The old man shook his head, his grin matching Fletcher's. "Well, when I rode along with you I sure figured life would never be dull. I guess I was right."

"We'll make it, Charlie. Don't ask me how, but we'll make it." Fletcher tipped his hat over his eyes again. "Now let's get some shut-eye. We got a full morning ahead of us."

Charlie was silent for a few moments, then said, "Only one thing, Buck: Promise me you ain't forgot about burying me in a tree. Damn it, boy, I want to lie there all peaceful and quiet-like, with my face to the stars so they can shine down on me."

"I promise, Charlie," Fletcher said. He said the words low and flat, and this time he did not look up.

Despite the cold, within moments both men were asleep. Fletcher's fight with the Apache had exhausted him, and his slumber was deep and dreamless. The snow continued to fall, rambling through the branches of the juniper, and the white wilderness was silent, waiting with a patience that stretched back millions of years for whatever was to come. Once, around three in the morning, the clouds parted and the moon touched the snow with silver, and a hunting wolf stopped in his tracks, looking around him, wondering at the enchanted beauty of it all, but aware with honed instincts that behind the loveliness lay the land's coldness and merciless cruelty.

Within the shelter of the trees Fletcher and Charlie slept on. Half an hour before the sun rose, Charlie stirred in his sleep and muttered the name of a woman who had drifted like smoke into his dream, then fell silent again and slept soundly.

The night shaded into day, the heavy clouds gathered, blotting out the sun that climbed over the White Mountains, but the weak morning light found its way into Fletcher's eyes and woke him with a start.

He shook Charlie awake and ran for his horse, calling out over his shoulder, "We overslept! It's after dawn."

Sensing the urgency, Charlie rose stiff and creaky but sprinted for his own mount. The two men trotted out of the juniper and back onto the flat, their struggling horses kicking up high, scattering fans of snow from their hooves.

Fletcher's face was grim as he rode, a knot in his belly telling him that all he'd find at the pueblo would be ashes, blood, and the sprawled, gray dead.

But when the two riders finally crested a gradual rise and had the pueblo canyon in sight, everything seemed normal.

Smoke rose from holes in the roofs of the pueblos, tying lazy bows in the still air, and children played in the snow, calling out to each other, red-cheeked from the cold.

Fletcher reined up his horse and Charlie eased alongside him. "Well, Buck, now what do we do? We ain't exactly welcome down there."

"Maybe the Apaches have moved on," Fletcher suggested.

"Could be." Charlie nodded. "Maybe there's sodjers in the area."

Fletcher sat slumped in the saddle, his chin on his chest, thinking the thing through. Finally he lifted his head and said, "That's way too many maybes. Let's go see for ourselves if the Apaches have left."

Charlie opened his mouth to object, but Fletcher had already swung his horse to the west and was riding toward the slope opposite the pueblos.

When he reached the base of the hill, he tied up his horse, and Charlie, muttering under his breath, did the same thing.

The two men climbed the rise, crouching low, and entered the cover of the pines along its summit. They slid through the trees like silent ghosts and reached the western slope of the hill.

Below them, the rise fell away to a narrow valley, a shallow creek running its full length without a single bend. Cottonwoods grew along both banks, and a single willow hung its branches over the creek where the Apaches were camped.

The Indians had no fire, knowing from hard-won experience that smoke in the Tonto Basin attracted soldiers, and each man was standing by his horse, listening to a warrior with gray in his hair who every now and then pointed in the direction of the pueblos.

The rest of the warriors were young, perhaps out on their first raiding party, but they were just as dangerous, and maybe more so, than older men.

Fletcher had seen enough. He eased back off the hill, then ran down the slope to his waiting horse.

"Now what?" Charlie asked as they swung into the saddle.

"Now we try again to talk some sense into those pilgrims."

The old man shook his head. "It won't work, Buck.

They didn't listen to you the first time and I don't reckon they will now."

"Maybe so, but I want to be there when the Apaches attack." He looked at Charlie with bleak eyes. "Old-timer, them young bucks are going to be seven different kinds of hell."

The two men rode to the pueblos at a gallop, attracting the usual interest as the Chosen One's people poured out of their blanket-covered doorways.

"Why did you come back? You aren't welcome here," the man called Emmanuel yelled, his face flushed with anger.

"Go away!" a woman called out. "Leave us."

She looked around at her feet, found a broken pottery shard, and heaved it at Fletcher. Now others joined in, pelting him and Charlie with bits of pottery and rocks.

A flying pottery shard opened up a cut on Charlie's forehead, and the old mountain man roared in anger, his rifle snaking out from the boot under his knee.

"No, Charlie!" Fletcher yelled. "Let them be."

"Damn these people, Buck!" Charlie said, a trickle of blood streaming down his face. "I don't give a damn if the Apaches kill 'em all."

More rocks were flying, but the Chosen One ran from the pueblo and stepped between his disciples and the riders. He raised his staff and yelled, "No! Stop this at once."

One by one the crowd let the rocks drop from their hands, though the eyes that were turned on Fletcher and Charlie were bright with anger and bitter resentment.

The Chosen One looked up at Fletcher. "You were told to leave us. Why did you come back?"

"To give you once last chance to listen," Fletcher said, his own anger flaring. "The Apaches were standing by their horses when we saw them just a couple of minutes ago. They'll be here soon, so get your people inside the pueblo and do it now. Me and Charlie can hold them off for a while with our rifles."

Fletcher looked around at the crowd of people, especially the dozen or so men. "If any of you men have weapons, arm yourselves. There isn't much time."

"Shame!" a man shouted. "You're bringing shame to all of us."

"Ride away," a woman said. "Leave us alone. You two are the very spawn of Satan."

"Listen to me!" Fletcher yelled. "You must listen."

"We listen only to the Chosen One," Emmanuel hollered. "He is our leader, not you."

Fletcher turned helplessly to Charlie, but the older man laid his rifle on the saddle horn and spread his hands wide. "Boy, I tole you it was a damn waste of time."

"You must leave us now," the Chosen One said. "And you must never come back here again. I am anointed by the Lord and so protected by his sword and shield, and I will deal with the Apaches."

Fletcher opened his mouth to speak but never said the words.

The Apaches came then. They trotted out of the valley and fanned across the flat, snow-covered ground in front of the pueblo cliff. Once in a long skirmish line, they slowed their ponies to a walk, rifles held ready across their chests.

There were thirty of them, lean as famine wolves, hard-eyed and merciless, all of them trained to be fighting men from birth, and they knew no fear, nor did they accept, or even understand, the concept of mercy.

The Apaches had been observing the pueblo for days and knew what they were facing: a ragtag, shirttail bunch of unarmed settlers.

But what they hadn't counted on was the presence of the two men they saw lead their horses toward the front of the lowest pueblo. Shrewd in the ways of enemies, the

Apaches recognized Fletcher and Charlie for what they were: fighting men like themselves and that gave them pause.

An Indian doesn't like to be surprised, and the sudden appearance of the two riders with their Winchesters surprised them. They slowed to a halt and began to talk excitedly among themselves, forming a rough circle around their gray-haired leader.

For his part, Fletcher watched the Apaches come, swallowing his fear like a dry bone in his throat. "How many cartridges you got, Charlie?" he asked, surprised that his voice was reasonably steady.

"What I got in the rifle and maybe another six, seven in my pocket. How many you got?"

"Not near enough," Fletcher said.

The Apaches spread out, wary now, but coming on at a trot.

"They'll attack all at once in a rush," Charlie said. "I don't think we're gonna stop them, Buck."

"Not out here we won't," Fletcher said. "Get into the pueblo."

He and Charlie left their horses and ducked into the room behind them. It was small, like all the rooms, with two tiny windows to the front and a smoke hole in the ceiling.

The walls would turn a bullet, but if the Apaches rushed the door, protected by nothing more than a Navaho blanket hung on a string, there would be no stopping them. Fletcher knew that in their last few hell-firing moments, he and Charlie could kill a dozen warriors, maybe several more, but that still left plenty to even the score.

That thought was confirmed when Charlie extended his hand. "Been real nice knowing you, Buck Fletcher," he said. "I got to say, you're one hell of a man."

"You too, Charlie," Fletcher said, smiling, taking the

old man's hand. "If it comes right down to it, I'll be right proud to die at your side."

But there would be no death that morning for Charlie and Fletcher. Dying aplenty there would be, but for others.

It was the Chosen One who saved them.

As Fletcher watched in horror, the man ran toward the Apaches, his staff upraised, the cross glittering in the cold morning light.

"My children," he yelled, "I come to preach Christ crucified. Prepare ye the way of the Lord."

Even as the Apaches circled him, the Chosen One seemed blissfully unaware of his danger. His face shone with that unholy light Fletcher had noted earlier, and the man's voice rose in what came close to a scream of passion.

"Doomsday is coming, my little ones, and you have been chosen by God to lead the people out of the valley of death and into light eternal."

The disciples, Estelle in the lead, were walking toward the warriors, their heads tilted back, eyes raised to the uncaring gray sky, singing a hymn Fletcher had never heard before.

> Lead your people to glory,
> The time of the end draws nigh.
> Chant the song of doom,
> Chant the song of doom.
> The Chosen One leads us to heaven,
> He shows us the righteous path.

Charlie spat through the pueblo window. "That ain't no kind of damn hymn a good Protestant should be a-singing. Hell, it don't even rhyme."

The Chosen One, perhaps inspired by the singing of his followers, made a fatal mistake. He reached out and grabbed the bridle of the older warrior, loudly urging him to be baptized and accept Christ as his savior. For several moments the Apache looked down at the man with cold glittering eyes; then he raised his rifle and chopped a short, vicious blow with the butt to the Chosen One's head. The man groaned and crumpled to the ground.

"I'd say," Fletcher said, his voice even and conversational, "that pretty much tears it."

The disciples were stunned, and the hymn they'd been singing staggered to a ragged halt, the last voice to fall silent that of a small child who had no real idea of what was happening. One by one the disciples drew back from the Apaches, their eyes wide, scared now that their leader had so mercilessly been cut down, stepping slowly and warily toward the pueblo.

But Emmanuel, the wattles under his turkey neck bobbing, ran toward the fallen man, calling out the Chosen One's name.

A bullet from one of the Apache rifles slammed into Emmanuel's chest, and the man rose up on his toes, then crashed his full length into the snow.

Wild war cries rose from the warriors' throats and they began shooting. Another man went down, then another. A woman was hit hard. She spun toward the pueblo, then fell, her face a sudden scarlet mask of blood.

The disciples turned and ran and the Apaches followed. The recent massacre of their own kinfolk by the army at Skull Cave fresh in their memories, the warriors shot down men, women, and children, whoever got in their sights.

A small white-haired man with round glasses balancing on the end of his nose was skewered through the chest by a war lance. He staggered to the pueblo, the forged iron point of the lance sticking a foot out of his back, and fell under the window where Fletcher stood.

Fletcher and Charlie had been unable to get a clear shot

at the Apaches, but now, as the disciples scattered, some of them falling, never to rise again, the warriors were drawing closer to the pueblo.

Fletcher fired, saw an Apache tumble backward over his horse, then fired again. He cranked another round into the chamber and watched as another warrior fell to Charlie's rifle.

A young Indian in a blue headband galloped his pony directly at the pueblo, his rifle spurting orange flame. His bullet chipped stone from the edge of the window close to Fletcher's head, and the gunfighter fired at the oncoming rider. The Indian screamed and threw up his arms, his rifle spinning away from him as Fletcher's shot slammed into his chest. Then Charlie fired and the warrior went down with his kicking pony, a grotesque sight as his entire lower jaw was blasted away.

The Apaches, badly burned, drew off, milling around at the base of the hill, steeling themselves for another charge.

The Chosen One rose groggily to his feet. He looked around for his staff, found it, and then staggered toward the warriors.

"Hey, Chosen, get back here!" Charlie yelled.

But the Chosen One didn't hear him, or if he did, ignored him.

The man walked unsteadily on his reeling path to the Indians, calling out again and again that he was the bearer of the message of Christ crucified.

A couple of young braves galloped to the Chosen One, hemming him in on both sides with their ponies. They leaned down and each grabbed the man by an arm and lifted him clear off the ground, riding back the way they had come.

"Yes, my children!" the Chosen One yelled, so loud that his voice carried all the way to the pueblo. "Carry me among you so that I may preach unto you the blessed message of the Lord."

The two Apaches carried the Chosen One toward their camp in the valley at a fast lope, and the man, still raving, was soon lost from sight.

A bullet buzzed through the window where Fletcher stood and thudded venomously into the wall opposite.

"Here they come again!" Charlie shouted, and his rifle was already firing.

Fourteen

When night fell, the people of the pueblo wandered outside and collected their dead.

The Chosen One had been screaming for a long time now. The Apaches were making his death a slow and long-drawn-out thing.

The Indians had attacked seven times throughout the day, but these had been long-range skirmishes and had not been pressed home. The Apaches had galloped back and forth across the open ground in front of the pueblo, firing their rifles at anyone who showed at a window or door, content to let Fletcher and Charlie expend their ammunition.

The warriors on their swift ponies had been fast, fleeting targets and had suffered no casualties except for a pony downed by Charlie and a man burned across the neck by Fletcher's Winchester.

At the pueblo a man named McKenzie had been hit as he glanced out of a window and had died an hour before, just as the sun was disappearing behind the Mazatzals. His wife was taking his death hard and her wails echoed eerily around the cliff above the pueblo. Another woman had been wounded, and so had a three-year-old girl, though the child had only been grazed by an arrow and seemed more frightened than hurt.

Inside one of the rooms, the disciples laid out the bodies of five men, three women, and two children, and Fletcher told Charlie, his voice edged by a vague, directionless anger, that many more would sure as hell follow.

One by one the disciples gathered in the room next to the one Fletcher and Charlie occupied, and furious voices were raised, more than a few of them cursing Estelle and the Chosen One.

"You both lied to us," a man's voice yelled, harsh and accusing. "He called himself the Chosen One, yet he was taken by the Apaches and God did nothing to save him."

The woman whose husband had been shot at the window screamed, "My man is dead, and all because we listened to you. The Chosen One was a false prophet. He led us into the fire."

Estelle's voice rose. "Listen to me! He will survive! The Chosen One will return to us. He cannot die until the hour of doomsday is upon us. This he was promised by the lord God."

"False prophet!" another woman yelled. "We should stone you for being the devil's harlot."

"Them folks is sure getting all riled up," Charlie said, feeding tobacco into the bowl of his pipe. "And I can't say as I blame them."

He looked to Fletcher for comment, but right then the gunfighter had other, more pressing concerns.

He was down to three shells for his rifle and a dozen cartridges in the loops of his gun belt for his Colts. Charlie wasn't in much better shape.

"I got five in the rifle and that's it," he said, his face gloomy.

"The Apaches tested us today," Fletcher said, "making us use up our ammunition. By this time they must know we don't have many shells left."

The Chosen One's piercing screams rang out again across the night.

Charlie swallowed hard. "Just make sure you save one for yourself, Buck. Them's words of wisdom."

Both their horses were in the room with them, standing heads down and miserable, Charlie's mustang bleeding from a stray round that had burned its shoulder.

Now Fletcher led the horses outside and staked them on a patch of grass at the bottom of the cliff that was relatively clear of snow. There was a small lean-to room at the northern end of the pueblo that had a good solid roof, and he laid both saddles in there.

When he came back inside, Charlie peered out at the gathering darkness and asked, "How long can he keep that up?"

The Chosen One's shrill shrieks had been shredding the fabric of the day since late afternoon. He had earlier interspersed his screams with pleas to the Apaches to repent and accept Christ. But his words were now an incoherent babble as pain that was beyond pain seared into his brain and set aflame every tormented nerve in his body.

"A long time, Charlie," Fletcher said, looking down at the smoke he was rolling. He lit the cigarette and added, "I reckon he'll scream like that all night. I'd say them young bucks are having themselves a good ol' time."

Charlie spat. "Damned Apaches. They got no consideration for a man's sleep."

Out of the corner of his eye, Fletcher saw a flicker of movement. He turned, glanced out the window, and saw Estelle run across the snow toward the valley and the Apache camp.

Without a word he pushed aside the blanket hanging on the doorway and ran outside, ignoring Charlie's startled cry of protest.

Awkward and heavy in her pregnancy, Estelle was stumbling across the snow, her skirt held high as she did her best to run.

"Wait!" Fletcher yelled.

The girl quickly glanced over her shoulder, her face pale and frightened, but she did not slow down.

Fletcher pounded after her, his long legs closing the distance fast. He caught up with Estelle and grabbed her by the shoulders, bringing her to a halt.

"Let me alone!" the girl yelled, struggling to get out of his grip. "I must go to him. The Chosen One needs me."

Fletcher spun the girl around and brought her face close to his own.

"They'll kill you too," he said, his voice low and urgent. "There's nothing you can do to help him now."

Estelle tried desperately to twist out of Fletcher's grasp on her shoulders, her eyes wild, but he held her all the more tightly, her huge belly pressing against him.

"Estelle," Fletcher said, "you heard those screams. You don't want to see him, not the way he is now."

"Let me go!" the girl shrieked. She opened her mouth, showing small white teeth, lowered her head, and clamped down hard on Fletcher's wrist.

The girl's teeth were sharp and they bit deep, and Fletcher let out an agonized "Ow!"

"Let me go!" Estelle yelled. And again her open mouth hungrily sought his wrist.

Fletcher shook his head and muttered under his breath, "I guess there's a first time for everything."

He let go of the girl's shoulder, drew back his right fist a couple of inches, and clipped her on the chin. Estelle's blue eyes flared wide in shocked surprise; then she went limp and Fletcher caught her in his left arm before she fell.

Fletcher glanced down at the girl's face and felt an instant pang of guilt. "Now you're beating up on pregnant ladies, Fletcher," he whispered to himself. "Maybe next you'll start kicking newborn puppy dogs."

But Fletcher had no time to explore those melancholy

thoughts further, because there was a sudden scuffle of moccasined feet near the base of the hill, and a piece of the darkness moved.

His gun flashed into his hand and Fletcher stepped backward in the direction of the pueblo, never taking his eyes off the now-shifting curtain of the dark.

Unlike many plains tribes, notably the Sioux, Cheyenne, and Comanche, the Apache were not keen on fighting at night, believing a warrior killed in the darkness was doomed to wander eternity in an endless gray mist.

But if put to it, they would. And did.

Here were a man and woman alone and isolated on the flat before the pueblo, and that was too good an opportunity to pass up.

The blackness moved again and Fletcher made out the shape of an Apache stepping warily toward them, his sturdy bowed legs testing the ground in front of him with each step.

Estelle lying limp and unconscious in his arm, Fletcher raised his Colt and fired, the snow around him flashing orange.

The Apache melted back into the darkness, and Fletcher did not know if he'd hit the man or not. A rifle crashed off to his left and he fired at the muzzle glare, then fired a second time. Once again he did not know if he'd scored a hit.

Feet pounded behind him and Fletcher spun, his gun coming up fast. It was Charlie.

The old man took in the situation in an instant and asked, "What happened to her?"

"I socked her," Fletcher said.

"Oh," Charlie said, "for a minute there I thought something bad had happened to her."

Covered by Charlie's rifle, Fletcher carried the unconscious girl back to their room in the pueblo. A few disci-

ples started to crowd around, but Charlie shooed them
away. "There are Apaches out there," he said.

The Chosen One's people had learned the terror of the
Apache and it had been a hard, bitter lesson. Now they ran
back into their rooms, a few of the men wielding hoes and
shovels as weapons.

But the Apaches had returned to the night and none
came near the pueblo.

As gently as he could Fletcher laid Estelle on a mat in
the corner of the room. The girl's eyes flew open and she
said groggily, "Wha . . . what happened?"

"You fell," Fletcher said, his voice even, "and hit your
chin on a rock buried in the snow."

The girl tried to rise to her feet. "I must go to him," she
gasped.

Fletcher gently but firmly pushed her back onto the rug.
"You're not going anywhere," he said. "There are Apaches
out there and they just did their level best to kill both of
us."

Out in the darkness where the valley lay, the Chosen
One screamed again, and he kept on screaming until he
could scream no longer and his terrible shrieks finally gur-
gled into silence.

Estelle covered her ears with her hands and sat rocking
back and forth, moaning wordless sounds, a primitive rit-
ual for the dead as ancient as woman's grief.

Fifteen

Before first light the two dozen surviving disciples buried their dead at a distance from the pueblo in a patch of open ground. The earth was winter-hard and difficult to dig, and of necessity the corpses were buried shallow, but hopefully, the people told each other, deep enough to deter scavengers.

Fletcher and Charlie stood guard with their rifles as men, women, and children lingered at the gravesides and did their best to pray, the light from a dozen lanterns casting pools of yellow and orange around their feet as falling snow, driven by an awakening wind, frosted their bent heads.

When the prayers were done and the burying over, one of the men turned to the others and said, "We must leave this place as soon as we can, because there is only death here and the honeyed words of the false prophet."

A ripple of agreement went through the mourners, and another heavily bearded man said, "Listen, all of you: Gather up what food you can and be ready to move out at daybreak."

"Where will we go?" a woman asked, a couple of youngsters clinging to her skirt, wide-eyed and scared since they had been unable to sleep away their fears.

"North," the bearded man said. "We will walk toward the soldiers."

Charlie took a step toward the crowd, his rifle in the crook of his buckskinned arm. "You won't make it," he said. "If a big snow doesn't get you, the Apaches will."

"The Apaches will get us if we stay here," the bearded man said, and again the rest of them voiced their agreement.

"Well, I can't argue with that," Charlie said. "But even if'n it's a slim one, which it is, you've got a better chance of getting out of this alive if you stay right here."

"You brought this misfortune down on us," a woman with a thick blond braid hanging to her hips said. "Why should we listen to you?"

"Because," said Fletcher, "we're the only men here with rifles."

The bearded man stepped belligerently toward Fletcher. "Maybe we'll just take those guns from you," he said, his fists clenching.

"Mister, try that and I swear to God you'll be digging more holes for dead men," Fletcher said, his voice flat and cold.

Estelle walked in front of Fletcher. She was wearing a pale blue dress embroidered with small white flowers, and she'd thrown a shawl around her shoulders. Her thick hair was pulled back in a bun, and in the lantern light a bruise showed black on her chin.

The girl threw up her arms for quiet as the disciples crowded around her, angry and spoiling for a fight. "Listen, as I've told you before, the Chosen One is alive. He cannot die until doomsday comes to pass. Stay right here. He'll come back to us, perhaps today, maybe tomorrow. But he'll come back. He would not leave his people stranded in this wilderness with no one to guide them."

"He screamed all night," somebody said. "He can die just like the rest of us."

"Yes, he can die," Estelle said, "like any mortal man.

But, since he is the Chosen One, he will be resurrected to glory and return to us."

Fletcher saw hesitation and doubt in the faces of many of the disciples, including that of the bearded man, and it was he who spoke next.

"Do you tell us the truth, Estelle? Will the Chosen One live again?"

"Oh, yes, oh, yes, he will. This I believe with all my heart and soul." The girl's eyes swept the crowd, her face shining. "He came to me in the night, after my grief for him was spent. He bent low and whispered in my ear, 'Grieve no longer. I shall return, for I have been granted the power over death itself.' "

The disciples were silent for a few moments, then began to talk among themselves. Finally the bearded man said, "We'll wait until this time tomorrow. If the Chosen One returns, he can lead us out of the wilderness."

Charlie leaned toward Fletcher and said in a hoarse stage whisper, "Ain't none of us gonna be here this time tomorrow."

Estelle rounded on Charlie angrily. "Oh, ye of little faith. The Chosen One will return and he will save us. You'll see."

"Lady, for your sake as well as mine, I hope you're right," was all Charlie said.

The Apaches attacked again an hour after dawn.

This time they walked their ponies toward the pueblo in a long skirmish line, firing as they came.

Dozens of bullets thudded into the wall near Fletcher and Charlie, and a flying chip of stone nicked Fletcher's cheekbone and drew blood.

Fletcher fired until his rifle ran dry, then went to his Colts. He stood at the window, his guns hammering, then ducked down again as bullets split the air around him.

Two Indians lay sprawled on the snow, but the rest kept on coming, a slow, inexorable walk toward the pueblo, firing as they rode.

"Buck," Charlie said, setting aside his empty rifle and drawing his bowie knife from his belt, "I think this is it. You got a bullet for me?"

Fletcher glanced out the window. The warriors were very close and he had only a few rounds left in his Colts.

"I'll save one, Charlie," he said, meaning every word of it.

Charlie brandished the bowie. "Just let me stand at the door and cut a few first."

Scattered firing broke out somewhere behind the advancing Apaches, in the direction of the valley. This was followed by a smashing volley as most of the warriors in front of the pueblo turned their ponies and began shooting.

"Now what the hell?" Charlie yelled.

More and more Indians were streaming away from the pueblo toward the valley, yipping their war cries.

The reason became apparent a few moments later when a small wagon drawn by a pair of mules galloped into the flat.

The mules were being driven hard, and Fletcher caught a fleeting glimpse of two men up on the box and the painted *U.S. Army* sign above crossed sabers on the side of the wagon.

One of the mules went down, but the impetus of the wagon dragged the dead animal with it to the front of the pueblo.

The two men, one in cavalry blue, jumped from the box, leveled their rifles, and blasted shot after shot at the Apaches, their firing accurate and deadly.

From the window Fletcher emptied his Colts at the galloping, whooping warriors, and the Indians, confused by this firestorm of lead and losing men, broke and streamed back to the valley.

They left six dead on the snow, their blood splashing red around them.

Fletcher and Charlie stepped out of the pueblo and walked toward the new arrivals, and beside him Fletcher heard Charlie's startled yelp of surprise.

One of the men was Sgt. Andy Wilson, the other Scarlet Hays.

And with that recognition the cold realization came to Fletcher that both had vowed to kill him.

"Well, well, well, fancy meeting you here," Hays said. "If it ain't the great Buck Fletcher." The gunman's fingers moved to his split lips. "Last time I seen you was at Fort Apache."

The threat was implied, and Fletcher took it as such.

"What are you doing here, Hays?" he asked as his eyes shaded to a cold gunmetal gray. Had this man come to murder Estelle?

The hatchet-faced gunman smiled, his teeth showing crooked and stained from chewing black plug tobacco. "Hell, we was driving south, heading down Nogales way, when we was jumped by Apaches. We came tearing in here and . . . well, here we are and there you are."

Acutely conscious of his empty guns, Fletcher said, "We're not out of the woods yet, Scar. Those young bucks will be back."

"Maybe so." Hays looked out at the Apache dead. "We hit 'em pretty hard, me and ol' Andy here."

Hays turned his head to the sergeant. "Oh, my sincere apologies; you two haven't been introduced. This is—"

"I know who he is," Fletcher said, cutting him off.

Wilson was a big man, huge in the shoulders and thick in the arms, his hands big-knuckled and scarred, the fighting mitts of a pugilist. His hair was cropped close to his head and a full cavalry mustache hung limp and untrimmed under a nose that had been broken many times. There was an air of casual, heedless brutality about the man, and this was reflected in his black, soulless eyes and the arrogant, aggressive way he held himself.

"We've met," Wilson said to Hays. He nodded at Fletcher. "Me and him have a score to settle, only this time he won't have a damn officer to hide behind."

Hays's smile was insolent as his fingers strayed to his lips again. "Yeah, well, we all got scores to settle, Andy."

Fletcher's eyes slid past Hays as though he was a thing of no importance and rested on the wagon.

"Pay wagon," Hays said, grinning. "Me and Andy here, we found it an' we're saving it for General Crook."

"Sure you are," Charlie said. "An' pigs fly."

If Hays was offended he didn't let it show. "Had three other boys with me, but they never showed," he said. "Told them to catch up, but they didn't."

"They're dead," Fletcher said. "Apaches got Clevinger and Gittings, and the Kid drew down on me."

"The Kid was greased-lightning fast," Hays said.

"I was faster," Fletcher said.

The disciples had poured out of the pueblo and, curious, surrounded the pay wagon, Estelle among them.

Hays saw the girl and a thin smile tightened his mouth.

"That's how I like them," he said to Wilson out of the corner of his mouth. "Once they swell they're available all the time, and they're all big butt and bobbers."

As Wilson guffawed, Hays set his derby hat at a jaunty angle and stepped beside Estelle. "How do, pretty lady?"

The girl looked at Hays and didn't like what she was seeing, and her eyes grew wide with something akin to fear.

"Hey, Scar," Charlie said, "that woman just lost her husband."

"Well, ain't it just too bad." Hays grinned. "Now she needs a real man to look after her."

Estelle tried to walk back to the pueblo, but Hays blocked her path. "Please step aside," she said. "I'm tired and I must rest."

Hays's face was ugly. "Don't you come the high-and-mighty fine Eastern lady with me," he said. "I got a feeling you and me is going to be heading down Nogales way together, an' that's a lot better than me leaving you to the Apaches. Well, some better, at least."

The girl's eyes held both fear and loathing, and Fletcher decided he could not let it go any further. "Let her be, Scar," he said.

The gunman whirled, his hands above his Colts, his eyes blazing with hate and fury.

Fletcher stood easy and relaxed, even as he knew he was running a desperate, dangerous bluff with empty guns. "Don't try it, Scar. You won't even clear the leather."

Hays thought about it—and for a single heart-pounding moment Fletcher believed he would say the hell with it and make the play.

But slowly the gunman relaxed, his fingers unclawing. "Damn you, Fletcher," he snarled, "once this is over and the Apaches have cleared out, me and you will go at it."

He turned to Estelle. "And you," he said, "pack a bag."

As the long day stretched into evening, there were no further attacks, though Charlie and Fletcher stood at the window of their room, empty rifles cradled in their arms.

Hays had vanished into one of the other rooms in the pueblo, but Wilson stood outside near the wagon, alert and watching the night.

Charlie nodded in the man's direction. "You figure the sergeant there tipped off ol' Scar about the pay wagon?"

"I'm willing to bet that's what happened," Fletcher said.

"I would say he was one of the escort and it was him who killed the major and the young trooper."

"How much do you reckon is in there?" Charlie asked.

Fletcher shrugged. "There's the best part of three cavalry regiments in the basin, not counting scouts. I'd say thirty thousand dollars, maybe more."

Charlie whistled. "Ol' Scar could have a time with that down in Nogales."

"He sure could." Fletcher nodded, saying one thing, thinking another.

"What's on your mind, Buck?" Charlie asked.

"Charlie, we've got to get some ammunition," Fletcher said. "We're powerless against Hays and Wilson with empty guns. When it comes right down to it, I don't want to go up against Scar's Colts when all I can do is throw rocks at him."

"Both them boys are carrying .44.40 Winchesters like yours, and Scar's revolvers are .45s," Charlie said. "That's where the cartridges be, if'n you can get to them."

"Getting to them, that's the problem," Fletcher said. "We can't tell Hays our guns are empty. He'd kill us both without even giving it a thought."

Charlie was silent for a few moments, then slapped the side of his head. "Buck, what we thinking about! There are all kinds of dead Apaches out there and they've got cartridge belts. Got to be our caliber among them."

Fletcher looked at Charlie, thinking it through. "Don't the Apaches always carry off their dead?" he asked finally.

"Mostly they do, but I'm betting those young bucks are still lying out there. I don't think the rest of them warriors will want to be slowed down by dead men until they take the pueblo, not with Georgie Crook's flying columns out after every Apache in the basin."

Fletcher nodded. "It's worth a try."

"Damn right it is." Charlie grinned.

The two men stepped out of the pueblo into the darkness. Behind them the windows glowed yellow from the light of oil lamps and candles, and Fletcher thought he heard Hays drunkenly yell something and then fall silent.

"Mescal," Charlie whispered.

"You heard him too, huh?"

"Ol' Scar, he's a terror when he's drinking," Charlie said. "You don't want to be around him, and you don't want your womenfolk around him either."

Off to their left, Wilson stood guard at the wagon, his Winchester in his arms. He was turned toward the sound of Hays and didn't look in the direction of Charlie and Fletcher as, crouching low, they made their way across the snow-covered flat.

The dead warriors were still there. Or at least one was, the prostrate form Charlie tripped over in the darkness.

The Apache was young, no more than sixteen by the look of his smooth face, but he had apparently not yet participated in enough raids to acquire a rifle. A quiver of arrows slanted across his back and his bow, the Osage wood shattered by a bullet, lay a few feet away.

Charlie motioned silently and he crept in the direction he'd pointed, Fletcher following. Another warrior lay flat in his back, the top of his head blown away. But this man wore a cartridge belt across his chest and another circled his hips.

"Hell, Buck," Charlie whispered, "we're in business."

Both belts held .44.40 shells, and Charlie and Fletcher quickly loaded their rifles and stuffed the remaining rounds into their pockets.

A search of the other bodies turned up just one belt of .45s, but it was enough for Fletcher to load both his Colts and fill half the loops in his gun belt.

Above them the clouds had parted and the moon rode high in the sky. The snow had been replaced by a hard frost and the breath of both men smoked misty white in the cold air.

"It's sure quiet out here," Charlie whispered. "You reckon maybe them Apaches decided enough was enough and pulled out?"

Fletcher shrugged. "I guess there's one way to find out." He nodded to the hill looming above them. "From up there."

He walked to the hill and began to climb, Charlie close behind him.

They reached the pines and moved through the restless trees to the western slope overlooking the valley. Fletcher dropped to his belly and studied the valley below.

Charlie dropped beside him. "See anything?"

"It's what I don't see that cheers me some," Fletcher answered. "I don't see any horses down there or men either. I think they've skedaddled."

"When?" Charlie asked. "*Más temprano?*"

"Yeah, much earlier. I think maybe right after Hays and Wilson arrived and they lost those six warriors."

Fletcher rose to his feet. "Let's go down there, Charlie. But step nice and easy."

The two men made their way down the slopes, rifles at the ready. But there was no need. The Apaches were gone.

Only the Chosen One remained.

Sixteen

The Chosen One hung between two closely growing cottonwoods, his spread out arms lashed to the trunks.

Before lapsing into agonized incoherence, he had preached to the Apaches of Christ crucified, and that had given the young warriors an idea. A braided grass rope had been rammed down on his head, its entire length spiked with a tangle of vicious cholla thorns, and blood from the wounds had dried in dull red streaks over his face and shoulders.

Hundreds of dry ocotillo thorns, slender and sharp, had been stuck all over his body and one by one had been set alight, burning down to the flesh, each one marked by a circle of black, scorched skin.

Fletcher counted seventeen arrows sticking out of the Chosen One's body, and each had struck a spot where it could inflict the most pain without killing. And finally, apparently impressed by his endurance, the Apaches had mercifully cut the man's throat before riding away.

Charlie looked over what was left of the Chosen One and spat. "That's a hell of a way for a man to die."

Fletcher nodded, his face grim. "Cut him down from there."

Charlie drew his bowie knife and did as he was told. "Now what?"

"Now we carry him back to the pueblo. I think it's time

Estelle and the rest of those people realize the Chosen One isn't coming back."

"Ain't that a shade harsh, Buck?"

"Maybe, but it's a sight better than staying here to be slaughtered by any Apache war band that happens to be riding by."

The Chosen One was a big man, and heavy, and both Charlie and Fletcher were breathing hard by the time they carried him to the pueblo.

Around them the disciples gathered, looking down at their fallen leader, his shattered body lit by the lanterns they carried. The people were silent, each knowing that there would be no resurrection, that this was the end of whatever strange, unreal dreams they had harbored.

Estelle stepped out of the pueblo and dropped to her knees beside her dead husband. "Come back," she whispered, tears streaming down her cheeks. "Come back to us."

Scarlet Hays, drunk and belligerent, clutching a jug of mescal, glanced down with bleary eyes at Estelle. "Don't you go grieving for him, woman," he said. "Tomorrow you're leaving with me."

"Let her be, Hays," Fletcher said, anger rising in him.

The gunman shrugged. "Just so you got it clear, Fletcher. She's riding out with me in the morning."

At that moment, Fletcher realized two things.

The first was that Hays had not been sent here by Falcon Stark to kill the girl. You don't plan to hold on to a woman you've been paid to murder. Hays had stolen the pay wagon and he'd told the truth about heading for Nogales, and only a wry twist of fate—and the Apaches—had brought him here to the pueblo.

The second was that Hays and Wilson would surely try to kill him before they left.

Women clustered around Estelle, their natural empathy

for another female's grief overriding their feelings of betrayal.

The girl was led, sobbing, into the pueblo, her face and the front of her dress stained red from her husband's blood. She looked to be all eyes, dark circles under them indicating a lack of sleep and her sorrow.

"You men," Fletcher said, "bury this man with the others."

They hesitated, and Fletcher said again, "Hell, you can't let him just lie there."

One of the men, younger than the rest, left and returned with a shovel, and this galvanized the others into action. A couple of the men lifted the body and carried it toward the burial place, and the remainder reluctantly followed.

"I'd say Mr. Chosen ain't gonna get much of a send off," Charlie said, spitting into the snow.

"They put their trust in the Chosen One and now they feel he deceived them," Fletcher said. "Not only about the Apaches but about doomsday itself. It's a bitter pill for anybody to swallow."

Charlie was silent for a moment, then said, "Buck, I don't think ol' Scar was sent here to kill Estelle. He wants that woman too bad for his ownself."

"I'd already come to that conclusion, Charlie."

"So what happens now?"

Fletcher shrugged. "I wish I knew."

"You could ride with her to Fort Apache, have her talk to Crook."

"About what? That her father hates her? I'd say that isn't going to cut any ice with Crook. Without proof that Stark is trying to murder his daughter, it would be my word against his." He turned to Charlie with bleak eyes. "If you were Crook, whose word would you take?"

Charlie nodded. "I see what you mean."

The old man hesitated, and Fletcher saw that he was trying to say something he couldn't quite frame into words.

"Let's hear it, Charlie. I got time."

"Damn, Buck, you always seem to know what I'm thinking."

"I'd say you were thinking about Scarlet Hays."

Charlie nodded. "I think he means to kill you."

"So do I, Charlie."

The men returned from burying the Chosen One, and gradually the pueblo fell silent. The women had done all they could for Estelle, and now they left her alone with her grief.

Fletcher and Charlie lay on mats in their room, their weapons close to hand.

Out in the darkness, unheard by those in the pueblo, a gray horse tossed its head, jangling the bit, and saddle leather creaked.

The night gathered around the cliff, and pack rats scurried in the upper pueblos. From the pines on the hill an owl asked a question of the horned moon and patiently repeated it again and again. The air was chill, heavy with frost, and a few stars glittered with a hard light, distant lanterns illuminating the way across an infinite universe.

Fletcher dozed, then woke with a start.

Had he heard something?

He lay on his mat, listening. Now he heard it again, a woman's sharp, frightened gasp, scarce begun before it was muffled.

Charlie was asleep, his rifle lying in his left arm.

Fletcher rose, pulled back the door curtain, and stepped into the darkness.

From somewhere to his left he heard a scuffle of feet and a man's voice, low and husky, but angry and slurred.

It was the voice of Scarlet Hays—and Estelle's room was in that direction. Fletcher sprinted across the snow, past the front of the sleeping pueblo. When he reached Estelle's room he slowed, then stepped to the window and looked inside.

The girl was naked, soapy water on her breasts and shoulders, and at her feet a large pottery basin and a sponge.

Hays had Estelle pinned against the wall, his left hand across her mouth, the other roaming all over her swollen body, exploring.

"You ain't gonna miss it one bit, little lady," he said, his voice hoarse with lust. "It ain't like you've never been done plenty times afore."

Hays fumbled with the buttons on his pants, and above his hand Estelle's eyes were huge and terrified.

He'd seen enough.

Fletcher threw back the door curtain and stepped quickly inside. His voice cut across the silence like the sharp blade of a knife. "Let her be, Hays."

The gunman whirled, the front of his shirt damp, and Estelle stepped away, catching up her bloodstained dress, holding it in front of her.

"Damn you, Fletcher," Hays said, "this is the last time you meddle in my affairs."

The gunman had been drunk earlier, but now he seemed stone-cold sober and dangerous. His hands were close to his guns, and in the shadow of his derby hat his eyes were glinting chips of ice.

"Walk away from it, Scar," Fletcher said. "Walk away from it now and we'll talk about it later."

"There ain't gonna be a later, Fletcher, at least not for you."

And Scarlet Hays drew.

His gun was out of the leather, leveling as he thumbed back the hammer, when Fletcher's first bullet crashed into his chest. Hays's eyes went big and he slammed against the wall, tipping over the basin at his feet, water splashing across his boots.

Hays shouldered off the wall, his gun coming up, and Fletcher fired again, the bullet hitting him an inch above his belt buckle. Hays screamed in terrible fury, desperately trying to lift a gun that now seemed too heavy for him, and Fletcher fired again and again.

The butt of Hays's Colt slipped out of his hand and the gun turned around on his trigger finger, then dropped to the floor. His eyes wild and staring, Hays took a step or two toward Fletcher, a strange grunting sound escaping his throat; then his legs buckled and he fell on his face.

His gun ready, Fletcher turned the gunman over with the toe of his boot. But there was no need for another shot.

Scarlet Hays was dead.

Fletcher punched the empty shells from his gun and reloaded from his gun belt. He looked at Estelle. "Are you all right?"

The girl nodded, her eyes huge and frightened as she looked down at the dead gunman.

People began to crowd into the room, and Fletcher walked through them and stepped outside. Andy Wilson was walking from the wagon, his rifle in his hands.

"Where's Scar?" he asked.

"Dead," Fletcher said, his voice flat.

Wilson read what had happened in Fletcher's eyes and didn't like what he saw. He laid the rifle at his feet, spread his hands wide, and said, "I ain't in this, Fletcher. I didn't know she was your woman."

"Oh, shut the hell up," Fletcher said, anger filling the emptiness inside him.

Charlie had walked into Estelle's room, and now he stepped to Fletcher's side.

"Damn it, Buck, you shot ol' Scar all to rag dolls," he said, grinning.

Fletcher ignored Charlie and said to Wilson: "You can catch up one of those Apache ponies wandering loose out there and leave here at first light. I reckon the army will catch up to you eventually and hang you."

Wilson's eyes slid to the wagon and Fletcher said, "That stays right here."

The sergeant bent to pick up his rifle but Fletcher's voice stopped him. "So does that."

Wilson straightened, swallowed hard, and nodded. "Anything you say, Mr. Fletcher. I'm not hunting trouble."

The man turned on his heel and walked away into the darkness.

Charlie put a hand on Fletcher's shoulder. "Buck, why don't you get some sleep. Me, I'm gonna stand guard on that wagon until daybreak so Wilson doesn't get any ideas."

Fletcher's eyes went to Estelle's room, where Hays lay, and Charlie said, "Don't worry; I'll take care of that." The mountain man smiled. "It will be a doggone pleasure to plant ol' Scar at last."

Suddenly weary, Fletcher nodded. "Thanks, Charlie. Wake me before first light so I can bid our friend Wilson a fond farewell."

Fletcher went to his room in the pueblo, stretched out on his mat, and within moments was asleep.

When he woke it was still dark, though when he looked out the window there was a suggestion of gray in the sky to the east.

Fletcher built a smoke from his dwindling supply of tobacco, a fact that gave him a twinge of concern, lit the cigarette, and stepped outside.

It was cold and he pulled the sheepskin collar of his mackinaw around his ears and walked toward the wagon, calling out softly for Charlie.

There was no answer.

"Some guard," Fletcher muttered to himself, smiling. "Probably sound asleep."

Charlie Moore was asleep. But it was a sleep from which he'd never waken.

The old mountain man lay flat on his face by the wagon, an 1860 model cavalry saber, useless against Apaches but an efficient murder weapon, sticking out of his back. The tracks of Andy Wilson's regulation boots lay around Charlie's body and led to the back of the pay wagon.

Fletcher pulled the saber free and turned Charlie over onto his back. The old man's eyes were closed and a slight smile showed on his mouth under his beard.

Fletcher knelt and placed the palm of his hand on Charlie's chest. There was no heartbeat, and death had already changed the tone of his skin and deepened the wrinkles around his eyes.

Charlie Moore was seven feet tall and wide in the shoulders, but now, somehow, he looked small and shrunken.

Rising, a terrible rage in him, Fletcher opened the back of the wagon and looked inside. The soldiers were paid mostly in paper money, and most of the sacks had been taken.

He left Charlie where he was and checked on the horses. The old man's mustang still grazed on a patch of thin winter grass, but Fletcher's big American stud was gone.

When he returned to Charlie's body there were a few people gathered around and a couple of the men helped him carry the old man into a room in the pueblo.

"Let him lie there," Fletcher said. "I'll be back for him."

"We can bury him," a man with tired, red-rimmed eyes said. "God knows we've put enough to rest around here."

Fletcher's face was hard and unyielding; he refused, at

least for now, to give in to his grief. "I'll kill any man who tries to bury him," he said. "I told you I'd be back for him."

The men around him drew back a step or two, reading his face, and the man with tired eyes said, "He'll be here, waiting for you."

"Make sure that he is," Fletcher said.

He walked outside, went to his room, and caught up his rifle. Then he saddled Charlie's horse, swung wide of the pueblo cliff and followed a trail of fresh horse tracks in the snow.

He was going to kill Andy Wilson.

With his bare hands.

Seventeen

Wilson's tracks led due south, toward the Gila River.

Fletcher calculated the man had maybe a four-hour start on him, but he was riding a stud with a distance-eating stride and that was no small thing.

Fletcher rode alert and ready in the saddle, his rifle across the horn, wary of an ambush.

This was mostly rolling hill country coming off the southern reaches of the Mazatzals, but beyond the Gila lay the Pinaleno, Santa Catarina, Santa Rita, Huachuca, and Chiricahua ranges, their rugged slopes thickly covered in pine, cedar, and juniper, and once among those peaks a man could lose himself forever if need be.

Fletcher put himself in Wilson's position, trying to guess the moves he'd make. He came to the conclusion the man would not veer from his set trail and continue to head due south, hoping to make Nogales and beyond that Mexico.

He rode on, the rage inside him replaced by a grim determination to stick to Wilson's trail no matter what happened.

For several miles there was no sound but the footfalls of Fletcher's mustang and the creak of saddle leather. Around him were the pine-covered hills, here and there vast outcroppings of ancient volcanic rock showing red or gray against the green.

Within view of Iron Mountain, Fletcher splashed into a shallow creek and let his horse drink, then urged the little mustang forward again.

Toward noon, as he topped a steep rise, the sun felt warm on his back, melting the frost from his bones. Above his head a buzzard turned lazy circles in the air, its wings hardly beating, and once a brown bear, wakened from hibernation, glared at him, sending him on his way with a surly growl as he rode by.

The mustang was tough and enduring and showed no sign of slacking his pace as the day wore on and the sun dropped lower in the sky.

Wilson's tracks in the snow were easy to follow, since nothing else was moving across that vast land. The coyotes, wolves, and deer and elk that were their prey had moved higher into the mountains with the coming of the first snows and would not be seen again until spring.

But once as the day was fading, Fletcher glanced at his back trail and thought he saw a flicker of gray vanish among the pines at the base of a saddleback rise.

Had an elk come down to graze lower on the slopes? Or was it a hunting wolf?

Fletcher rode on, dismissing the incident from his mind.

It had been an elk, nothing more.

The day shaded into night and Wilson's tracks became harder to follow. But Fletcher rode south, reading the man's mind.

Wilson would keep on riding through the night, not daring to stop, and Fletcher would follow.

The sky was clear but for a band of black cloud, and around it the night birds were pecking at the first stars. It had grown colder and Fletcher huddled in his mackinaw, thinking of hot coffee and blankets by the fire, both of them as out of reach as the stars above him.

A long wind, blowing chill from the north, teased the

surrounding pines, bringing with it a few scattered flakes of snow.

Reluctantly, knowing it was his last, Fletcher stopped in the shelter of some trailside spruce and built a thin cigarette with the remaining few shreds of his tobacco.

He smoked gratefully until the cigarette burned to his fingers, then, with a pang of regret, dropped the butt into the snow.

Fletcher swung the mustang again to the south, his breath steaming around his mouth in the cold air, and rode deeper into the night.

At one point he lost his way and had to backtrack for an hour after he found that he'd ridden into a wide box canyon. He rode out of the canyon, then swung south again, and after a couple of miles he caught a glimpse of Wilson's tracks. They led down a shallow rise and onto a wide, tree-rimmed, and snow-covered valley that was probably carpeted thick with sage and black grama grass in the spring.

Fletcher rode down the rise and reached the valley floor. He swung out of the saddle and cast around looking for tracks. After a few minutes he found them, angling across the valley toward a long line of spruce and cedar.

Was that a lantern bobbing among the trees?

Fletcher wiped the back of his hand across tired eyes and looked again. What he saw was just a pinpoint of light against the surrounding darkness, a light that flickered among the pines.

It was a campfire!

Fletcher shook his head. It couldn't be Wilson. The man didn't shape up to be that stupid . . . or confident.

Or did he?

Fletcher recalled Wilson's arrogance when he first arrived at the pueblo. Did he think that no one would dare follow him into this wilderness?

It was possible, Fletcher decided. Unlikely, perhaps, but possible.

There was also the chance that he was seeing an Apache fire, and if that was the case, he'd be in a world of trouble if he rode closer.

Fletcher sat his horse, turning the probabilities over in his mind, then came to a decision.

Maybe it was Wilson and maybe it was not. He had to find out for sure.

Fletcher urged his horse forward, trusting to the dark to keep him hidden, angling across the valley to a point among the trees just to the north of the fire. When he reached the pines he swung out of the saddle and led the horse among the close-growing trunks. Thick brush lay underfoot, some of it covered by areas of snow, and here and there tufts of coarse, yellowish grass stubbornly shoved up from the ground.

Fletcher left the mustang—far from a picky eater—near a patch of this grass and slid his rifle out of the boot. He unbuckled his spurs and hung them on the saddle horn and on silent feet made his way through the trees toward the fire. It was rough going in the darkness, and thorns and brush tugged at him, slowing him down.

He crept closer to the campfire, now dying to an orange glow in the darkness.

Closer still.

Wilson sat with his back against a tree in a small clearing among the trees and he did not look up when Fletcher stepped into the circle of the firelight, his rifle pointing at the man's chest.

"Get on your feet, Wilson," he said, his anger flaring. "I intend to beat you to within an inch of your life, then turn you over to the army. That is, if you're lucky."

The man didn't answer, but kept his stony gaze on the guttering fire.

Fletcher stepped closer and kicked the man's feet and Wilson slid to his left, his head hitting the ground with a thud. Something small and white slid off his chest and landed beside him.

Wilson's eyes were wide open, shocked and unbelieving, and he was dead.

The handle of a bowie knife stuck out from his back, its eight-inch blade buried deep between his shoulder blades.

Fletcher bent and picked up the white object that had fallen from Wilson's chest. It was a sack of Bull Durham tobacco rolled up in a piece of paper, and on the paper Fletcher read the hastily scrawled, penciled words: *I knowed you was out of tabbaka.*

Fletcher looked around at the surrounding trees, his knuckles whitening on his Winchester. But there was only silence and the mocking rustle of the wind among the pine branches.

Someone had beaten him to Wilson. But how?

Then he recalled the box canyon that had cost him an hour. Whoever had killed Wilson had taken advantage of that lost time to get to the man first.

The other question running through Fletcher's mind was, Who?

Old Charlie had told him maybe he had a guardian angel, but angels didn't go around sticking bowie knives into people's backs, even into the back of a lowlife like Andy Wilson.

Fletcher felt his skin crawl. This was not the work of an angel. Wilson had been murdered quietly and efficiently by someone who knew his business.

This was more the work of a devil, and Fletcher had a feeling that down the line the man would exact his price—and then there would be hell to pay.

Fletcher was not one to look a gift horse in the mouth,

especially when it came to tobacco. He rolled a smoke, then lit his cigarette with a brand from the fire.

Wilson's battered coffeepot had been neatly pushed to the side of the flames, where it would stay warm without boiling further, and the same thing had been done with several strips of thick bacon, each cooked and skewered on its own stick.

After he'd finished his cigarette, Fletcher poured coffee into a cup that was lying nearby and ate the bacon.

After he finished eating he looked around Wilson's camp. The money sacks were gone but Fletcher's stud was tethered back in the trees and seemed to be in good shape for the trail.

There were tracks in the patches of snow surrounding the camp, mostly of Wilson's cavalry boots, but here and there were the smaller, neater footprints of a man wearing high-heeled boots, the heel underslung and the toe squared off in the current Texas fashion.

Fletcher poured himself another cup of coffee, smoked a cigarette, then, after a last, cold look at Wilson's body, led his stud out of the trees, swung into the saddle, and rode back for the mustang.

He had to get back to the pueblo.

There was a burying to do.

As the night brightened into morning and even before the pueblo came in sight, Fletcher knew something was wrong.

Like a man can tell by a sudden shift in the atmosphere that a thunderstorm is due, he sensed the taut, strung-out tension in the air.

Fletcher spurred his stud, trailing Charlie's mustang after him, and worked his way around the southern rim of the hill and rode out into the flat in front of the cliff.

He swung the stud toward the pueblo just as several people left the building and came toward him.

As he reined up the woman who wore her hair in a long braid stepped close to him, a fluttering piece of paper in her hand.

"Estelle is gone," the woman said. "Two men came here just before sunup and took her. One of them left you this."

She handed the paper to Fletcher. It was written in the same hand as the one left on Wilson's body, and the spelling was just as bad.

Fletcher—We have the girl.
Kum and get hur
If you want hur

Fletcher read the note, then looked down at the woman. "What did these men look like?"

The woman shrugged. "What does any man look like? One was big and bearded, the other smaller and meaner and he did all the talking. They both wore big Texas sombreros like yours . . . and had guns like yours." The woman hesitated, then said, "The men said you should head northwest toward Mazatzal Peak."

Fletcher sat his saddle and thought this through.

The men who had taken Estelle badly wanted him to go after her. The question was why?

There was only one possible answer: Falcon Stark had sent these men to the basin to kill his daughter, and they wanted to draw Fletcher to them when the deed was done.

A quick bullet in the back; then they could tell General Crook that Buck Fletcher had murdered Estelle, that they'd caught him in the act and killed him after a desperate gun battle.

It was neat, efficient, and well planned. And it was typical of Senator Falcon Stark's warped thinking.

Any man who would sacrifice his own daughter to preserve his reputation and keep alive his hopes for the presidency had to be insane.

It wasn't power that had corrupted Stark—it was the wielding of that power, and with it the knowledge that he could crush anyone who stood in his way and if necessary move mountains to achieve his aims.

He had patiently set up Fletcher for the murder of a sheriff, worked behind the scenes to make sure he was convicted and sent to prison, then had him quickly released so Estelle's murder could be blamed on a notorious gunfighter out for revenge.

There were loose ends to be tied up for sure, like taking care of the soldiers who had escorted Fletcher to Lexington. But those men were only pawns to be moved across Stark's chessboard and sacrificed when the time came.

Such a man should never become president of the United States, and Fletcher, though he realized he was just another pawn, vowed he would do everything he could to stop Stark—even at the cost of his own life.

A man was talking to him, and Fletcher swung his mind back to the here and now.

". . . so what do you want to do? Do you want us to help you bury the old man?"

Fletcher looked down at the man from the saddle. "No," he said, "I'll lay him to rest." He nodded toward the highest pueblo. "Up there."

"What? Are you crazy?" the man asked, his face shocked. "Man, that's six hundred and fifty feet, and it's almost straight up."

"Charlie didn't want to be buried in the ground," Fletcher said, his voice even. "He wanted to lie where he could see the stars. Well, he can see the stars from up there."

The man shook his head. "Mister, we're all pulling out

of here in an hour. There's nothing to hold us here now except memories of death and lies." He shrugged. "You're on your own."

Fletcher smiled, bringing a fleeting softness to his hard, tough, and unhandsome features. "Charlie would have it no other way."

Fletcher unsaddled the horses and staked them out on the grass. He was kicking aside as much of the snow as he could when the man he'd spoken to earlier brought a bucket of grain, saying that was the last of it, and Fletcher divided it between the horses.

He had to go after Estelle, no matter what the risk. But that would have to wait. He would take care of Charlie first.

The old mountain man lay wrapped in a blanket in one of the empty rooms in the pueblo.

Fletcher lifted the blanket from Charlie's face. The aging of death was on him, and its quiet. A strand of gray hair had fallen over Charlie's forehead, and Fletcher gently pushed it back into place.

"Old-timer," he whispered, "you and me have a journey to take."

Fletcher was a big man, and strong, but even so Charlie Moore was a heavy burden.

The path to the uppermost pueblo, once climbed by the Salado Indians who had lived here hundreds of years in the past, wound up the steep canyon hillside through a thick forest of saguaro, cholla, palo verde, and ocotillo cactus.

Charlie lay across Fletcher's shoulder, but the climb was long and hard, and Fletcher's legs were soon scraped by hundreds of thorns. Despite the cold of the morning, sweat trickled down his back and stung his eyes.

Fletcher stopped and gently laid Charlie on a patch of brush clear of cactus and shrugged out of his mackinaw.

He laid the coat on the path where he would find it on the way down and wiped sweat from his forehead.

"Old-timer," he said, breathing heavily, "you really set me a task."

He picked up Charlie again and climbed higher.

Three hundred and fifty feet above the canyon floor, Fletcher reached ruins set into an alcove in the cliff. He counted sixteen ground-floor rooms and three on a second story.

Fletcher carried Charlie into one of the rooms and set him on hard mud floor. He stepped to the doorway and saw the canyon spread out below him, the hill opposite covered in pine, snow whitening their branches.

He rolled a smoke and stood in the doorway, enjoying the stillness and rugged beauty of the morning. Out there somewhere was Estelle Stark, and the girl was in deadly danger. He would have to go after her and face the two men who had taken her.

It would not be easy, and before it was over he might be as dead as old Charlie lying cold and quiet behind him.

Fletcher finished his cigarette and ground out the butt under his heel.

"Hell," he said aloud, "it's just another hill to climb."

He went back into the room and picked up Charlie again.

Now the slope rose steeper and the way harder.

Fletcher slipped and fell heavily, and Charlie's body rolled away from him, tumbled among the cholla cactus, and came to rest at the base of a giant saguaro.

He walked back down the slope and sat beside Charlie, his breath coming in great, gulping gasps as the air around him thinned.

But there could be no stopping. Not yet.

Wearily, Fletcher again hoisted his burden onto his shoulder. He glanced up at the ruins two hundred feet above him, set into a shallow cavelike depression in the cliff.

The distance seemed impossible, but he set his chin and climbed, placing one foot in front of the other like a mechanical man, climbing . . . climbing higher . . . and higher . . .

His legs shaking from the ascent and the strain of Charlie's great weight, Fletcher reached the upper ruins, a complex of thirty-two rectangular rooms, eight of them with a second story.

It was there Charlie would rest.

An ancient ladder still stood against the front wall of the pueblo, leading to one of the higher rooms. Fletcher put his foot on the first rung, testing its strength with his weight.

Old and dried-out though it was, the ladder held.

Fletcher shifted Charlie on his shoulder, holding the old man's body with his left arm, and climbed, taking it slowly, one rung at a time.

When he reached the roof he laid Charlie down as gently as he could and covered the old man with the blanket. The rocky overhang above the pueblo cut off the view of the sky, but Fletcher moved the blanket away from Charlie's face and turned the old man's head to the north.

"The stars are that way, Charlie," he said.

Fletcher was not a praying man, nor did he know any words to say. But he took off his hat and stood in silence with his head bowed.

After a while he replaced his hat, took one last look at Charlie, and said, "*Hasta luego*, old-timer."

Then he went down the ladder and down the slope and back to the flat.

Eighteen

When Fletcher descended to the canyon floor, the pueblo was deserted. The Chosen One's disciples were gone, their footprints tracking to the northeast, a tribe of nomads who had come to the pueblos in search of doomsday and their Lord's return but found only death, despair, and disillusionment.

One of them was riding—the one who had taken Charlie's horse—but Fletcher felt no inclination to go after him.

That would take too much time and he had none to spare.

He searched the pueblo and found a dozen roasted mescal cakes, and these he stuffed in the pockets of his mackinaw. The Apaches carried the flat, dry cakes as their principal means of sustenance on their periodic raids into Mexico. Tasting somewhat like boiled beets, the cakes were both filling and nutritious and they kept fresh for a long time.

Fletcher saddled the stud and swung out of the valley and headed toward the Mazatzal Peak, fifty hard, broken miles to the northwest.

The shadowed canyon country around him gradually gave way to the rolling, pine-covered foothills of the Mazatzals. Fletcher saw no open ground and everything around him was built on a vast scale, the boulders, the

trunks of the spruce, and the pine-choked ravines between the hills.

He had earlier picked up the tracks of two horses. One
left a deeper imprint, suggesting that the mount was carrying two riders, one of them presumably Estelle, surely
a jolting, uncomfortable ride for a pregnant woman.

Around noon Fletcher rode into a narrow divide between the hills where the trees stretched a canopy of
leaves on each side, almost blotting out the sky. A stream
ran through the length of the valley, one of the hundreds
of runoffs from the Salt River. Although sheets of pane
ice extended from each bank, the water bubbled free in
the middle over a mossy, pebbled bottom.

Fletcher let the stud drink, then led him to a patch of
grass and chokecherry within the tree canopy. He sat with
his back to a juniper and, without appetite, ate a couple of
the mescal cakes, then built and lit a cigarette.

It was peaceful here among the trees, the only sound
the rushing water and the breeze rustling among the
branches. When he looked up and caught a glimpse of the
sky through the pine needles it was blue and cloudless,
but the sun held no warmth and frost clung thick to the
north-facing bark of the tree trunks.

The air smelled fresh, of sage and cedar, and when
Fletcher tilted his nose to the wind he thought he could
detect the scent of buffalo grass buried under the snow.

He finished his cigarette, rose to his feet, and swung
into the saddle.

The men who had taken Estelle had also ridden
through this valley, perhaps not two hours before, and
Fletcher knew the time of reckoning was getting close.

Now, as he cleared the divide and worked his way
across hilly, broken country, he rode alert in the saddle,
his eyes never still.

Ahead of him in the distance he saw rugged Mazatzal

Peak, the foothills sweeping away from him, rising higher and higher to meet the mountain's lower slopes.

As Fletcher topped a low rise, the horse tracks stretched out in front of him and disappeared within the walls of a narrow, high-walled canyon about a quarter of a mile distant. A jumble of rocks was scattered on top of the canyon rim facing him, and here and there grew spruce, identifiable as dark arrowheads of green against the sky. To his right rose a gradual slope ending after thirty yards at a band of mixed pine and low-growing greasewood that in early summer would be covered in yellow blossoms.

The gulch seemed innocent and peaceful enough but Fletcher's survival instincts were clamoring. Something didn't seem right. . . .

He leaned over to slide the Winchester out of the boot—and that motion saved his life.

Fletcher felt the bullet burn across the side of his head before he heard the racket of the rifle.

Stunned, he toppled out of the saddle and hit the ground hard. Another bullet kicked up snow inches from his right leg; a third pounded into the ground close beside him.

He had to get away from here!

Fletcher climbed to his feet and stumbled toward the tree line, firing as he went, cranking and triggering the Winchester as he ran. He saw no target except for a fleeting puff of gray smoke atop the canyon wall. He fired at the smoke, then to the left and right of it, and kept running.

Without slowing his pace, Fletcher dived into the trees, landing headfirst in a wild blackberry bush that tore at his face and hands with vicious thorns. Fletcher rolled out of the bush and scrambled higher up the slope, taking up a position behind the wide trunk of a spruce. Heart pounding in his chest and dizzy from his head wound, he waited, the salty, metallic taste of blood in his mouth.

A slow ten minutes ticked past, and out in the snow where his horse stood, reins trailing, nothing moved.

A jay flapped into the tree beside Fletcher, saw him, and took exception to his presence, protesting noisily and furiously before it indignantly fluttered away.

Fletcher's horse pawed at the snow, seeking grass, and he heard its bit chink softly in the quiet.

Something was moving out there.

A huge, bearded man in a long buffalo-hide coat was walking out of the canyon, heading toward the horse. Beside him stepped a tall, thin man in a wide-brimmed black hat and sheepskin mackinaw, a red muffler wrapped loosely around his neck and the bottom half of his face.

But for Fletcher there was no mistaking that arrogant tilt of the head and the way the man wore his guns—it was Wes Slaughter.

As he studied the gunman, the dawning realization came to Fletcher that here was the guardian angel Charlie had spoken about. Everything Slaughter had done, from the shooting of the Apache back at pueblo to the killing of Andy Wilson, had been done to preserve Fletcher for this moment . . .

. . . the moment he could be killed alongside Estelle Stark and her father's vile scheme finally completed.

Was Estelle already dead? That seemed unlikely. Falcon Stark, such a meticulous planner, would want them both murdered at the same time.

Slaughter's voice rose among the trees where Fletcher knelt hidden.

"You sure you got him good, Woody? He looked right spry to me."

The man called Woody pointed at the surface of the

snow with his rifle muzzle. "See that blood, Wes? I tole you I hit him hard." The man pointed in the direction of the trees with his bearded chin. "He's probably in there dead, or dying."

Fletcher recognized the bearded man. He was Woody Barton, a sure-thing back shooter, scalp hunter, and piece of white trash out of the Cumberland Plateau country of Tennessee. His usual fee for a murder was fifty dollars, and he didn't much care if the victim was man, woman, or child.

Slaughter was talking again.

"You go in there and get him, damn it. I want Fletcher a-laying dead alongside that pregnant sow when we get Crook or one of his officers down here."

Barton hesitated. He was long on bullying those he considered weak or old or scared, but short enough on the courage to face a man like Buck Fletcher, even if he was wounded and dying.

"What if he ain't hurt so bad, Wes?" he asked. "I could be mistook."

"Then go in there and get him, or I swear, Woody, I'll gun you down myself." Slaughter took a step toward Barton. "Go ahead. Hell, I'll be right here covering you."

Fletcher saw Barton's throat bob under his beard as the man swallowed hard. But he walked slowly toward the trees, his rifle at a high port. A few feet away from the tree line he stopped and looked back at Slaughter.

"You got me covered real good, Wes?"

"Depend on it, Woody."

Woody Barton stepped into the trees, his head swiveling this way and that, knuckles white on the stock of his Henry.

"Wes," he called out without turning his head, "you still there?"

"Right behind you, Woody. Now go get Fletcher."

Barton started to climb the slope. He was about ten feet from Fletcher's position. Nine . . . eight . . . seven . . . six . . .

Fletcher stepped out from behind the spruce. "You looking for me, Woody?"

The man's rifle swung on Fletcher fast. But not nearly fast enough.

The Colt in Fletcher's right fist hammered, three shots so close together they sounded like one.

Each bullet hit Barton in the middle of the chest and the man screamed, his face wild, and he fell backward, crashing down the slope.

Fletcher threw himself to his right as Slaughter thumbed off a couple of quick shots into the trees, scattering branches and pine needles. Both missed.

Gray gunsmoke drifted through the trees as Fletcher crouched, heart thudding, and punched shells into the empty cylinders of his gun.

Behind him, higher up the slope, the jays were scattering, frightened by the gunfire, and something larger crashed through the underbrush in panicked flight.

"Woody!" Slaughter's hushed voice came from somewhere among the trees to Fletcher's right. "Are you there?"

"Poor Woody ain't with us no more, Wes," Fletcher said. "He caught a bad case of lead poisoning."

He quickly moved his position, moments before Slaughter sent another shot crashing into the trees where he'd been standing.

"Buck, did I get you?"

This time Fletcher didn't answer, knowing the gunman was using his voice to direct his shots.

A few minutes passed in silence; then Slaughter called out, "Buck, we don't have to snipe at each other. Let's me and you settle this thing like gentlemen."

"You're no gentleman, Wes. Or has nobody told you that before?"

Fletcher moved again. But this time there was no shot from Slaughter.

"Buck?"

"Yeah?"

"Know that sheriff you was blamed for shooting back to Wyoming?"

"Yeah?"

"Well, that was me, Buck. I got to the livery stable just before you did and put a bullet into that rube. Then I ran back to the saloon and spread it around that you'd just killed the sheriff. They caught you red-handed, Buck."

"How much did Stark pay you for that, Wes?"

"It were considerable. See, it wasn't something I could set up real easy, though Stark wanted it done real fast. After our little disagreement in Cheyenne, I had to follow you around for quite a spell, waiting for the right moment. Who was to know it would come in a hick cow town that didn't even have a name?"

"I got twenty years for that, Wes."

"I know, and all on account of me." There was a few moments' pause; then Slaughter said, "Now, knowing all that, why don't you come out and face me like a man instead of hiding in them trees like a damn lily-livered skunk?"

"How you want to play this, Wes?"

"Hell, man, the usual procedure. We meet face-to-face and make our play. Fastest man wins. Ain't that always the way of it, Buck?"

"That's always the way. At least it is with me."

"Well, come on down and I'll meet you out on the slope. Just you and me, Buck, the way it should be."

"I'm coming down."

Fletcher cleared his mackinaw from the holstered Colt

on his hip, letting it show. He drew the gun from the cross-draw holster, held it behind his back, and made his way down the slope to the edge of the tree line.

Fletcher stepped out of the trees, just as Slaughter appeared about twenty feet away, his rifle coming up fast to his shoulder.

The gun streaked from behind Fletcher's back and both men fired at the same time.

Slaughter's bullet tugged at Fletcher's mackinaw; then the gunman tried to work the lever again. He did not have the strength. Slowly he sank to his knees, his face chalk white and shocked, a scarlet stain widening on the front of his coat.

Fletcher stepped closer, his gun ready. Slaughter looked up at him, his mouth under his mustache twisting into a grim, agonized parody of a smile.

"Hell, Buck," he said, "you're just as downright lowdown and sneaky as I am."

"Not hardly," Fletcher said.

Blood stained Slaughter's lips and mustache, and his gray eyes were fading fast.

"You got the makings?" he whispered. "I reckon I left you some."

Fletcher's hand slipped under his mackinaw to his shirt pocket as Slaughter opened his mouth to speak again. But his words died with him and he pitched faceforward into the snow.

"Wes," Fletcher said, "you're right. I plumb forgot to thank you for the tobacco."

He stepped down the rise, gathered the reins of his horse, and walked toward the canyon.

Was Estelle still alive?

Fletcher led his horse into the ravine. He cupped a hand to his mouth and shouted the girl's name. There was no answer, just the bouncing echoes along the canyon walls repeating, "Estelle . . . Estelle . . . Estelle . . ."

Mocking him.

Rocks and thick brush carpeted the floor of the ravine. The horizontally growing Mexican mule clipper with its cruel thorns formed impassible barriers that Fletcher many times had to walk around. The going was slow, the footing treacherous, and his stud didn't like it one bit, jerking at the reins, irritably tossing his head.

But in the end it was the horse that led him to Estelle.

The big stud lifted his head, read what was written in the breeze, and whinnied. An answering call came from the canyon wall to Fletcher's right. He walked closer and discovered a shallow cave gouged out of the red rock, two horses standing close together, tethered to a fallen spruce.

Estelle was deeper in the cave, sitting with her back to the rock. She was bound hand and foot and her mouth was gagged by a filthy bandanna.

The girl's eyes were huge and frightened as Fletcher stepped closer. He knelt beside Estelle, found his pocketknife, and cut the ropes around her feet and wrists, then gently untied the bandanna.

"Are you all right?" he asked when the girl was free, knowing how totally inadequate it sounded.

Estelle nodded, saying nothing.

There was a canteen looped to the saddle horn of one of the horses. Fletcher stood, brought it to Estelle, and let her drink.

The girl swallowed a few sips, then said, "Please help me up."

Fletcher raised her to her feet and she clung to him desperately, despite her swelling belly that pressed awkward and hard against him.

"Those dreadful men . . ." she began.

"Dead," Fletcher said. "They can't hurt you anymore."

The girl raised her tearstained face to Fletcher's. "He must hate me very much. More than I ever knew."

Fletcher cast around in his mind for the right words, then said, "Your father seems to have a tremendous capacity for hate. It eats at him like a cancer."

Estelle's eyes searched Fletcher's face as though trying to find an answer to a question she had not yet asked. "But why all this? If he hates me so much why did he not just send someone to shoot me and get it over with? That man, that Woody, told me he'd have done it for fifty dollars."

Fletcher shook his head. "Estelle, that's not Falcon Stark's way. I think this was all a game with him. He had the power and he wanted to see how far it could take him. He wanted it to be efficient, neat, without leaving any loose ends."

Fletcher's smile was thin. "If Slaughter had accomplished what he set out to do, Woody Barton would never have left this canyon alive. He would have been passed off as another victim of the murderous Buck Fletcher."

"But why you, Buck?"

The girl's eyes were puzzled, her limited intelligence groping to understand the complex motives of a man with an intellect far greater than her own.

"Hate. It's not only that Falcon Stark hates me personally, though indeed he does; it's that he hates everything I stand for, men who make their living with a gun. He told me when he becomes president he'll rid the West of men like me, and the Indians too, and he meant every word of it."

"He'll never become president," Estelle said, her eyes blazing. "I won't let him."

Fletcher nodded. "Maybe so," he said, his voice totally lacking in conviction.

Estelle stepped back from him. "Where are my people?" she asked.

"There are no people, Estelle. They've all gone home. There's only one old man there, looking at the stars."

The girl stood in silence for a few moments, studying Fletcher, and with a rueful twinge he knew what she was seeing—a big, rawboned man, homely as a mud fence, his mustache holding up a great beak of a nose.

But to his surprise, Estelle leaned over and kissed him on the cheek. "Thank you for saving my life, Buck. And my baby's life."

Fletcher smiled. "Hell, I'd do it more often if that was my reward."

He hesitated, then said, "Estelle, I want to take you to Fort Apache. Your baby is due soon and you should be around womenfolk."

He'd expected Estelle to argue, to say she wanted to go back to the pueblo, but, like the others, it seemed her dream had died with the Chosen One.

"I'll tell General Crook all I know," she said. "Buck, I want justice for you—and for me."

One of the horses ridden by Slaughter and Barton was a mustang, the other a Montana-bred roan that went over sixteen hands. Fletcher unsaddled the mustang and let him go. There were wild horse herds in the basin and he'd make out.

The dead men had been well supplied with coffee and bacon, and these Fletcher stashed on the back of his saddle with his blanket roll.

That done, Fletcher looked over Estelle's swollen figure doubtfully. "Do you think you can ride that roan?" he asked.

"I can ride him," she said. "But you're going to have to help me up—and then let's just take it at a walk."

They were seventy-five miles from Fort Apache across rough and broken country swarming with hostile Apaches.

It was, Fletcher considered, going to be an interesting ride.

Nineteen

Three days later, without incident, Fletcher and Estelle crossed the Salt and as night was falling caught sight of the distant outline of Fort Apache.

Estelle rode slumped and weary in the saddle, her huge belly pressed against the horn.

Throughout the trip, the girl had been uncomplaining and undemanding, enduring much.

Born to great wealth and privilege, she had nonetheless shared Fletcher's overcooked bacon and muddy coffee without comment and had quietly tolerated his cigarette smoke, a small thing that had enormously raised her esteem in his eyes.

Now, as they made out the yellow glitter of the fort's oil lamps, Estelle swayed, her hand straying to her head, and Fletcher heard her whisper, "Buck . . . I . . . I don't feel very well."

Alarmed, Fletcher kneed his horse next to the girl's roan and she almost fell into his arms. Fletcher lifted her onto his own saddle, and when he glanced at her horse he saw blood trickling down the stirrup leathers.

Estelle's saddle was slick with blood, and when he touched the back of her dress his hand came away wet and red.

Fear spiking at him, not for himself but for the girl, he

spurred his stud toward the fort. Soldiers were running toward him and he yelled, "Get the post doctor!"

Fletcher reined up near Crook's headquarters as a man with gray hair walked quickly in his direction, pulling his suspenders up over his shoulders. The man had yellow cavalry stripes on his pants and carried a small black bag.

"Doctor?" Fletcher asked.

The man nodded. "Captain Milton, at your service."

Fletcher slid Estelle from the saddle into the doctor's arms. "This woman is very sick," he said.

Captain Milton, helped by a couple of soldiers, carried Estelle toward a cabin across the parade ground. Soon they were joined by several women who crowded around the girl, one plump, motherly-looking woman holding Estelle's hand as she walked beside her.

Fletcher sat his horse, watching them go, then reached into his shirt for the makings.

A door banged open to his left and Fletcher turned and saw Crook stomping toward him, his shirttails flying. "What in tarnation is all the fuss about?" he yelled.

The general stopped and looked up belligerently at Fletcher. Then a dawning recognition flared in his eyes.

"Officer of the guard!" Crook bellowed without turning his head. "Arrest that man!"

The hours hung heavy on Buck Fletcher.

He sat on the cot in the same cabin where he'd been held before. Only this time the guard was doubled and there would be no Charlie Moore at the window.

He'd been here for three days and already it felt like a lifetime.

Fletcher rose and looked up at the sky though the barred window. It had snowed earlier, but now the clouds had cleared and he could tell by the light that somewhere the sun was shining.

His only contact with the outside world was with the corporal who brought him his meals. But the man was sullen and uncommunicative and handed Fletcher his tin plate and cup without comment, taking them away later in the same silent manner.

Fletcher had asked the corporal for news of Estelle, but the soldier had ignored him.

Earlier that morning he'd bribed one of the privates who stood guard at the door to bring him tobacco from the sutler, and now he sat back on the cot again and began to build a smoke.

He rolled the cigarette slowly and carefully, the way of a man who knows he has all the time in the world.

Fletcher had smoked one cigarette and was considering building another, when the door slammed open and two soldiers, bayonets fixed, stepped inside and then made way for a young lieutenant.

"General Crook's compliments, and could he please see you in his office," the officer said.

Fletcher smiled at the hidebound military mentality. He'd once been a major in the United States Army, and because of that, despite being a prisoner, he was entitled to at least this much courtesy.

"I would be honored to see the general," Fletcher said, rising to his feet.

The lieutenant led the way across the parade ground, Fletcher boxed in by the four-man guard detail.

Crook sat behind his desk, wearing his canvas suit, and he waved Fletcher into a chair. This time there was no gun in evidence.

"How is Estelle?" Fletcher asked, the question that was uppermost in his mind.

The general shook his head. "Bad news, I'm afraid. She lost the baby. It would have been a boy, I'm told."

"And Estelle?"

"She's recovering. At least her body is. I'm not so sure about her mind."

Crook sat in silence for a few moments, studying Fletcher, his fingernails tapping a drumbeat on the desk. He seemed to make up his mind about something and said, "She's been making some very serious accusations, very serious accusations indeed."

Fletcher nodded. "About Falcon Stark, you mean?"

"Yes, about her father, a highly respected senator."

"What she told you is true. I know, because I was a part of it."

"The whole story seems highly unlikely. Why would a man go to all that trouble to kill his errant daughter?"

"Because he's Falcon Stark. He doesn't think like normal people, at least not like you, General, or me."

"Where's your proof, Fletcher?"

"What proof I had, a man named Weş Slaughter, is lying out there dead in the snow."

"Ah, yes, I know; Estelle told me that also."

Crook glanced out the window where a cavalry troop was trotting past, Indian scouts to the fore, then the fluttering red and white guidons.

He turned to Fletcher again and said, "She plans to travel to Lexington, you know. She says she wants to confront her father in front of witnesses and expose him." Crook shrugged. "A wild enough scheme, but, wilder still, she wants you to go with her."

"I'm a prisoner here," Fletcher said. "And that's surely stating the obvious."

Crook leaned over and reached inside a drawer on his desk.

"General," Fletcher said, his voice low and hard, "I'd take it kindly if you don't come up with a gun. You did that before and I didn't care for it then. I'd care for it even less now."

But Crook ignored Fletcher, and when his hand reappeared it was holding a small scrap of paper. "This arrived in a bunch of dispatches from Washington this morning. Most of them I ignore, since they're from deskbound warriors who know nothing about fighting Apaches. However, this one caught my eye. It's a routine message, sent out to army posts all over the country, and the only reason I read it was that the name Lt. Elisha Simpson jumped out at me."

"That's the young officer who escorted me to Lexington," Fletcher said.

"You'd better read it," Crook said.

Fletcher took the paper and read. It was short and couched in cold, formal military language.

On December 31, a six-man woodcutting detail of the Fourteenth Infantry was engaged by a renegade band of Sioux north of Fort Lyon in the Wyoming territory. The action occurred on the southern bend of Bear Trap Creek. Killed were Lt. Elisha Simpson, son of Col. William Simpson, Corp. James Pearson, and Privates John Gallagher, Jacob Hayden, Noble Engel, and Richard Cribbs.

Fletcher read the dispatch, read it again, then dropped it on the desk.

"I hardly think you can blame Senator Stark for that," Crook said, his right eyebrow crawling up his forehead.

"Perhaps not," Fletcher said. "But it makes me wonder if Lieutenant Simpson volunteered for the woodcutting detail. Or was he ordered out there on that creek with just five men? Stark's tentacles spread wide."

Crook shrugged. "I do not care to comment on that hypothesis. Fletcher, I have nine columns of cavalry in the field, and my business is fighting Apaches. I can't devote time to this matter, nor can I bring myself to fully believe what Estelle Stark has told me. Yet I must admit her words have the ring of sincerity about them and they've sown a seed of doubt about Senator Stark in my mind."

The general steepled his fingers. "I have given this some thought and I've prayed for guidance. As a result, I've decided to release you as of this moment. I just hope to God I'm doing the right thing."

"You won't regret it, General," Fletcher said. "An old Apache told me I'd face evil in the Tonto Basin, and I did. But I think the greater evil is not here—it's in Lexington."

"Then I hope to God you're right too," Crook said.

Fletcher asked a soldier the way to Estelle's cabin, and the man pointed out a low log building to the west of the parade ground.

"She's been living with the doc's wife," he said.

Fletcher crossed to the cabin and rapped on the door. The woman he'd seen take Estelle's hand opened the door and smiled. "Recognized you right off. You must be Buck Fletcher. Estelle's been asking for you."

The woman looked past Fletcher's shoulder, as though expecting to see something, and he smiled. "There's no guard. I've been released."

"Well, I'm glad to hear that for your sake," the woman said.

She led Fletcher into a bedroom off the parlor, and to his surprise Estelle herself answered his tap on the door. She was fully dressed in borrowed gingham a size too small for her, but she seemed rested and pretty, and her figure seemed almost back to normal.

Fletcher stood with his hat in his hands, curling the brim, a habit of his. Finally the words came to him. "I'm sorry about the baby," he said. "I took it hard."

Estelle raised her chin, her eyes angry. "My father

killed my son, just as surely as though he'd taken a knife and plunged it into my belly."

"Slaughter pushed you mighty fast and far," Fletcher said. "That was no ride for a pregnant lady."

"I want you to go to Lexington with me, Buck. I want to confront my father in front of witnesses and get him to confess what he's done."

"From what I've seen of the senator, that's a tall order," Fletcher said. "He doesn't seem the type to break down and 'fess up to his crimes."

"Then if that fails, I'll go to the newspapers. He told you he wanted no scandals; well, he's going to get plenty. When I'm finished with him and I'm through muddying the waters, he'll never be nominated for president."

Fletcher was silent for a few moments, then said, "General Crook told me you want me to go to Lexington with you."

"I'd like that, Buck. I'd like that very much. I want to clear your name too, you know."

"It's a long trip, Estelle. Are you sure you're up to it?"

"I have to be," the girl said. "For my murdered son's sake." She hesitated and rubbed away a tear falling on her cheek. "And for the sake of the Chosen One, his father."

Fletcher wanted to tell her that the Chosen One was at best delusional and at worst completely insane and that he'd caused the deaths of a lot of equally deluded people.

But he said none of these things.

"I have money," he said, biting back the bitter comments he so badly wanted to make, "enough to get us and our horses to Lexington and enough"—he smiled—"to buy you some clothes at the sutler's store."

Estelle nodded. "Thank you. But after I buy the things I need I want to leave here. I mean today."

Fletcher nodded. "So do I."

An hour later, his guns belatedly and reluctantly returned to him by Crook's adjutant, Fletcher rode out of Fort Apache, Estelle next to him wearing a new split riding skirt of canvas and a wool mackinaw.

It was snowing.

Twenty

A thick fog curled over Lexington, drifting off the Missouri, pooling yellow around the guttering gas lamps that lit the main streets of the city.

Carriages clattered along cobbled roads, the hooves of the horses clanging loud, and people on the sidewalks stepped hurriedly, coat collars pulled up against the clammy evening chill so only their eyes showed above red, pinched noses.

None spared a glance for the train that had brought Fletcher and Estelle on the last leg of their journey to Lexington.

The iron monster hissed and steamed, billowing white clouds escaping from under its wheels, competing with the fog.

Fletcher and Estelle coaxed their horses down the ramp from the boxcar and led them around the station and Main Street, the cold nipping at their faces and hands.

The horses had been a trial and a tribulation on a journey of close to a thousand miles that began on the northern side of the Mogollon Rim and had taken them across parts of New Mexico, Oklahoma, and Kansas.

Horses were difficult to transport and expensive to feed, and in the past nineteen days much more money had been spent on their grain than on food for Fletcher and Estelle.

But a man without a horse could not travel fast and far

if the need arose, and Fletcher had not sufficient money to buy another.

They'd traveled by train where they found a railhead, by stage where such was available, and by horseback where there was neither.

For hours they'd kicked their heels waiting at railroad stations that were sometimes no more than an old boxcar and water tank set at the end of a lonely spur, and all too often a stage ride represented cramped hours of jolting misery, choked by dust or frozen by cold winds, their horses trailing behind.

Through it all, Estelle had held up well, a sense of grim determination driving her.

Now she mounted her horse and gathered the reins. "I can sense him," she said to Fletcher. "I can feel his presence."

As for Fletcher, he felt only the chill that bit at him and the depressing lightness of the money belt around his waist.

In a few minutes he and Estelle would confront Falcon Stark. How would the man react? That he would break down and confess his transgressions in front of others, Fletcher doubted. More than likely he'd fight. But how?

Fletcher eased the guns in his holsters and decided to cross that particular bridge when he came to it.

Estelle led off, her big roan up on his toes, tossing his head, eager for the trail after being confined for four days in the boxcar. Fletcher trotted after her and together they made their way along Lexington's busy main thorough-fare, two riders lost amid the swirling fog and a churning, bobbing sea of carriages, wagons, other horsemen, darting pedestrians, and swaggering, half-drunk riverboat men, painted, hard-eyed women with scarlet mouths hanging on their arms.

Stark's house was as Fletcher remembered it, a sprawling white mansion fronting the street, every room aglow with lamps and candles.

He and Estelle tied their horses to the hitching posts, small black boys made of cast iron, resplendent in a livery of blue and yellow.

Fletcher followed Estelle to the door, recalling the last time he'd been here, a time that already seemed an eternity ago.

Estelle rapped on the door and a few moments later it was opened by the same high-nosed butler. The man stood there for a few moments, disdainfully looking them over, apparently not liking what he saw.

"Good evening, William," Estelle said finally.

It took the butler a while; then his frozen face melted into a smile. "Why, Miss Estelle! It's wonderful to see you again."

"Thank you, William," Estelle returned with the practiced, offhand ease of someone who grew up with servants.

The butler ushered the girl inside, reluctantly doing the same for the tall, grim, and unsmiling Fletcher.

"Mattie!" the man called out over his shoulder as he took Estelle's coat. "Mattie, Miss Estelle's home!"

The plump cook bustled out from the kitchen, grinned wide, and took Estelle in her arms, holding her tight in huge arms. "Honey," she said, when she finally let the breathless girl go, "I swear you're as skinny as a rail."

She turned to Fletcher. "I can see you ain't been eatin' too good either, young feller."

Fletcher opened his mouth to speak, but Estelle cut him off. "William, tell Father I want to see him in the library immediately, and I want you and Mattie there too."

The butler shook his head. "But the senator isn't here, Miss Estelle."

"Where is he?" Estelle asked, her face stricken.

"Why, he's in Kansas with the president, another senator, and a Russian nobleman and his lady," the man replied. "Shooting wild buffalo on the plains, I believe."

"Who's guiding them?" Fletcher asked, such things always of interest to him.

"A frontier person," the butler said, sniffing as his nose tilted higher. The man's forehead wrinkled as he tried to remember. "Ah, yes, a quite famous scout named Hitchcock."

"You mean Hickok? Wild Bill Hickok?"

"Yes, exactly, that's the person's name."

Fletcher shook his head and Estelle asked, "What's bothering you, Buck?"

"Nothing. It's just that Bill can be all kinds of trouble on a buffalo hunt or anywhere else. He's hard to handle."

"When did Father leave?" Estelle asked the butler.

"The day before yesterday," the man replied. "He and his guests took the early morning Union Pacific, bound for Fort Hays."

Estelle looked at Fletcher, her eyes bleak. "We've missed our chance."

"No, we haven't," Fletcher said. "Estelle, we're going after him."

The girl looked at him, puzzled, her slow thinking trying to catch up.

"Estelle, study on this—we wanted to confront your father and corner him into a confession. I still don't think it's going to happen, but if we'd managed to do it here tonight, any smart lawyer could later discredit the testimony of two servants, one of them a black cook. I don't think that could happen with President Grant and another senator."

Fletcher smiled. "And around Kansas, Wild Bill's word goes a long way."

Understanding dawned on the girl and she nodded enthusiastically. "Of course, that's so much better."

Fletcher put a hand on her shoulder. "Just don't get your

hopes up, Estelle. Like I just said, I don't think it's going to happen."

The butler and Mattie had been following this exchange, their faces showing growing bafflement, but it was the cook who brought it to a close, grasping onto something she understood and could handle.

"You two," she said, "get on into the library. There's a fire there and I'll bring you both some food. I swear, you both look like you could each eat a chicken, feathers, beak, cluck and all."

The next morning, well fed and well rested, Fletcher and Estelle loaded their horses into a Union Pacific boxcar heading west.

The train made frequent stops along the line to take on water and the coal the engine burned at the rate of forty to two hundred pounds a mile, depending on the grade.

Once they were clear of the Missouri, the remaining one hundred and eighty miles to their destination took Fletcher and Estelle across the Big Blue and the Republican and Saline rivers. There were stops at Kansas City, Abilene, and finally Salina, where the cars were hitched to a new engine for the seventy-mile haul to Hays across rolling, snow-covered prairies, the massive escarpment of the Rocky Mountains lifting their peaks above the flat three hundred miles to the west.

Two days after leaving Lexington the train pulled into the station at Hays, with its thirty-seven saloons and dance halls and a restless, shifting, and often violent population of army scouts, buffalo hunters, railroad workers, soldiers, gunmen, pale-faced gamblers, and prostitutes.

The town was a ramshackle collection of false-fronted buildings and cabins along the railroad track with nothing around in all directions but endless, windswept prairie.

The stock pens lay close to the rails to the east, ready

for the spring herds from Texas; the homes of the town's more respectable elements, the bankers and businessmen, lay upwind to the north, where the rowdy drovers were not allowed to go. Beyond the main street lay the shacks of the girls on the line, and beyond those a cemetery, a Boot Hill that did a rousing, if mostly seasonal, business.

The fort lay a few miles farther along the track to the west, but Fletcher and Estelle unloaded their horses and led them toward the town's muddy main street.

It was yet early afternoon but Hays was up and roaring, the saloons crowded from bar to warped timber walls, an out-of-tune piano in one of the dance halls gallantly trying to compete against the racket of drunk men and laughing women.

Riders and wagons crowded the street, churning the already thick mud and slush into a rutted, clinging swamp.

Fletcher and Estelle led their horses across the street and looped the reins around a hitching post outside a restaurant with a painted sign that proclaimed: *Ma's Sideboard*.

Inside it was steamy and hot, the glass panes of the two windows facing the street misted. There were a dozen tables, each covered in a checkered red-and-white cloth, but only one was occupied, by a man in railroad engineer's overalls who left shortly after Fletcher and the girl entered.

Fletcher felt gritty and his eyes smarted from the soot and sparks that penetrated every window of the car he and Estelle had ridden, all of it made worse by the smoke of the potbellied stove at one end of the aisle.

He was sure Estelle felt the same, but somehow she managed to look fresh and pretty despite the rattling ordeal of the long train ride.

Ma turned out to be a sour-faced stringbean of a man who had the look of the trail cook about him. But he was quick with the coffeepot and recommended buffalo steak, potatoes, and boiled onions, an easy matter since those were the only items on the menu.

Fletcher had tested his coffee and was rolling a cigarette when the door opened and a soldier in a bearskin coat stepped into the restaurant, slapping his gloved hands together against the outside cold.

The man glanced at Fletcher, his cool eyes dismissing him as yet another rootless Hays gunman, saw Estelle, and, his interest pleasurably roused, smiled.

"Chilly out," he said, taking his seat at a table next to her.

"It is indeed," the girl said. "But seasonally so, I suppose."

The soldier shrugged out his coat, revealing captain's straps on his shoulders.

This time the man looked at Fletcher with renewed interest, obviously wondering what this hard-faced gunman was doing here with a young and obviously well-bred girl.

"Capt. Anthony Ferrell, at your service," he said, speaking to Estelle but still studying Fletcher. "Tenth Cavalry, stationed here at Fort Hays."

Fletcher had heard of the Tenth, a regiment of black buffalo soldiers that had already built an enviable combat record in dozens of battles against the plains tribes. They had white officers and Ferrell must be one of them.

Estelle introduced herself and then Fletcher, but the captain's brow was furrowed in thought.

"Are you by any chance related to Senator Falcon Stark?" he asked finally.

"He's my father," Estelle replied, her voice cold.

"Ah," Ferrell said, apparently content to say no more as he tasted the coffee the cook had poured for him.

"Have you met him, Captain?" Fletcher asked, speaking for the first time.

"Indeed," Ferrell said. "The senator is out on the plains

right now with President Grant, Senator John Gray and his wife, and last, but certainly not least, Count and Countess Boris Vorishilov, straight from the Russian imperial court." The officer smiled. "I'd say that was a very distinguished company."

"How large an escort?" Fletcher asked.

It was a soldier's question and Ferrell was eager to answer it. "None. The president said he didn't want a clanking cavalry troop—his very words—scaring away the buffalo. He told the colonel there were four hunters in the party, including himself, all superbly armed and good enough shots to beat off any Indian attack."

The captain grinned. "And besides, they have about a dozen servants with them, maybe half that many skinners—and Wild Bill."

Fletcher nodded. "Bill can make a difference." He paused, then asked, "How long do they plan to be out?"

"Two weeks, maybe three. I'd say it depends on how quickly Hickok can locate a buffalo herd, how long the snow holds off, and how badly they're slowed by their wagons. That's the best-equipped hunting party I've ever seen. The five wagons are packed with fine linens, crystal and silverware, to say nothing of cases of wine, champagne, bourbon, and cigars. They've even got silver candelabras. It's the Russian count more so than the others who loves to travel in style."

"Indians?"

Captain Ferrell shrugged. "Normally the Sioux and Cheyenne like to hole up somewhere snug in the winter. But a week ago four buffalo hunters were ambushed and scalped about sixty miles south of here down on the Santa Fe Trail at the bend of the Arkansas River. With Indians you never can tell. When you least expect them, that's when you'll find them, or rather, that's when they'll find you."

"And Senator Stark, where does he figure in all this?" Fletcher asked.

"The trip was his idea." He turned to Estelle. "I'm sure you know your father plans to run for president. I believe this is his way of winning hearts and minds—mainly the support of the president and another very influential Republican senator."

The food came, and while Fletcher and Estelle ate they talked to the soldier of other things, mainly the harsh winter weather on the plains, the much-anticipated arrival of the spring cattle herds, and the dearth of decent officers' quarters at Fort Hays.

When they'd finished eating, Fletcher built a smoke and poured more coffee for himself and Estelle.

"Do you intend to join your father, Miss Stark?" Captain Ferrell asked.

Estelle nodded, saying nothing, and Fletcher stepped into the conversation. "I think we'll stay at a hotel here tonight and move out at first light tomorrow."

"The best hotel in town, and that's not saying much, is the Cattleman's Haven at the eastern end of town. At least the beds are clean and free of unwanted guests."

Estelle caught Fletcher's eye and they both rose. The girl extended her hand and Ferrell bowed over it gallantly.

"You've been a great help, Captain," she said.

Fletcher dropped money on the table, then asked the soldier, "What direction did the president and Senator Stark take?"

"Due south from right where you stand. Hickok says he plans to scout all the way to the Santa Fe Trail, then swing west well before he reaches the Cimarron."

Fletcher nodded. "Much obliged, Captain."

He and Estelle took their leave of the officer and stepped out of the restaurant and back into the rowdy street.

They were untying their horses when a commotion at the end of town toward the stock pens attracted their attention.

Five riders, buffalo hunters by the look of them, were surrounded by a cheering, laughing crowd, and the man in front was brandishing a bloody scalp above his head.

"Boys, we caught the damned savages camped at Twin Butte Creek and we had at 'em," the buffalo hunter yelled. "By God, when we lit into them with our Sharps they didn't know what hit them."

The hunters stopped at a saloon and were carried inside shoulder-high by the crowd, the man with the scalp still waving it as he ducked his head under the door.

"Buck," Estelle whispered, her face pale, "how horrible."

Fletcher nodded, lips a tight, grim line under his mustache. "I got a feeling there's going to be hell to pay out there on the long grass," he said. "That was a woman's scalp."

Twenty-one

Buck Fletcher lay on top of his bed in his room at the Cattleman's Haven Hotel, a strange, echoing restlessness tugging at him.

Earlier he had seen Estelle settled in the room next to his. The girl was completely exhausted and badly needed sleep.

"I'll wake you at first light," Fletcher had told her. "Best you try to get some shut-eye and rebuild your strength."

Hays was a wide-open, exciting town with plenty to see, but Estelle made no objection. Dark circles stained the pale skin under her eyes, and it was obvious to Fletcher that the strain of the past weeks was beginning to tell.

"Buck," she'd said before he closed the door to her room, "be careful."

Fletcher smiled. "I will."

"Buck."

"Yeah?"

"I don't know why I said that. I don't know why I told you to be careful."

Fletcher shrugged. "A man can't be too careful, Estelle. I'm not on the prod, and, believe me, I've no intention of borrowing trouble."

Now he stared at the ceiling, listening to the noises from the saloons, the roar of men, the laughter of women, the whirring click of roulette wheels and always the tinny, out-of-tune pianos dropping notes like bad coins into the night.

Over the years, how many towns had he known like this one? Hundreds maybe? And how many more would he see before it all ended for him? A thousand? More that that?

Often he'd pause for only a night or two in such a town, just riding through. But there were other times, using his Colts for pay—the hard chink of gold in the palm—when he'd met belted men in gunfights who were every bit as fearless, skilled, and tough as himself.

Those were days spent along the dangerous, ragged fringes of hell, blazing, searing days, when men died, falling behind a cloud of gray gunsmoke, Colts blasting in teeth-bared defiance, battling until the very end.

Fletcher closed his eyes against the echoes, reaching for sleep, but saw only the wild, reckless, and laughing faces of men he'd known who lived by the gun. Men like Wes Hardin and Cullen Baker and Clay Allison, men he'd ridden with, men magnificently, vibrantly alive because, every single day of their lives, they lived so close to death.

Sleep would not come to him.

Fletcher swung his long legs off the bed and rose to his feet. He stepped to the window and looked outside.

Along the boardwalks oil lamps had been lit against the gathering darkness, casting dancing pools of yellow and orange on the rough pine planks, lights that could be seen for miles out on the plains.

Men came and went, heels pounding, leaving one saloon, heading for another.

The scent of cigar smoke and rye whiskey and women's perfume hung in the air, and overlaying it all another, subtler odor—the smell of excitement. The restlessness pulled at Fletcher, refusing to let him be.

He ran a hand through his thick, shaggy hair, trying to reach a compromise with himself.

A glass of rye, maybe. Just one. Then long enough to stand in a saloon to bring it all back and no longer.

He scrubbed a hand over the harsh stubble of his cheeks but decided a shave could wait. He also thought to trim his mustache, but that too could be put off until later. Besides, he knew there was little he could do to bring even a remote suggestion of handsomeness to his saddle-brown, hard-boned features.

Fletcher put on his hat, then tugged on his boots. He picked up his gun belts, but decided against wearing them. A belted man could be seen as a threat—or a challenge.

The short-barreled Colt he slid from the holster and stuck in the waistband of his pants, covering the gun with his mackinaw so it would not show.

He checked in his shirt pocket to make sure he had his tobacco, and then studied himself briefly in the flyspecked mirror above the washstand.

What he saw did little to cheer him, but then it seldom did.

Fletcher stepped out of his room and closed the door quietly behind him. For a brief moment he stopped outside Estelle's room but heard no sound. The girl must be sound asleep.

He went down the stairs, ignored the lifted, quizzical eyebrow of the bored night clerk, and stepped onto the boardwalk, his spurs ringing.

There was a saloon a short distance away. Like most drinking establishments in Hays it had a false front, twice as high and twice as wide as the real single-story timber shack hiding behind it. A faded sign hanging on rusty chains proclaimed the place to be Chris Riley's Saloon. It looked as good, or as bad, as any other, and Fletcher made his way toward it.

He opened the door and stepped inside.

The saloon was a long, low room, dimly lit by oil lamps strung along the entire length of the vee-shaped ceiling that valiantly tried to penetrate the fog of cigar and pipe smoke. A mahogany bar at least forty feet long dominated the room, the rest of the space taken up by tables and chairs.

The saloon was crowded with the usual flotsam and jetsam of the frontier. Buffalo hunters, huge and shaggy in hide coats, rubbed shoulders with ragged miners, drifted in from God knows where, both noisily rejoicing in their youth and great strength. Long-limbed cowhands in from surrounding ranches stood, one high-heeled boot hooked on the brass rail, drinking rye, telling each other lies about deserts they'd crossed, blizzards they'd known, and horses they'd ridden. Gamblers of high and low degree went about their business with careful eyes and handled the pasteboards with white, sensitive fingers.

The tables were crowded with people of both sexes, playing poker, drinking, smoking, talking all at once at the top of their voices. The women were no longer in the first flush of youth, painted faces hard and knowing, drinking vinegar and water bought for them by lustful admirers at champagne prices.

Here and there pasty young clerks in celluloid collars and grinning farm boys in ill-fitting suits were getting their first lessons in sin, the tantalizing joys of hard liquor and the soft flesh of women.

At a table set apart from the rest were five black troopers of the Tenth Cavalry, barely tolerated and for the most part ignored.

A piano player was hard at work in one corner, competing with flush-faced waiters calling, chairs shuffling, drunken men shouting, women's voices joining in, the

clash and chink of glasses and the noise of the street outside, all of it blending together in one deafening din.

All this Buck Fletcher saw, heard, and smelled with
considerable joy. He managed to find a space at the bar
long enough to order a rye, then took his drink to an out-
of-the-way corner, already feeling the tensions of the past
weeks slowly drain from him.

He held his glass in an elbow jammed into his side and
built a cigarette. Then he smoked and sipped his whiskey,
an interested observer of what was going on around him
but carefully making himself no part of it.

Much of the crowd's excited talk centered around the
recent visit of President Grant, two distinguished senators,
the Russian count and countess, and Wild Bill Hickok—
and there was much speculation as to whether or not the
buffalo herds had already drifted too far south into the
sheltering buttes and ravines of the Bear Creek country
and spoiled the hunt.

This heated conversation muted and staggered to a
ragged halt when Chris Riley, a round-faced man with
muttonchop whiskers, a white apron tied around his waist,
stepped beside the piano and held up his hands for silence.

After he'd called out, "Ladies and gentlemen, please,"
several times, all talk died away into quiet, and the man
beamed and yelled so that everyone could hear him, "As
you are all aware, our fair city was recently honored by the
visit of President Grant, that gallant hero of the late War
Between the States."

There was some scattered applause and more than a few
boos and catcalls, the war still a festering wound that refused to heal.

Nonplussed, Riley continued: "With the president were
a distinguished senator, members of the Russian aristoc-
racy, and that peerless prince of pistoleers, that paladin of
the plains, the one we lesser mortals, rejoicing when a god

deigns to make one of his periodic visits to Hays, have yclept Wild Bill."

Again there was applause and a few boos and Fletcher heard a man's voice yell, "God, my ass! Hickok ain't much."

Alone among a mostly good-humored crowd, this voice was unnecessarily belligerent and aggressive, gratingly out of place, and Fletcher recognized it as such. Without turning his head, his eyes sought the man who had spoken.

He was not hard to find.

Sitting at a table to Fletcher's right was a big, wide-shouldered man, his ruggedly handsome face revealing an ominous hint of brutality around the mouth and hard blue eyes. He wore two Colts low on his thighs, as some professional gunmen were starting to do, and there was no doubt in Fletcher's mind that the man could use them well. He knew the type. Here was a bully and a braggart who had killed before and would kill again without even giving the death of another human being a second thought.

The man beside him was cut from the same mold, a little older, with a sweeping dragoon mustache above a wide, thin-lipped mouth that was now curled in a cold smile, eyes gray, glittering in the lamplight like steel blades.

On the table in front of them was an almost empty bottle of whiskey. They had been drinking heavily and the alcohol had made both men mean and hostile, stirring the inner anger that drove them. Now, confident, combative, and eager, they were very much on the prod and looking for a fight.

Fletcher had run into men like these in the past. Clay Allison for one. An affable, pleasant enough man when sober, he was a touchy, dangerous demon in drink and best left strictly alone.

Accepting his own counsel in this matter, Fletcher rolled himself another cigarette, fading as much as he was able into the background. A man might die here tonight, shot down by the guns of the two at the table, but that was no concern of his. It was for the law to handle.

What Fletcher, from long experience, had heard, seen, and evaluated, passed unnoticed by the saloon patrons. All eyes were on Riley, who was speaking again.

"Ladies and gentlemen, I am not here to talk of Wild Bill—"

"Yeah," the older of the two men yelled, "shut your trap about ol' duck beak!"

A few of the people around the two gunmen laughed nervously, but the four black cavalry troopers, vulnerable in this place, were suddenly wary and alert, taking notice.

"Before," Riley said, refusing to be intimidated, "I was so rudely interrupted, I was saying that I'm here not to speak of our former town marshal, but of our other distinguished visitors, those glittering scions of the Russian nobility, those blue bloods from the steppes"—he finished with a flourish—"Count and Countess Vorishilov."

The crowd, half-drunk and ready to cheer anybody, applauded wildly, and again Riley held up his hands for silence.

"To commemorate this auspicious occasion, the first visit to our city of any royalty, Russian or otherwise, I have the honor to present to you the famous tenor Mr. Francis Fitzhaugh, recently returned to us from Boston town, who will sing a ballad in honor of that illustrious couple."

"Let's hear it, Frank!" the younger gunman yelled, and his companion laughed and slapped him on the back.

Fitzhaugh was small and portly, a perfectly round belly protruding from the opening of his frockcoat. His hair was black, parted in the middle and slicked down on both sides with pomade, a carefully arranged kiss curl at each temple, and he sported a narrow mustache cultivated into points that stuck out on each side of his face.

Fussy and fastidious, the tenor was the kind of man who would cut quite a dash among the ladies, and indeed, the women in the saloon were regarding him with more than a passing interest.

"Ladies and gentlemen," Fitzhaugh said, "this is a serenade to the count and countess and to all our Russian friends o'er the foam, as the poets say. The ballad is sung to the tune of 'Old John Brown.'" The man turned to the piano player and gave a little bow. "Maestro, if you please."

Fletcher was thoroughly enjoying this unexpected treat. He had a great affection for singers of all kinds, his own voice being so unlovely that during a brief stint as a puncher a few years back he was excused night hawk duty for fear his caterwauling would stampede the herd.

Now he took a step closer to the piano, eagerly anticipating the song as the pianist pounded out the opening chords with a deal more enthusiasm than skill.

Fitzhaugh clasped his hands together and laid them on the top of his round belly and in a fair, high tenor sang:

> Mid the grandeur of the prairies, how can youthful
>   Kansas vie
> With her Russia-loving sisters, in a fitting welcome
>   cry?
> With her heart give full expression, and the answer
>   echo high
> The Czar and Grant are friends!
> Ho! For Russia and the Union
> Ho! For Russia and the Union
> The Czar and Grant are friends!

There were other verses in the same vein, and after the song was over Fletcher applauded as loudly as the rest, and was even moved by Mr. Fitzhaugh's touching rendition to give the man a resounding "Huzzah!"

As Fitzhaugh bowed his way through a door at the rear of the saloon, a bevy of squealing women chasing after him, it was Fletcher's intention to call it a night and return to the hotel.

But then he looked around him and saw the trouble coming.

Later Fletcher would be unable to determine why he'd decided to stay where he was for a few minutes longer that night. Had it been mere curiosity? Or his gunfighter's instinct telling him that he might have to get involved?

He would never find the answers to those questions, though many a time he would think about them, wondering.

During the singer's performance, a tall, gawky farm boy in a homespun butternut shirt, bib-front overalls, and a threadbare wool coat three sizes too small for him had been talking and giggling with one of the saloon girls, spending his hard-earned money on beer for himself and "champagne" for her.

The younger of the two gunmen rose slowly to his feet, the menacing chime of his spurs on the rough pine floor and the purposeful way he walked hushing the people nearest him into an uneasy silence.

Riley saw it coming as clearly as Fletcher did. "Here," he said, stepping to the edge of the bar, "we'll have no trouble in here."

"No trouble," the gunman said. "All I want is this pumpkin roller to sing the song again. He spoiled it for me the first time with all his damn yakking."

Now the entire crowd was quiet, waiting for what was to come, some faces concerned, others grinning and eager.

A man beside Fletcher, a freighter by the look of him, in a plaid shirt, his pants tucked inside mule-eared boots, leaned closer and whispered, "Now there's going to be hell to pay. The farm boy is about to dance with the devil, because that there is Arkansas Jack Dunn, and the one with him is Will French."

The names meant nothing to Fletcher. He'd known gunmen with local reputations as hard cases all over the West, and usually they amounted to nothing.

But even so, Dunn was more than a match for any farm boy. Dunn knew it and apparently so did the kid, a skinny youngster with big hands and wrists, no more than eighteen, freckles scattered over his cheekbones and nose.

The boy's face was flushed, but whether from fear, beer, or anger, Fletcher could not guess.

"I don't know the song," the boy said, his voice unsteady. "An' I never did learn how to sing except maybe a hymn or two."

"Then you'd better learn real fast," Dunn said. "I want to hear the song."

"You heard the song, mister," the boy said. "The man already done sung it oncet."

Dunn smiled, a thin, hard grimace that didn't reach his eyes. "Boy, I swear, you just called me a liar."

The saloon girl, experienced in such matters, moved quickly away from the boy, as did the crowd around him. Now the kid was standing at the bar alone.

Fletcher turned to the freighter. "Where's the town marshal?"

The man shook his head. "He ain't here. He escorted the president's wagons part of the way and he ain't expected back until tomorrow. Maybe the day after that."

The freighter looked Fletcher up and down, measuring him. "You thinking about taking a hand in this?"

"No," Fletcher said. "It isn't any of my business."

The freighter nodded, dismissing him with a scathing,

209

sidelong glance. "Jack Dunn is no bargain. All you'd do is get your fool self kilt."

The railroad clock hanging on the saloon wall ticked loud in the silence; then Dunn said again, "Did you get my drift, boy? You called me a damned liar."

The kid swallowed hard, his throat bobbing. "I didn't mean to, mister. Honest I didn't."

Dunn shook his head. "It's too late for that now." He jutted a chin toward the boy. "When you call a man a liar, all you can do next is haul your iron and get to your work."

"I don't have a gun," the kid said, looking around the room like a cornered animal, his eyes wild.

Fletcher knew the boy was desperately trying to find a way out of this situation. He'd walked into the saloon to drink beer and talk to a pretty girl, and now he was going to die—and for nothing.

"Somebody give this man a gun," Dunn said, not taking his eyes off his victim.

One of the black troopers rose from his seat and stepped to the boy's side. He unfastened the flap of his holster and laid his blue, long-barreled Colt on the bar.

"Take mine, kid," he said with rough kindness. "She shoots true to the point of aim."

"I ain't never used a Colt's gun before," the boy said, looking down at the revolver as if it was a living thing that might rise up and bite him. "Had me a Kentucky squirrel rifle one time, but my folks never could get together twelve dollars for a Colt's gun."

"Well," Dunn said, "you got one now, sodbuster. Pick it up."

The boy knew he was trapped. He swallowed hard, and Fletcher saw him tense as he summoned his courage, determined, now that the chips were down and there was no way out, to die like a man.

Fletcher nodded his admiration. The final measure of

any man, even one as young as this, is how well he acts when he stands on the threshold of eternity.

But with cold certainty Fletcher knew that as soon as the kid's fingers touched the Colt, Dunn would draw and shoot him. And later he'd giggle and cut another notch on his gun handle or whatever tinhorn trick he used to keep count of his dead.

The boy's hand moved slowly toward the gun and, silently cursing himself for being a meddling fool, Fletcher dealt himself a hand in the game.

He walked quickly to the middle of the floor, past the gawping crowd of onlookers, and said, "Hey, Dunn."

Surprised, the gunman's head turned in Fletcher's direction, his eyes snake cold. "Who the hell are you?"

Fletcher shrugged. "Just a man who wants to buy you a drink."

"I buy my own drinks," Dunn said. "Now get the hell away from me."

Trying a different tack, Fletcher said, "The boy didn't mean anything. He was just having a good time like the rest of us. Take that drink, Dunn, and let him be."

"Well spoken, stranger." Riley beamed. "We're all friends here."

Fletcher stepped closer to the bar and laid down his empty glass. He turned to Dunn. "Care to join me, friend? I can recommend the rye."

At first the gunman was taken aback, but he very quickly recovered his composure. "Step away from the bar, mister," he said, his eyes ugly. "Unless you want to die alongside the sodbuster there."

Fletcher shook his head. "It makes me downright sad that there's so much incivility in this world. Dunn, let's you and me be friends."

Two things happened very fast.

The first was that French, smiling thinly, rose from his

chair and stepped beside Dunn. French saw what Dunn saw. Facing him was a big, homely man with a wide grin under a straggling mustache, his clothes shabby, boots down at heel, his entire, slightly stooped posture seemingly awkward and unhandy. What he didn't see, but should have, was that the man's eyes had changed from blue to a cold gunmetal gray, and that he showed no trace of fear.

The second was that the kid tried to pick up the gun.

Fletcher could do little about the first, but he took care of the second, stiff-arming the youngster away from the Colt, hurling him backward into the onlookers.

"Keep him there!" Fletcher yelled.

Dunn's face was livid. "I'm going to kill you for that," he said.

Fletcher sighed and picked up the trooper's Colt in his right hand. He did a fast border shift and drew his own gun from his waistband, the trooper's long-barreled Colt thudding into his left hand.

Dunn, stunned at Fletcher's speed, quicker than the eye could follow, was momentarily frozen into immobility.

Fletcher smiled pleasantly, letting the Colts hang loose at his sides. "Right, Mr. Dunn, you've insulted me by refusing my offer of a drink, and for that I'm calling you a low-down, dirty, no-good, lying skunk. You've proved yourself real good at frightening farm boys, so now why don't you try to scare me."

"What name do you want on your tombstone?" Dunn asked, smirking even as he tensed for his draw.

"Most folks call me Buck Fletcher."

A ripple of surprise went through the crowd. This was a known name and one to be reckoned with, and Dunn had heard it before.

The gunman hesitated, and French, suddenly looking a

little green around the gills, stepped back and moved quickly away from him.

"This isn't my play," he told Fletcher, his hands wide, away from his guns. "I don't want any part of this."

"Stay in or sit this one out," Fletcher said. "It's all the same to me."

French slumped into his chair on unsteady legs, poured himself a drink, gulped it down, and poured himself another, his hands trembling.

"What about you, Dunn?" Fletcher asked. "Ready for that glass of rye now?"

"Damn you!" Dunn screamed. And he went for his guns.

The trooper had been right—his army Colt shot to the point of aim, and Fletcher's aim was the middle of Dunn's chest.

His bullet crashed into Dunn, staggering him. The gunman tried to bring his Colts up and Fletcher fired again, this time with his own revolver. The second bullet took Dunn a few inches lower, another flower of red suddenly blossoming below the first, and the man cartwheeled backward and crashed against the wall. Dunn straightened, fired once, twice, his bullets wild, slamming into the front of the bar, scattering tiny chips of wood. Then, approaching death robbing him of strength, his Colts slipped from his hands and thudded one by one onto the floor.

The gunman went to his knees, his face shocked, unable to believe that it was he who was dying, then sprawled his length on the pine boards, his eyes staring into darkness.

Fletcher stepped out of a gray cloud of gunsmoke, looking for French. The man hadn't moved. He kept his hands on the table in front of him and said again, his voice cracked and urgent, "For God's sake, Fletcher! I'm not in this play."

The farm boy moved up beside Fletcher and looked

down at Dunn's blood-splashed body. He opened his mouth, eyes wide with horror, and tried to say something. The words wouldn't come and he turned quickly away, retching uncontrollably, all the beer he'd drunk suddenly leaving him in a heaving gush.

Fletcher strolled over to the cavalry troopers and gave the gun back to the man who had loaned it to the kid.

The soldier grinned and slid the Colt into his holster.

"Mister," he said, "Jack Dunn killed eight men, but he only picked on them he figured were a lot slower than himself, or scared stiff maybe. He made a mistake this time, was all."

Fletcher nodded. "All I wanted was a rye whiskey and a quiet corner to drink it in. It wasn't any of my business."

Another trooper smiled, his teeth very white against the dark brown of his skin. "Mister, my name is Johnson, and the next time you decide something ain't your business, I sure hope you tell me. I want to be around when the lead starts flying."

Twenty-two

Fletcher woke before daybreak. He rose and gave himself a hurried sponge bath, then shaved as best he could with cold water from the cracked pitcher in his room.

He dressed, then stepped into the corridor and rapped on Estelle's door. The girl was already awake and she opened the door almost immediately.

She looked pretty and fresh this morning in her canvas riding skirt and pale yellow shirt, and Fletcher's breath caught in his throat.

"Are you here to take me to breakfast?" Estelle asked, smiling, sparing Fletcher the need for speech.

Fletcher nodded. Then, at last finding his voice, he added, "After we eat we'll buy some supplies and ride on out. Estelle, Kansas is a big place. Finding your father might not be so easy."

"We'll find him, Buck," the girl said, her face set and determined. "If I have to, I'll search hell itself for him."

"That's a big place too, I guess," Fletcher said.

A few moments later he and Estelle stepped onto the boardwalk after asking the desk clerk directions to the nearest restaurant, preferring to forgo the buffalo steak of Ma's Sideboard.

It was still full dark, and the lamps, running low on oil, guttered in a strong, cold wind blowing off the plains that smelled of buffalo grass and the tall pines growing among the foothills of the Rockies three hundred miles to the west.

Hays was quiet, most of the population sleeping off hangovers. A freight wagon trundled past, drawn by a mule team, then turned toward the cattle pens by the railroad and faded into the darkness.

The restaurant cast a welcoming rectangle of yellow light onto the boardwalk, and with every step Fletcher's spurs rang loud in the morning quiet as he and Estelle walked to the door and stepped inside.

There were a dozen tables, none of them occupied at this early hour, and Fletcher and Estelle took seats by the window.

A young girl, a pretty redhead in a blue gingham dress, stepped out of the kitchen, a coffeepot in hand. "You two are early risers," she said, her smile bright and practiced.

Fletcher nodded. "Riding out this morning."

The waitress's face changed. "Didn't you hear? There's been a lot of trouble with the Indians."

"Lately I've had all the Indian trouble I can stand," Fletcher said. "We'll ride careful."

As the girl poured coffee she told them cavalry patrols had been sent out into the plains from Fort Hays. "They've been told to find the president and his hunting party and bring them back to the fort," she said.

"From what I hear, the president has more than enough fighting men with him to take care of any war party," Fletcher said. He smiled. "And he was a general."

The waitress nodded. "Oh, I know. But still, don't you think it's a very worrisome thing?"

"From where I sit it is," Fletcher said. "But I don't know how Grant feels about it."

What was more worrisome to Fletcher was the possibility that, once on the plains, he and Estelle could miss Falcon Stark entirely. If one of the patrols escorted his hunting party back to Fort Hays they might have to follow the man all the way to Lexington again, or even Washington.

Fletcher and Estelle ordered bacon and eggs, and while they waited for the food the gunfighter built himself his first cigarette of the day and smoked it with his coffee.

He was about to crush the butt into an ashtray brought to him by the waitress when the door swung open and a man bundled up in a sheepskin mackinaw stepped inside. He was tall and thin-faced, his sweeping cavalry mustache gray against the sunburned, mahogany brown of his skin. When his eyes went to Fletcher and Estelle they were green, shot through with golden brown, the eyes of a hawk.

The man wore a deputy marshal's badge pinned to his coat, and he carried a rolled-up poster under his arm.

"'Morning, ma'am," the lawman said to Estelle. Then, several degrees colder, "How are you, Buck?"

"I'm fair to middling, Dan," Fletcher replied, his eyes wary.

"Mind if I sit?" the deputy asked. Without waiting for a reply he dropped into a chair opposite Fletcher, laying the now-open poster printed side down on the table.

Fletcher turned to Estelle. "Estelle Stark, this is Dan Cain."

"Pleased to meet you, ma'am," Cain said, smiling faintly.

"Never expected to see you wearing a tin star, Dan," Fletcher said. "Last I heard, you were riding with Jesse and Frank and the Younger boys over to Missouri way."

"Times change, Buck," Cain said. "And sometimes change is forced on a man." He hesitated then said: "After Jesse shot that bank president in Russellville four years back, I felt a noose tightening around my neck and figured it was time I left the James boys and found me a new line of work."

The lawman shook his head. "The way things are, there

just ain't no future in bank robbing anymore, Buck, and that's a natural fact."

Fletcher's eyes went to the poster, and Cain, seeing this, covered it with a gloved hand, his fingers spread wide. The waitress poured the lawman coffee and said to Fletcher, "Your breakfast will be ready in a few minutes. The cook had trouble getting the fire started in the stove."

Cain tested his coffee, said, "Hot," then leaned back in his chair, stretching. "Got to bury a man today." He yawned, looking hard at Fletcher, his arms above his head. Finally Cain let his hands drop to the table. "Of course, I'm not telling you something you don't already know."

"It was a fair fight, Dan," Fletcher said, his voice even. "Jack Dunn drew down on me."

Cain nodded. "That's the way I heard it. Heard too that you was standing up for some sodbuster."

"He was just a kid. He was scared of that tinhorn."

Estelle turned to Fletcher, her eyes wide. "Buck, you never told me this."

"I know," Fletcher said. "But I was meaning to tell you over breakfast." He looked back toward the kitchen. "If we ever get it."

"Buck here did the city of Hays a favor, Miss Stark," Cain said. "Jack Dunn was a lowlife, and so was his sidekick, Will French. Frenchy pulled his freight for parts unknown last night, by the way."

Cain suddenly sat upright in his chair. "Wait a minute. Estelle Stark! I knew I'd heard that name before, or part of it, at least. Are you any kin to—"

"Senator Stark is my father," Estelle said quickly.

"A fine man," Cain said. "Told me he plans to bring law and order to the West, and now I've changed my ways, I sure can't fault him for that."

Estelle was spared the need to reply because the waitress suddenly showed up with their food, apologizing for the delay.

The bacon was good and the eggs were fresh, and, despite the disturbing presence of Cain, Fletcher and Estelle found they each had a ravenous appetite. As they ate, the lawman spoke to them of other things, how high the prices were in Dodge for everything and how ridiculous were the size of women's bustles in the town, even those of the respectable sort.

"Saw one gal, and I swear she was carrying around six inches of snow, just a-setting there on top of a bustle as big as a shed roof," Cain said. "It's a wonder she didn't freeze to death."

When Fletcher finished, he pushed away his plate and began to build a smoke.

"Dan," he said, "you didn't come here to talk about bustles." He looked at the lawman, his eyes hard and cold. "Get it over with. Say your piece."

Cain nodded. "Buck, you and me go way back. We rode the same trails, knew the same men, stepped from one side of the law to the other when times were hard. You even saved my hide a time or two."

"Never made any complaint about you, Dan," Fletcher said. "When the shooting started you always stood up and did your share."

Fletcher knew Dan Cain to be fast and deadly with a gun. A man who rode with Jesse and Frank could be no other way.

"That's good to hear, coming from you, Buck," Cain said. "And I surely do appreciate it." He gave an apologetic shrug of his shoulders. "You told me to speak my piece. Well . . . there's this. It's part of it."

Cain turned the poster over and handed it to Fletcher. "The drawing is from the picture they made of you in

prison. It's a good likeness, though it ain't real pretty."
Cain smiled. "But then, neither are you."

"Thanks," Fletcher said, taking no offense.

He glanced down at the poster, a reward dodger routinely sent out to lawmen throughout the West at that time.

Fletcher, his face bleak, read it aloud: " 'Buck Fletcher. Wanted dead or alive. For the murder of a sheriff and a prison guard.' " Fletcher looked at Cain. "This dodger is offering a reward of a thousand dollars—in gold."

Cain nodded. "That about says it all."

"Would it make any difference if I told you I was set up, that I didn't commit these murders?" Fletcher asked.

"It might. But then, that's for a judge to decide."

"You planning to arrest me, Dan?"

Fletcher opened his coat, clearing his guns, a motion Cain noticed, recognizing its significance.

"Buck," the lawman said, his voice steady, "in my time I've known a lot of men, some of them I called friends, who were killed so some bounty hunter could collect his blood money. That's not my style, and it surely discourages me that you would think otherwise."

"I know you're no bounty hunter, Dan. But you're a lawman. You have a duty to perform."

"You don't have to preach to me about my duty. I know my duty."

Cain looked from Fletcher to Estelle and seemed to make his mind up about something. "Buck, you rid Hays of Jack Dunn, and I'm beholden to you for that, and once, maybe twice, I'm beholden to you for my life."

He took the poster from Fletcher hands. "This dodger arrived yesterday and it isn't common knowledge in town yet. Now, it's not for me to figure the right or the wrong of these murders. Like I told you, that's up to a judge.

"But I've thought this thing through, rassled with my conscience, you might say, and I've decided to let you ride

on out of here. I don't want to see you get shot in the back
so somebody can collect this reward, and I don't want you
to dangle at the end of a rope. Let's just call it professional
courtesy, or something I'm doing for old times' sake. Take
it any damn way you want."

Fletcher felt relief flood over him. "Dan, I appreciate it.
The only way I can clear my name is to get the man who
set all this up to confess. I know that sounds thin, but it's a
chance and I've got to take it."

Cain rose to his feet. "Buck, you do whatever you have
to do. All I know is I owe you a favor from the old days
and now I'm repaying it. I'm going to have to square this
with the marshal when he gets back, an' that won't be easy,
but whatever lay between us is now over. There won't be
a second time."

The lawman walked toward the door, then stopped.
"There's one more thing," he said, turning to Fletcher.
"Like I told you, this dodger isn't common knowledge, but
the word is getting around that it was Buck Fletcher who
killed Jack Dunn over to Riley's last night."

"What are you telling me, Dan?"

"Only this—Hank Crane is in town."

"Do you think he knows?"

Cain nodded. "It's his business to know."

After Cain left, Estelle said, "Buck, who is this Hank
Crane?"

"Bounty hunter, maybe the best there is. He's good with
a gun but usually shoots from ambush and he doesn't believe in bringing his captives in alive. He says there's more
profit in killing a man—he doesn't have to feed him."

"Will he come after us, Buck?"

"Estelle, I think we can bet the farm on it."

Fletcher and the girl left the restaurant and walked to
the general store near the stockyards. The night was shad-

ing into a gray dawn and there were more people in the street, respectable citizens mostly, the shadier element seldom rising before noon.

The day was starting out bitter cold, the wind biting, and the smell of snow was in the air. People walked bundled up in coats and mufflers, their breath smoking, telling each other that surely a blizzard was on the way.

The store, when Fletcher and Estelle walked inside, was warm and welcoming, a potbellied stove in the middle of the floor glowing cherry red.

A burlap bag of green coffee stood by the door and near it a barrel of sorghum, leaking, as they always did, black drops onto the floor. Bright candy canes stood on end in jars along the front counter next to rounds of yellow cheese, some of them cut into thick, vee-shaped slices. A barrel of crackers, the lid off, shouldered against a hogshead of sugar, and on its other side a barrel of pungent sauerkraut was surrounded by open boxes of gingersnap cookies.

Slabs of smoked bacon on iron hooks hung from the ceiling, and beneath them were piles of hickory shirting in stripes and plaid and bolts of calico and gingham cloth.

On the back shelves were rows of shoes, coffeepots, bags of gunpowder, canned goods, and boxes of rifle and pistol ammunition.

Fletcher made his purchases—bacon, coffee, salt, flour, and shells for his rifle and Colts—from the rapidly dwindling money he'd been given by Falcon Stark. A generous man by nature, Fletcher was unusually careful with money, knowing it was hard to come by and harder to keep. Somehow, as he counted the coins in his money belt, he was missing twenty dollars that he could not account for and did not recall spending.

In the scheme of things, it was a small loss, and Fletcher

shrugged it off, thinking that he must have lost the double eagle, probably at the pueblos.

He had no way of knowing it then, but that missing twenty dollars would play a significant role in what was to come—not for its own sake, but for what it was used to buy.

With a word of thanks and the gift of a free sample of cheese, small enough but nonetheless welcome, the store-keeper sacked up the supplies and Fletcher and Estelle walked back to their hotel.

Thirty minutes later they rode out of Hays, heading south into the Kansas plains.

Twenty-three

Keeping Big Creek to his east, Fletcher planned to ride to the Arkansas River, a distance of about seventy-five miles, and then swing west.

Hickok would be slowed by the wagons, and Fletcher doubted he'd push all the way to the Cimarron before making his own westward turn to reach the migrating herds in the sheltered, shallow canyons near the Colorado border.

If they had any chance of catching up to Falcon Stark, it would have to be west of the Arkansas, in that flat, open country where a man on a tall horse could see for miles.

The gently rolling land around them was covered in buffalo and blue grama grass, and here and there Fletcher and Estelle rode past bright green bushes of tumbleweed with its purple-and-red-striped leaves. Come summer, sunflowers would bloom on these plains, and colorful masses of columbines, daisies, goldenrod, and wild morning glory would stretch to the horizon.

But now, in the depths of winter, the landscape was bleak, the grass scorched by snow and frost to a dull brown, and willows and leafless cottonwoods clung to the banks of the partially frozen creeks. The cold was icy and penetrating, the kind of cold that made a man huddle into his mackinaw and think the fires of hell would be a welcome relief.

To the southwest lay the 2,400-foot peak of Round House Rock, and just ahead was the south fork of the Smoky Hill River, a barrier Fletcher and Estelle would soon have to cross.

When they were an hour out of Hays, Fletcher picked up the wheel ruts of heavily loaded wagons heading due south toward the Arkansas.

"I'd say that's our buffalo hunters," he told Estelle. "The ground was still fairly soft when they rolled across here and they've left a pretty obvious trail. I'd say they're maybe three days ahead of us."

The trail led to the Smoky, then swung east toward its junction with the north fork.

Fletcher dismounted and studied the tracks. Hickok had been looking for a place to cross, either a shallow ford or a ferry, of which there were several scattered up and down both banks of the river.

He stepped into the saddle and again followed the wheel ruts. The Smoky had not yet frozen, though patches of ice clung to the rocks along its banks and there was a thick hoarfrost on the trunks and branches of the cottonwoods.

It was getting colder, and Estelle shivered and pulled her mackinaw closer around her, only her eyes showing above the sheepskin collar.

"As soon as we're across the river, we can stop and boil some coffee," Fletcher told the girl, trying to bolster her sagging spirits. "Heat you up some."

Estelle lowered the collar of her coat and gave Fletcher a grateful smile, immediately covering her mouth again.

Fletcher noticed scattered buffalo tracks along the bank, and he recalled hearing that in the summer drought of 1868 a vast herd of a million animals, stretching thirty-five miles from point to drag, had drunk this river dry.

The wagon ruts led through a shallow valley between two saddleback hills, then, as the valley opened out, headed back to the river again. Ahead Fletcher saw a small shack, an iron pipe belching black smoke sticking out of its roof, and a ferry tied up to a ramshackle wood dock.

He and Estelle rode to the shack, and Fletcher yelled, "Ho, the house!"

After a few moments a man stepped outside. He was big and burly, dressed in greasy buckskins decorated with ornate beadwork, and a matted red beard spread thick to his belt buckle. A young Indian woman hung shyly in the background, her braids plaited in the northern Cheyenne style with blue trade ribbon, her face revealing bruises from blows old and recent.

"We want to cross," Fletcher said. Now that he'd seen the woman he was unwilling to be civil. "Right now."

The man stood scratching under his beard, studying Fletcher closely as he tried to figure how much the traffic would bear. "Two bits for man and horse," he said finally. "Each."

Fletcher nodded his agreement. "Anybody else cross recently?"

The ferryman smiled, his teeth showing yellow and broken under his beard. "I guess you mean the president and the senators and them foreign fancies."

"How long ago?"

The man's face screwed up in thought. "Three, four days. Four maybe."

"Did they say which way they were headed?"

"South, then west. That's all they tole me."

Fletcher swung out of the saddle, and Estelle did the same.

The ferryman looked at the girl, his tongue running over his top lip, eyes suddenly hot. "Been a long time since I saw a yeller-haired woman," he said. "Been a long time since I had me any white woman."

"Yeah, times are tough all over," Fletcher said. "Now let's get going."

"Name's Jones, little lady, Red Jones," the ferryman said, his grin sly. "A name you mought care to know real well."

Estelle ignored the man and led her horse onto the ferry, following Fletcher up the ramp. The ferry itself was a roughly made raft of pine logs, a low plank rail running along each side.

Jones, the huge muscles of his arms bunching under his buckskins, grabbed the rope that looped around a pulley on the other bank about ninety feet away and began to pull. He gave Fletcher a single, surly glance, then went back to his task. Slowly the ferry inched away from the bank and headed out to midstream.

Fletcher stood with Estelle at the rail, looking at the river as it wound away to the east, toward its junction with the north fork.

"See those cottonwoods lining the banks?" Fletcher asked the girl. Estelle nodded and he continued: "The Indians say that in summer the gray-green leaves of the trees look like smoke, and that's how the Smoky Hill River got its name." He smiled. "Well, that's one story anyway."

"How did you know that, Buck?" Estelle asked.

Fletcher shrugged. "I read a lot. Newspapers, local histories, Dickens, Scott, Cervantes, Shakespeare, the labels on peach cans." He smiled. "I guess any reading material I can lay my hands on."

"Buck Fletcher, you're quite a remarkable man. I think you— Look out!"

Fletcher turned quickly as the girl screamed her warning. Jones was right on top of him, the man's eyes blazing, a wicked-looking hickory club in his upraised fist.

Fletcher tried to step to his right, his hands flashing to his guns as he moved.

He was too late.

The club crashed onto the top of his head, and the last thing he remembered before darkness took him was blinding pain and the brown torrent of the river rushing up to meet him.

Buck Fletcher woke to cold.

He lay among ice-covered rocks along the bank of the river, his booted feet still in the water.

Shallow pools among the rocks, driven by the current, lapped around his chest, and when he raised his head the water under him was stained red.

Fletcher tried to rise to his feet but couldn't muster the strength to make it. He sank back to the rocks and lay there for several minutes, his head spinning, waiting for the world around him to right itself.

Having learned from his mistake, he made no attempt to get up again. Instead he crawled toward the grassy bank, dragging himself over rocks that gouged cruelly into his chest and belly.

It took Fletcher the best part of fifteen minutes to clear the rocks and scramble higher onto the bank, where tufts of buffalo grass spiked among thick, tangled brush surrounding the trunks of the cottonwoods.

He was soaked to the skin and freezing cold. Shivering uncontrollably, Fletcher burrowed into the brush like a wounded and hurting animal, trying to find shelter away from the worst of the wind.

Covered by brush and feeling a little warmer, he lay flat on his belly and pillowed his head on his forearm. It was time to sleep, and he told himself that when he woke up he'd be sure to feel better.

Fletcher closed his eyes. He had no idea where he was or how he had gotten here. Nor did he care. He knew only that if he could sleep, the terrible, jarring pounding in his head would go away. . . .

Above him the sky was a pale blue dome stretching from horizon to horizon, streaked with narrow bands of hazy white cloud. A bluegill splashed in a shallow pool near the bank, sending out a widening circle of ripples. A single, shriveled leaf drifted from a branch of the cottonwood above where Fletcher lay, its fall making a tiny sound that passed unheard and unnoticed in that vast wilderness.

Fletcher slept. . . .

The copper sun slid lower in the sky as the day wore on and touched the gathering clouds with scarlet. A few flakes of snow spiraled in the restless prairie wind, and the hushed, shadowless land braced itself for the long, cold night to come.

Fletcher woke with a start. He lay still for a few moments, his eyes open, trying to remember. . . .

He forced himself to think. Then it came to him.

Estelle!

Ignoring the pounding in his head, he backed out of the brush and used the trunk of a cottonwood to help him struggle to his feet. He was cold and wet, his body stiff, and when he attempted to walk, his knees gave way and he fell flat on his face.

Fletcher lay still until the hammering in his head subsided; then, more slowly this time, he rose and walked to the riverbank. Kneeling, he splashed icy water on his face, the sudden jolt of coldness helping to revive him.

Fletcher got stiffly to his feet, his hands searching for

his guns. They were both in place, secured by the rawhide thongs over the hammers.

Shivering, he looked up and down the riverbank. Something black was wedged among the rocks about twenty yards away, and when Fletcher reached it he saw it was his hat.

Like the hat, he must have been pushed to the bank by the current. Swollen by melted snow, the river was running fast enough that it had shoved him along, refusing to let him sink and drown.

Fletcher knew he had been lucky. Very lucky.

His hand strayed to the top of his head and found a deep gash crusted with hard blood. Fletcher cursed softly and bitterly, remembering Red Jones and his hickory club. He had turned his back on the man like a green pilgrim, and he had paid the price.

Absently he reached for his tobacco. The sack was soaked and shredded, the makings useless, a gloomy fact that immediately filled Fletcher with a dull rage. It had been personal before between him and Jones; now it was even more so. The ferryman had denied him even the small consolation of a smoke—and that was something he could not forgive.

Fletcher rubbed his temples, his head throbbing. There was something else . . . something he had forgotten. . . .

Jones must have taken Estelle!

He recalled the bruises on the face of the Cheyenne woman and how the man had looked at Estelle, the lust in his eyes naked and cruel. Jones's intentions had been clear from the start, and Fletcher cursed himself for not recognizing that the man would act on them. He had taken Jones too lightly, dismissing the ferryman as just a dirty, unkempt woman beater. It was a mistake—and one he vowed he'd never in his life make again.

Now Estelle was in terrible danger . . . and he was just standing there, mourning his tobacco.

Wincing, Fletcher settled his hat on his head. How far downstream had the current taken him? He had no way of knowing. The ferry might be just around the next bend of the river—or a hundred miles away.

The day was slowly dying, shading into night, and a few flakes of snow tumbled in the air. Fletcher shivered. He had to make it to some kind of shelter before the temperature dropped much further or he could freeze to death in these wet clothes.

How far away was that damned ferry?

There was only one way to find out.

Fletcher glanced toward the last dim glow of the setting sun, gauging the time, then turned to the east and, unsteady on his feet, his head spinning, began to walk upstream.

The riverbank was lined with cottonwood and willow and was mostly flat, though in many places the underbrush grew thick, slowing Fletcher's progress.

Here and there where the bank had crumbled under the relentless pressure of the current, the rushing waters had gouged great semicircles out of the land, the bottoms covered in rock-strewn sand and massive boulders, and these obstacles also took time to cross.

The rising temperature of his own body as he struggled forward was rapidly drying Fletcher's clothes, at least those nearest his skin, but amid the gathering darkness the night was getting colder, and very soon he would be unable to see where he was going.

Up ahead there was a bend in the river where a spit of land jutted into the water. It looked to be mostly hard-packed sand, but there were cottonwoods growing among scattered boulders at the point nearest the bank.

Fletcher stumbled forward and rounded the spit, tak-

ing the easiest route across the sand. When he cleared the
promontory he saw what he'd been hoping to see. About
two hundred yards away was the ferry, smoke still belching from the chimney of the shack.

There was only one problem.

It was on the other side of the river.

Twenty-four

Fletcher stood on the bank, stunned by this melancholy development. In his befuddled state he had never even considered the possibility that he might have been washed up on the bank opposite the ferry.

He sat on the grass under a cottonwood, trying to get his brain to work. He had to think this thing through.

After a few minutes he realized there was only one solution to the problem—he'd have to swim for it.

But that solved one problem and created another. He was a poor swimmer, and the river at this point was wide.

Fletcher's hand strayed to his shirt pocket and it took him several moments before he remembered his makings were ruined. Again he directed his growing rage at Red Jones, angrily cursing the man under his breath.

He had to get across the river and soon—but how?

The answer finally came to him.

Back at the spit he'd seen the skeletal trunk of a dead cottonwood lying half-buried in the sand. If he could get the trunk into the water, he could float across.

It wasn't going to be easy, but Fletcher knew he had no alternative. He had to save Estelle, and that dead tree could be her salvation—and his.

Wearily he rose to his feet and retraced his steps to the sandbar.

The cottonwood was easier to move than he had feared,

mainly because it had been stripped of its branches in some ancient tumble down the river when it was in flood and there was nothing left to dig deep into the sand.

Fletcher lifted one end of the log free, then the other. The trunk was heavy and awkward to handle, but after several attempts he managed to pry it loose from the sand and drag it to the water's edge. He stripped off his mackinaw, then his boots and gun belts, and bundled them up inside the coat, using the arms to tie it all together.

Fletcher placed his wet package on top of the trunk and pushed it into the river, holding on with his right arm. He kicked out with his feet, and the log floated slowly into the current.

The water was cold and its icy slap made Fletcher gasp. He kicked out harder and the trunk, with agonizing slowness, nosed further into the wide Smoky.

The current was strong and he was slowly being swept downstream of the sandbar, but his steadily churning feet kept the trunk on a steady, if slanting, course for the opposite bank.

It took the best part of fifteen minutes before Fletcher felt the trunk grind across rock and come to a sudden halt. He was still about ten yards from the bank, but here the water was shallow, and he managed to splash his way to shore, holding his precious bundle above his head.

Fletcher clambered up the steep side of the bank and fell on the grass, numb from cold and teetering on the edge of exhaustion. After a few moments he climbed slowly to his feet and pulled on his boots, then buckled on his gun belts.

He shrugged into his wet mackinaw, then checked his Colts, punching out each round and drying them one by one, or as much as he was able to get them dry, on his damp shirt.

Reholstering his guns, Fletcher removed his spurs,

shoving them into the pockets of his mackinaw where their jingle would not betray him, and walked toward the ferry and Red Jones's shack.

The reckoning was coming, and the anger in Fletcher was a growing thing, building inexorably with each stiff, painful step he took. Jones had played his hand well and thought he had the game won.

But very soon now Fletcher would up the ante—betting all he had on a pair of Mr. Sam Colt's sixes.

When Fletcher got close to the shack, he drew the gun from his cross-draw holster. There was no one around, and, luckily, Jones did not seem to own a dog that would bark an alarm.

The shack had one small, uncurtained window to the front. On cat feet, Fletcher stepped quietly to the window, dropped to one knee, and looked inside.

Estelle was sitting on a cot opposite Jones. Her shirt was unbuttoned and hung over her waist, exposing creamy, pink-tipped breasts that were still full and swollen from her pregnancy.

The ferryman sat at a table, a whiskey jug to his lips, never, for a single moment, taking his eyes off the half-naked girl as he drank.

It seemed that eager anticipation played a major role in Jones's perverse sexual appetite, and he appeared to be in no hurry to throw his unwashed body on Estelle.

Fletcher shook his head. There was just no accounting for people.

A sudden shuffling noise to his right made him duck back from the window, his gun coming up fast.

The Cheyenne woman, her arms loaded with firewood, had walked around the corner of the shack. Now she stopped in her tracks, her only reaction to Fletcher's presence a slight widening of her dark eyes.

Fletcher put a finger to his lips and whispered:

"Sssh . . . " The woman stood where she was, saying nothing.

It was now or never, Fletcher decided. The Cheyenne might open her mouth and scream at any moment.

He stepped quickly to the door of the shack, judged its strength, then kicked it in with his right boot, following through when timbers splintered and the door crashed open.

Jones, his face all at once managing to register fear, surprise, and shock, let the jug slip from his hand. It crashed onto the table, spilling whiskey across the rough pine boards. The man roared a vile oath and dived for Fletcher's rifle standing near the stove.

He never made it.

Fletcher's Colt barked once, twice, three times, and Jones slammed heavily into the wall, rocking the flimsy shack to its foundations. He sank to the floor, three bullet holes forming a perfect ace of clubs dead center in his chest.

"I finally played my hand, Jones," Fletcher said, talking to a dead man. "And I reckon you've cashed in your chips."

"Help me," Estelle said, without a glance at Jones's body. She pulled up her shirt and turned her back to Fletcher.

"What do you want me to do?" Fletcher asked, smoke drifting around him. He punched out the spent shells from the cylinder of his Colt, reloaded, then holstered his gun.

"Button my dress, unless that filthy animal ripped them all off. I'm too shaken to do it myself."

"They're all there," Fletcher said, his face troubled. He could handle a gun or a rope and in a pinch a blacksmith's hammer, but women's fixings were usually beyond him.

The buttons were small and round, covered in the same fabric of the shirt, and there seemed to be a hundred of them. It took Fletcher's big, fumbling fingers a long time to get them all fastened.

When he finished, Estelle turned to face him. "I knew you'd come for me, Buck," she whispered. "With all my heart and soul, I knew it."

"Did he . . . " Fletcher stopped, trying to find the right words.

There was no need. "No, he didn't. Buck, I am protected by the shield of the Lord, and had that animal tried to force himself on me, I would have called down the terrible thunder of His wrath."

Fletcher nodded. "Well, I guess there's more than one way to skin a cat." He glanced at Jones's body without sympathy. "Or in his case a skunk."

Estelle looked at Fletcher as if seeing him for the first time. "Buck," she said, "you're soaking wet!"

"Some," Fletcher admitted.

"Let's get you out of those wet clothes before you catch your death of cold."

Fletcher nodded toward the dead man. "I'll get rid of that first."

He grabbed Jones by the feet and dragged the body outside. There was no sign of the Cheyenne woman, the wood for the stove lying where she'd dropped it.

Fletcher dragged Jones's body into some deep brush on the riverbank, then returned to the shack.

Tired, wet, and irritable, he insisted Estelle turn her back while he stripped off his wet clothes. These he spread in front of the stove, then wrapped himself in a blanket from the cot.

"Can I look now?" Estelle asked, a barely suppressed laugh in her voice.

"Yeah," Fletcher answered gruffly, annoyed at the girl and the way all women seemed to have of making a naked man feel foolish about his modesty.

Estelle looked around the shack and found the coffeepot and a sack of Arbuckle. There was water in a jug, no doubt brought in by the Cheyenne woman, and she filled the pot and placed it on top of the stove.

Sitting back on the bed, Estelle leaned over and moved Fletcher's shirt and mackinaw closer to the fire. "Where is the Indian woman?" she asked.

Fletcher shrugged. "Gone."

"Gone where?"

"I don't know, back to her people maybe. I guess living with Red Jones was no picnic and she was glad to get rid of him."

The girl reached down and pulled a sodden wad of sack, paper, and tobacco from the pocket of Fletcher's shirt and threw it into the fire.

Fletcher followed her movements with unhappy eyes. "I wasn't killing mad at Jones until I discovered that," he said. "Then it became real personal between him and me."

Estelle smiled. She rose and picked up her coat that Jones had thrown on the floor in his haste to strip her. She held up the mackinaw and reached into a pocket, coming up with a tobacco sack and papers.

"How the hell—" Fletcher began.

"You know, Buck," the girl said, interrupting him, "sometimes the way you talk to me, explaining every little thing, I get the impression you don't think I'm very intelligent."

Stung and embarrassed, Fletcher fumbled for words. "I don't think that. I mean—"

Estelle shook her head. "It doesn't matter; really it doesn't. But early on I was clever enough to figure out that a smoking man without tobacco would be like a grizzly bear with a toothache." She smiled and handed sack and papers to Fletcher. "That's why I bought these back at the sutler's store at Fort Apache. I thought it might be real prudent to have some spare."

"Estelle," Fletcher said, grinning, meaning every word, "you are an angel."

The girl rose and found matches and scratched one alight, holding it up to Fletcher's cigarette. He drew deep and long, then, smoke trickling slowly from his nose, sighed. "Ahh . . . that was good."

"Nasty habit," Estelle said, her nose tilting. "I don't approve of it."

Fletcher and Estelle both decided to forgo the dubious cleanliness and comfort of Red Jones's cot, preferring to sleep on their own bedrolls. Fletcher, shivering in his blanket, found them stashed with their horses and saddles in the dead man's small barn behind the shack.

Fletcher hotfooted it back to the shack, threw the bedrolls on the floor, and was glad to return to his coffee and the welcoming warmth of the stove.

In the early hours of the morning, he rose and brought in the wood the Cheyenne woman had dropped, and fed the fire.

Outside the night was bitter cold and a frosty moon rode high. There were a few stars scattered across the sky, but the horizon toward the north was black with building clouds. The coyotes had begun calling, and down by the riverbank a large animal crashed through the brush.

Fletcher lay on his blankets again, listening to Estelle's soft breathing, wondering at the girl's dry-eyed grief for her dead husband and baby and her determination to even the score with her father.

Restless, thoughts crowding on thoughts, Fletcher built himself a smoke and lit the cigarette with a brand from the stove.

Despite the still-visible wagon tracks, trying to find Fal-

con Stark in the vast, featureless wilderness would be like
looking for a needle in a haystack. And if it snowed heavily or a cavalry patrol escorted the senator and his hunting
party to Fort Hays they would have to turn back and start
the search all over again. That is, if they survived. Getting
caught in a blizzard on the Kansas plains was no bargain.

And Dan Cain was in Hays. The city marshal would
have returned by this time and Cain had made it clear that
any debt he owed Fletcher for past favors had been paid in
full. Next time he would do what the law demanded of
him.

Fletcher had nothing against the lawman. Cain must do
his duty as he saw it, and he could not be blamed for that.

Then there was no going back to Hays. Maybe he and
Estelle would head for Ellsworth and ride the boxcars of
the Union Pacific east. But to where? Lexington? Or
would they have to follow Stark all the way back to
Washington?

It seemed the chances of clearing his name were slender and growing more so all the time. Falcon Stark was a
powerful, respected man in the nation's capital, and exposing him for the liar and murderer he was would not be
easy and, indeed, might be impossible. Fletcher felt a pang
of despair deep in his belly as he took a last drag on his
cigarette and threw the butt into the fire.

All he could do now was play the cards where they fell
and hope he could put together a winning hand.

But that was mighty cold comfort, as cold as the night
outside, and just as dark and as fraught with danger.

Fletcher woke as dawn changed the light inside the
shack from scarlet-streaked black to a watery gray. He
rose, shivering, and piled more wood into the glowing
stove. The water jug was empty, so he dressed and filled
the coffeepot at the river.

When he returned Estelle was also awake, and the girl seemed refreshed by her sleep and greeted him with a smile.

Fletcher threw a handful of coffee into the pot and placed it on the stove to boil.

"We'll head south and see where the wagon tracks take us," he said. "Just hope the snow holds off or we'll lose the tracks and our way."

"What will we do if that happens?" Estelle asked, her face troubled.

Shrugging, Fletcher made an adjustment to the position of the coffeepot.

"If that happens we head to Ellsworth and try again some other day in another place."

"That's not going to happen, Buck," the girl said. "We're going to find my father. I know we will. Believe me, Buck, the Lord is on our side."

Fletcher nodded, smiling. "That's good, because right about now we can sure use all the help we can get."

After a breakfast of coffee and broiled bacon, Fletcher and Estelle saddled their horses and led them onto the ferry.

They walked past where Red Jones, unburied and unmourned, lay in the brush, his bearded face turned to the sky, unseeing eyes wide open.

Neither of them felt the slightest pang at leaving the man there. You don't take time to bury a dead coyote.

Fletcher grabbed the rope, his strong arms nosing the ferry into the river. It took him ten minutes of steady hauling to cross to the opposite bank, and after they led their horses down the ramp, Fletcher tied the raft securely to a tree.

"The way the weather is, I doubt there will be other travelers in need of this ferry," he said. "But we might want it in a real hurry on the way back."

He and Estelle swung into the saddle and rode south, onto flat, rolling land cut through by innumerable shallow creeks. The tracks of Stark's heavy supply wagons still scarred the grass, but even a few inches of snow could cover them completely, leaving Fletcher to find the trail like a blind man groping for the way.

He glanced at the sky. To the east, the sun was lifting itself above the horizon, painting the edges of gathering clouds a pale rose, and the air was crisp on the tongue, tasting of frost and early morning. A few snowflakes tumbled in a fretful prairie wind that set the buffalo grass to rippling, and ahead of him Fletcher saw the parallel ruts of the wagons stretch away into the distance like phantom railroad tracks laid to nowhere.

Estelle kneed her horse close to his and Fletcher turned to the girl and smiled. He lifted his hand and brought it down in a chopping motion, directing the girl's attention to the wagon path.

"That's where we're going," he said. "Wherever the tracks lead."

"If those tracks marked the milestones along the turnpike to hell, I'd still take it," Estelle said, her face set and defiant, no trace of surrender and less of forgiveness in her.

Fletcher nodded, his smile fading until his mouth became a grim, straight line. "Young lady, hell might be just where we're headed," he said.

Twenty-five

At noon, Estelle and Fletcher stopped in the shelter of cottonwoods along Sand Creek and ate some cold bacon washed down with creek water.

A buffalo cow, a yearling calf walking at her flank, came to the creek. The cow watched the two humans warily, white arcs showing in her eyes as she dipped her nose into the cold water and drank.

After a few minutes the huge buffalo, shaggy and ragged in her winter coat, scrambled back up the bank, the calf following, and, humpbacked and watchful, walked to the southwest.

The calf showed evidence of recent wounds on his legs and back, and Fletcher figured he and his mother had been involved in a scrape with wolves. Sometimes such an attack could last for several days, and that must be the reason why the cow had dropped so far behind the rest of the herd.

Nature in this harsh land had a cruel indifference to the fate of a single buffalo calf, but with perseverance and more than his share of luck he would make it.

Fletcher hoped he did, feeling the natural sympathy of one hunted creature for another.

He and Estelle swung into the saddle and followed the wagon's tracks south. For now the snow was still holding off, though from horizon to horizon the sky was dark and ominous, the clouds curling like great sheets of gray lead.

They cleared Walnut Creek and rode into country even more cut through by narrow creeks and washes. Here and there buffalo wallows, ancient and used by countless generations, were gouged deep into the ground, some of them holding thin patches of snow at their lowest levels.

As the day wore on to late afternoon, Fletcher caught sight of a rectangular black rock rising above the plain like a block of basalt about a mile ahead of them. As he and Estelle rode closer they saw that this was no rock, but the blackened ruins of a settler cabin.

Three walls still stood, supporting part of the roof, and a creek ran close to the place, providing a ready supply of water.

There was no way to tell when the cabin had burned or who had burned it, but Fletcher suspected it had happened years before and was probably the result of an Indian attack.

His impression about the age of the place was confirmed when Estelle, staking out the horses close to the cabin, found a wooden grave marker half-buried in the grass. The wood had rotted considerably, but she and Fletcher made out the name, Annie, and the date, 1868. Under that was a single word: *Cholera.*

Death for cholera victims was so certain on the Kansas plains, their graves were dug while they yet breathed, and later they were laid to rest wrapped only in a blanket, wood being scarce and expensive in a treeless land.

Maybe the people who once lived here had burned the cabin themselves, then picked up and left to dream other, better dreams in a safer, less hostile place.

Fletcher had no idea of what had really happened. But whoever had built this cabin had done him and Estelle a favor, because here they would spend the night.

There was plenty of dry wood in the cabin, most of it already charred, and Fletcher built a small fire. The remaining walls sheltered him and Estelle from the worst of the wind, and as night fell they ate a supper of broiled bacon, pan bread, and coffee.

After he finished eating, Fletcher built a smoke and studied Estelle for a few minutes, framing in his mind what he was going to say. Firelight touched the girl's face, adding color to her cheeks and a reddish tone to the blond hair that fell in shining waves over her shoulders.

Finally Fletcher said, "Estelle, you ever think about what you're going to say to your father if we catch up to him?"

"Not if, Buck, when." Estelle was silent for a moment or two, then added, "I'm going to tell him he tried to have me killed and failed, mostly because of you, someone else he wanted dead. But, more importantly, I'm going to tell him he murdered my son and that I'll never forgive him for that. All this, and more, I'll tell him in front of President Grant and those who are with him."

"It might not wash, Estelle," Fletcher said gently. "Grant and the other senators may not believe you. They know your father; they don't know you."

Estelle nodded. "I realize that. But at the very least some of the dirt will stick, enough perhaps to sow a seed of doubt in Grant's mind. Enough to make sure my father never gets a chance to run for president."

Fletcher sighed and shook his head. "It's thin, Estelle, mighty thin." He hesitated, about to say their chances of evening the score with Falcon Stark didn't amount to a hill of beans and that they were both hopelessly clutching at straws. But he thought better of it and instead asked, "And after that, I mean when it's all over, what will you do?"

"Do what my husband would want me to do, of course. I'll go back to the Tonto Basin and continue the work of the Chosen One, bringing the Apaches the word of the Lord, preparing them for the terrible day of doomsday to come."

The girl looked at Fletcher, her blue eyes shining and alive in the fire-streaked darkness. "This is my calling, Buck. I can no more turn my back on it than I could the good Lord Himself."

Fletcher tossed his cigarette butt into the fire. "It's fine to have a dream, Estelle, kind of like the people who once lived in this cabin. But look around you, when the dream is gone all that's left is ashes and a grave out back where your hopes lie buried."

Estelle took it without even blinking. "That won't happen to me, Buck. I am doing God's work and He will keep the dream alive in me. This the Chosen One told me, and this I believe."

"The Chosen One's dream ended with the Apaches," Fletcher said, trying to slap this girl across the face with his words and bring her back to reality. "About the same time they ended his life in the worst way they could."

If Estelle felt any hurt, she didn't let it show. "Yes, Buck, the Chosen One is dead, but his spirit dwells in me. I can feel it. He knows I will preserve and in time fulfill his dream. I speak with his voice and I am his prophet." She joined her hands together and raised her eyes heavenward. "Amen and amen."

Fletcher let it go. Despite her youth and vulnerability, Estelle Stark was a fanatic, and there is no reasoning with a zealot. For her, his words were empty of meaning, just noise, like so many rocks falling on a tin roof.

"Better get some sleep," Fletcher said, his voice gentle, not allowing himself to blame this misguided young woman for anything. "We've got a long day on the trail tomorrow."

*   *   *

Fletcher and Estelle rode out at first light.

They crossed Pawnee Creek at the rocky shallows fifty miles due west of Fort Larned and headed southwest, following the trail of the wagons. Stark's party had swung well wide of the fort, built on the upper reaches of the Pawnee close to the Arkansas to protect travelers on the Santa Fe Trail.

Confident of his heavily armed hunting expedition's ability to defend itself against any Indian attack, Stark had obviously ordered Wild Bill Hickok to lead them directly to the buffalo herds before the threatening weather worsened.

Fletcher and Estelle rode all of that day and camped by a wide, frozen creek where there was evidence that Stark's wagons had also stopped for the night.

The wagons had been pulled into a defensive circle, no doubt Hickok's idea, and several large fires had been lit.

Fletcher knew that the always cautious Bill would not have approved of the blazing fires so deep in Indian country. But scattered, empty champagne bottles, littered cigar butts, and gnawed steak bones revealed Stark's intention that his influential guests have a good time.

If Bill had made an objection, he had been ignored.

The creek had a steep-cut bank as tall as a man that curved away a good hundred yards to the south, most of its length lined with cottonwoods. The creek bottom was sandy, and only a narrow ribbon of water, covered in pane ice, ran through it. Fletcher brought the horses down to the creek and staked them on the sand. He gathered up armfuls of buffalo grass and threw it down for the horses; then he had Estelle huddle in the hollow of the cutbank out of the wind.

There were enough twigs and branches lying around among the roots of the cottonwoods to start a small fire.

There would be little smoke, and the fire itself would be hidden from any passing Sioux by the creekbank.

Over this hatful of fire Fletcher boiled a pot of coffee and broiled a few strips of bacon. After he and Estelle had eaten and finished the coffee between them, he scattered the fire and stomped out any remaining embers.

The fire may have been hidden, but it was better to take no chances. Even a pinpoint of light could be seen for miles across the plains in the darkness.

As the night gathered around them and the temperature dropped, Fletcher and Estelle huddled together, taking what comfort they could in their closeness and body heat.

The prairie wind sighed among the branches of the gaunt cottonwoods and set the buffalo grass to rustling . . . promising that it was going to be a long, cold night.

Shortly before midnight Fletcher woke after a few hours of restless sleep and gathered more grass for the horses.

He scrambled back down the bank and scattered the grass at the horses' feet, then sat close to Estelle and built a smoke.

He had made up his mind.

The weather was getting more threatening by the hour and the smell of snow was in the air. If they did not overtake Stark's wagons by sundown tomorrow, they would give up the chase and head for the safety of Fort Larned. He did not want to get caught out here on the plains in a blizzard. As it was, they might already have cut it too fine. The fort was maybe seventy, eighty miles away across wide-open country with little shelter, and their supply of food was rapidly dwindling.

Fletcher nodded, agreeing with himself. It would have to be tomorrow. He would tell Estelle that when the time came.

Just before daybreak he lit another fire and put the coffeepot in the middle of the coals. When the coffee boiled he shook Estelle awake and the girl shivered, blinking her eyes against the light of the gray dawn.

"How did you sleep?" Fletcher asked, knowing it was a ridiculous question, but hard-pressed to say anything.

"I was cold," Estelle said. "You?"

Fletcher nodded. "Cold." He poured steaming coffee into a cup and handed it to the girl. "Here, drink this while I saddle the horses."

He did not mention his decision. That would come later.

The sun was yet to appear above the horizon when Fletcher and Estelle took to the trail again. The icy wind had risen, slapping at their faces with wintry fingers, and snowflakes tumbled, many more of them than before.

Ahead of them the tracks pointed across the endless grass, beckoning them onward . . . yet mocking them for their foolishness.

Two hours later they found the wagon.

It was Estelle who saw it first. She reined up and pointed directly ahead of her. "Buck, is that one of the wagons?"

Fletcher squinted his eyes against the wind and falling snow. There was something there and it was a wagon. It was tipped over on its side and there was no sign of the team or the driver.

Sliding his Winchester from the boot, Fletcher ordered Estelle to stay back. He rode forward at a walk, the rifle in his right hand, the butt resting on his thigh.

Tense and wary, he swung wide to the east and circled the wagon at a distance. There was no sign of life.

He rode closer and listened, hearing no sound but the wind and the rustle of the grass.

What had happened here?

Fletcher, the Winchester now ready across his saddle

horn, cut across the grass directly for the wagon. He stopped when he was about thirty yards away. Just in front of his horse there was a wide splash of scarlet blood, another to the right of the first. Someone had been hit by a heavy-caliber bullet here and had staggered to his right, only to be shot a second time.

And the man could only be an Indian.

Riding closer Fletcher saw that the wagon had been looted, then overturned. Around it lay the mutilated bodies of four men, three of them bearded and dressed in buckskin shirts, low-heeled boots, and heavy wool pants.

These had been Falcon Stark's skinners. They had made a fight of it, judging by the brass shell casings lying around them.

One man, younger than the others, smooth-faced and looking to be no more than seventeen, had been pinned to the wagon by a war lance, the blade driven into the wood too deeply to be removed. The shaft of the lance stuck out from the boy's chest, and he hung there, scalped, dead eyes still wide with his terror at the manner of his death.

The other three bristled with arrows, most of them fired into their bodies when they were dying or already dead, and two of them had been scalped. The right cheek of one skinner, who had sported a magnificent pair of bushy red side-whiskers, had been cut away, the only trophy available since the man was completely bald.

Estelle rode up beside Fletcher, her face chalk white from shock.

"What . . . what happened, Buck?" she whispered, knowing what she was seeing, but wanting Fletcher to tell it and perhaps find a way to somehow quell the horror of it.

But there was no easy way around what had taken place here.

"They were caught out in the open and didn't have a

chance," Fletcher said, his eyes bleak. He nodded toward a wheel at the rear of the wagon, one of the spokes broken. "They stopped to fix that, probably told the others they'd catch up. Then the Indians hit them." Fletcher pulled an arrow from the side of the wagon. "I'm not an expert on these matters like Bill Hickok is, but I'd say this is Sioux, and over there"—he nodded toward the young skinner— "judging by the otter fur and eagle feathers, that war lance is Cheyenne."

Fletcher swung out of the saddle, knelt and felt the neck of one of the men. He looked up at Estelle. "He's still warm and the blood on him hasn't dried. I think this attack happened no more than an hour ago."

"My God, Buck," Estelle whispered. "The president."

Fletcher nodded, rising to his feet. "Yes, Estelle, the president. And us."

He searched the wagon, but the Indians had taken everything of value. Ammunition boxes had been smashed open and their contents removed, and the gun belts had been stripped from around the waists of the dead men and their rifles and skinning knives taken.

The Sioux and Cheyenne had no love for buffalo hunters and their indiscriminate slaughter, and the dead men had been mutilated badly, ensuring that they would wander the afterlife maimed and crippled, unable to exact vengeance on the warriors who had killed them.

Swinging into the saddle, Fletcher turned to Estelle. "We'll catch up to the wagons very soon, maybe in a couple of hours." He tried to smile, managing only a joyless grimace that never reached his eyes. "Better get your speech ready."

"I'm ready," the girl said, her face rigid. "My speech has been ready since my son was murdered."

Fletcher nodded. "So be it. Let's ride."

Twenty-six

The way across the grass was still clearly marked by the remaining wagons.

It was snowing, but not yet hard enough to cover the tracks, though white showed on the blades of the buffalo grass, and a shifting haze that looked like a tattered lace curtain blowing in the wind shrouded the distance.

It was an hour before noon, but the moody day had gathered a depressing gloom around itself, made gloomier still by heavy, lowering clouds, their black billows touched here and there with streaks of rust. The flat, featureless land seemed empty of life, and there was no clear dividing line between earth and sky, both merging into a single, drab backdrop of gray and white.

A man could lose himself in this land. He would no longer believe that he knew north from south, east from west, and here he would die, to be buried by the wind and snow, uncaring undertakers for a passing that would go unmourned and unnoticed but for the ravenous coyotes, unwelcome guests at his funeral feast.

But somewhere ahead were the wagons, and Buck Fletcher knew his showdown with Falcon Stark was very close.

Would Grant listen to Estelle? Would he care? It was an uncertain thing. Falcon Stark was a smooth, polished, and practiced talker, and his honeyed words could prevail over any accusation his daughter made.

And what of himself? What of Buck Fletcher? If Estelle failed to convince the president, all that might be left to him would be to shoot his way out of there and spend what little remained of his life as a hunted fugitive.

And, inevitably, that thought brought Fletcher to Wild Bill Hickok.

In this situation Bill was an unknown quantity. High-strung, unpredictable, and lightning-fast on the draw, he might be the deciding vote. And, like he always did, Hickok would make his mark on the ballot paper with his guns.

Fletcher told himself he was riding with Estelle Stark into more trouble than a man could reasonably be expected to handle. The outcome was uncertain, and perhaps even now his life was measured, not in years or months or days, but in hours.

Beside him Estelle rode with her head high, eager for what was to come, her need for vengeance driving her.

Fletcher smiled at the girl. "How are you holding up?" he asked.

"I'll make it," Estelle said. "He's very close now, isn't he, Buck?"

The big man nodded. "Those wagon tracks are fresh and so are the horse droppings. I'd say we're real close."

They were—close enough to hear a sudden burst of gunfire.

From where Fletcher and Estelle sat their horses, the plain rose away from them in a gentle rise for about two hundred yards. Too shallow to be called a hill, the slope was yet high enough to conceal what lay beyond—and the gunfire was coming from that direction.

Fletcher swung out of the saddle and silently indicated to Estelle that she should stay where she was.

He slid his Winchester from the boot and, crouching low, made his way up the slope. Before he reached the crest, he dropped to all fours and crawled to where he could look over the rise at what lay below.

As it did on Fletcher's side, the slope fell away gradually for several hundred yards, but here it ended at the bend of a creek, where there was a thick stand of willow and cottonwood.

Stark's wagons, five of them, had been drawn into a rough semicircle around the trees, the rear wheels of each of the outer wagons resting on the creekbank.

Fletcher saw at once that the site had been well chosen for its defensibility, perhaps by Grant himself. The trees gave cover from anyone attempting to attack from the other side of the creek, and the wagon mule teams and riding horses had been taken inside the wagon circle.

Mounted Sioux and Cheyenne warriors, about thirty of them, had drawn out of rifle range and were milling around, brandishing their guns, yelling at the men behind the wagons as they worked themselves up to launch another attack.

If no one had yet been hit, Fletcher calculated there were at least four fighting men holding the wagon circle, Hickok, Stark, Grant, and presumably the Russian count, who would have had military training. There were servants with them, and muleskinners, but he had no way of knowing how many of them could use a gun.

When the attack came, Fletcher could add his fire from the crest of the rise, but up here, out in the open with no cover, he'd quickly be ridden down and killed.

He brushed snow from his mustache, thinking it through, then made up his mind. He would have to get inside the wagon circle and add his guns to the defense.

A dead Falcon Stark would be of no use to him or Estelle.

Fletcher backed down the slope, then rose to his feet and caught the reins of his horse. "Get ready," he told the girl, his voice brusque. "The wagons are under attack and we're going to join them."

Estelle did not question Fletcher's decision. The gunsmoke-streaked air was full of trouble, and her father must remain alive, at least long enough for her to confront him. Wordlessly she swung her horse around, obediently following Fletcher's beckoning hand, and reined up on his right.

The snow had stopped, at least for now, but the temperature had dropped, and Fletcher's breath hung in the air like mist as he talked.

"When we go charging down that slope, stay here, on my right side," he said. "That way I'll be between you and the fire from the Indians." He studied the girl's face closely for a couple of moments. "Think you can do this?"

Estelle nodded. "The Lord is my buckler: He will protect me."

Fletcher nodded. "Maybe so, but He's not the one getting shot at." He grinned. "Let's do it."

He spurred his horse and, startled, the big stud galloped up the rise, Estelle's mount keeping pace. They crested the slope and charged toward the wagons. Fletcher threw his Winchester to his shoulder, cranked the lever, and fired into the Indians, who were still crowded close together. He saw a warrior fall, then fired again and again.

The Indians had been taken by surprise. But now they yelled their war whoops and came on Fletcher at a run. He and Estelle were still a hundred yards from the wagons.

Fletcher slowed his pace, trying to match the speed of the girl's horse, keeping his body between her and the Indians. He fired at a warrior in a red blanket coat riding a spotted pony and the man threw up his arms and toppled backward off his mount. A bullet tugged at Fletcher's sleeve and he heard another split the air just inches above his head.

Fifty yards to the wagons . . .

The warriors, all of them by their braids Sioux and Cheyenne, were closing the distance, coming at Fletcher and Estelle hard.

Ahead Fletcher saw two men step out from the wagon circle. One, judging by his long hair and buckskins, was Wild Bill, the other a bearded teamster who dragged a wounded leg behind him.

Both men opened up with rifles and an Indian fell, then another. The teamster took a bullet in the chest and dropped and Hickok moved to cover him, standing straddle-legged over the man's prostrate form as he calmly cranked and fired his Winchester.

Twenty-five yards . . .

Puffs of powder smoke showed between the wagons as the defenders laid down a supporting fire.

A warrior, two eagle feathers slanting behind his head, charged directly at Fletcher, his rifle hammering. Fletcher cranked his Winchester and fired directly at the man's chest, holding the rifle in one hand like a pistol.

Hit hard, the Indian bent over, his pony slowing to a walk, and then Fletcher was beyond him.

A few yards more . . .

Someone, stocky and bearded, a cigar clenched in his teeth, opened a space in the defensive circle, moving boxes off a wagon tree. Fletcher reined up and motioned Estelle forward. The girl jumped her horse into the space and Fletcher followed. He winced as a bullet burned across the thick muscles of his right shoulder as he jumped off his horse. A quick glance told him it was not a serious wound, and he ran to help the bearded man replace the boxes.

"Need some help, General?" Fletcher asked.

Grant nodded, smiling around his cigar. "I guess I do,

but there's no need to call me General. I'm just plain Mr. President now, Major Fletcher."

That last surprised Fletcher. Grant remembered him!

The president, a perceptive man, read the astonishment on Fletcher's face and said, "When I pin a medal on a man, especially one of my most daring officers of horse artillery, I remember his name."

Grant's brow wrinkled as he started to form a question, but as it was smashed by a bullet, wood splintered from the rim of the wagon near the president's face and all conversation ceased.

The Indians were attacking again.

Their charge was not pressed with determination, and the Sioux and Cheyenne drew off and began to argue loudly among themselves. This attack was proving costly and they'd already lost almost a third of their strength. Yet the prize was great: horses, mules, guns, and supplies, to say nothing of the young women within the wagon circle.

Fletcher was in no doubt they'd charge again.

The snow that had slacked off for the past half hour was back again, the white flakes tossing around in a rising wind. As he stood at the wagon, Fletcher got a chance to look around him.

Wild Bill stood to his right and beyond him a slender young man who would be Count Vorishilov. The Russian was dressed in a blue uniform, red at his cuffs and collar tabs, and he held a large-caliber hunting rifle, the stock heavily inlaid with mother-of-pearl and silver.

To Fletcher's left a teamster stood, a Sharps at the ready, looking intently at the milling Indians, and beyond him Grant and a man Fletcher didn't know, probably the other senator, judging by his gray hair and the way he and the president talked with easy informality.

At the other end of the circle was Falcon Stark. The man was looking hard at Fletcher, his cold eyes bright with a strange mix of anger, hate, and malice. And something else—something Fletcher recognized as the first hatching of madness.

There was no doubt Stark knew why he and Estelle were there, and the man was ready for them, obviously eager to finally bring it all to an end.

Estelle stood with an elegant woman in a blue velvet riding habit who could only be the countess, and with them were a couple of young blond girls with high Slavic cheekbones, dressed in the black and white of maids.

A flunky in a butler's suit was propped against a wagon wheel, his face ashen, an arrow sticking out of his left shoulder. Several other men, cooks and servants, stiffened by a single bearded teamster who abused them with profane relish, were on uneasy guard among the trees, looking scared and awkward as they clutched unfamiliar rifles to their chests.

After a measuring glance at the Indians, Hickok left his position and strolled over to Fletcher, moving relaxed, easy, and loose-limbed the way he always did. The gunfighter wore two Navy Colts, butt forward in carved black holsters, and his eyes were guarded and wary.

"A fair piece off your home ground, ain't you, Buck?" Hickok asked. "Last I heard you was riding with John Wesley and them wild ones down in Texas a ways."

"That was a spell back, Bill," Fletcher said, keeping his voice even, sensing the danger in Hickok. There was no telling how this man would react in any given situation. But if he did decide to act, he was almighty sudden, certain, and deadly.

"All right," Bill said, "enough of being sociable. I'll put it to you as a direct question—What are you doing here?"

A sudden anger flared in Fletcher, and for a moment he thought about telling Hickok to go to hell. But that would have only created another problem and solved none of the others.

Taking a deep breath, calming himself down, Fletcher nodded in the direction of Estelle. "That's Senator Stark's daughter. I brought her here"— he hesitated, groping for the right words, then managed only—"to meet her father."

Hickok wasn't buying it.

"Buck," he said, "me and you go way back, a lot of years, too many maybe. A man trained to the gun like you doesn't track across a wilderness, then ride into a wagon circle under Indian attack, unless he's on the prod and there's something he means to do."

Fletcher opened his mouth to speak, but Hickok's raised hand silenced him.

"I don't want to hear it, Buck. Know only this: I'm responsible for the president and the others on this expedition, and if something were to happen to any of them, I'd take it mighty hard and downright personal."

Fletcher nodded. "You've said your piece, Bill, and I don't hold anything against you for that. But there's a reckoning coming and I guess we'll all have to choose sides."

"I just told you the side I'll be on," Hickok said. "It pains me considerable to say this because I like you, Buck. But if I have to, I swear to God, I'll gun you like I'd gun any other man."

"So be it, Bill. A man should do what he thinks is right."

"Just so you know."

Hickok, wide-shouldered and narrow in the hips, turned on his heel and strolled back to his position behind the wagons, and Fletcher watched him go.

If it came right down to it, was he faster than Hickok? It was not something he cared to prove, but it might happen in the very near future, and right now it was a worrisome thing.

Fletcher turned and saw Falcon Stark staring at him.

The man had heard every word that had passed between him and Wild Bill, and there was a look of sneering triumph on his face.

Stark had seen his daughter ride in, and he must be aware that the showdown was coming. He would also know that when it happened he could appeal to Hickok for protection against Buck Fletcher, a wanted murderer and dangerous gunman. Wild Bill's lightning-fast Navy Colts stood ready to tilt the scales in his favor.

But Fletcher wouldn't let it go, the man's smug grin making sudden anger boil up in him as it had with Hickok.

"One way or another, Stark," he called out to the senator, "it will all end here, but you won't walk away from it, damn you!"

Fletcher was aware that Grant and the senator with him were looking at him, puzzled and shocked by his outburst. Even Count Vorishilov snapped his head around, trying to figure out the significance of what he had just heard.

Grant opened his mouth to speak, but a bullet thudded into the wagon near Fletcher's head. The Indians were attacking and the time for talk was over—at least for now.

The Sioux and Cheyenne warriors had learned from their mistake.

This was no reckless, mounted charge. The warriors were on foot, advancing in a loose skirmish line, disappearing every now and then as they took advantage of every scrap of cover they could find.

Fletcher heard the boom of the count's heavy rifle and the sharper crack of Winchesters. He aimed at an Indian darting closer to the wagon circle and fired twice, missing each time, his aim thrown off by the gusting wind and swirling snow.

Count Vorishilov's rifle boomed again, and the warrior threw up his arms and went down. Then Hickok's rifle hammered, Wild Bill cranking and firing so fast his right hand working the lever was a blur of motion.

The attack was broken up and ended as quickly as it had begun, the Indians drawing off again out of range.

At least two warriors lay dead in the snow, this fight costing the Sioux and Cheyenne war party a higher price than they ever imagined.

Throughout the remainder of the gray afternoon, the Indians were content to snipe at the wagons from a distance.

For the most part, their fire was ineffective, but just before nightfall one of the cooks manning the defenses among the trees was burned across the neck by a stray bullet. The man slapped a hand to his wound and squealed like a piglet caught under a gate until the teamster beside him cursed him for being "a damned boogered pilgrim" and scowled him into a whimpering silence.

As day shaded into night, the immediate danger of an all-out attack seemed to be over. The Indians continued to fire into the wagon circle, but their shots were growing fewer and even more wildly inaccurate because of the darkness and thickening snow.

Hickok strolled around the wagons and ordered that no fires should be lit and that the defenders should stand by their arms at their positions.

One danger had lessened for now, but for Fletcher another had taken its place. He fixed Stark's position. The man stood at his post between two wagons, kneeling behind a pile of boxes and flour sacks. He wasn't looking in Fletcher's direction, all his attention seemingly fixed on the surrounding darkness.

But Fletcher knew Stark was capable of putting a bullet into his back, and it could be explained away later as a lucky shot from an Indian marksman.

Earlier Stark had been shrewd enough to realize that

they needed every rifle for the defense of the wagons, but now that threat had passed, Fletcher was fair game.

The gunfighter loosened his Colts in their holsters, his eyes on Stark. If the man made any sudden move with his rifle he'd be ready . . . and to hell with Hickok.

Shortly before midnight the women, including the countess and her maids, delivered food to the defenders. Estelle brought Fletcher a thick beef sandwich and a bottle of Bass Ale, Wild Bill Hickok's favorite brew.

The girl looked pale and drawn, the strain of the past days beginning to tell on her.

"Stay close to the other women, Estelle," Fletcher whispered, his gaze on Falcon Stark. "There are a lot of stray bullets flying around."

The girl grabbed at his meaning and nodded. "I caught him looking at me, Buck. I saw only hate in his eyes. He looked like a . . . a . . . demon."

Fletcher bit into his sandwich and chewed thoughtfully for a few moments, then said, "If you can't convince Grant, I don't think either of us will get out of here alive. I believe your father will manufacture an incident and Bill Hickok will make his play. Maybe the teamsters will join him, and that will make for some long odds."

Fletcher's face was bleak. "Estelle, I don't know if I can shade Hickok, and I sure as hell don't care to try unless I'm really put to it."

Estelle's face was stiff, her eyes accusing. "Do you want me to back off, forget the whole thing?"

"I don't. We've come this far and we might as well let the cards fall where they may." Fletcher forced a smile. "Hell, we've been in tighter spots than this and come through."

"No, we haven't," Estelle said.

Head held high, she turned on her heel and walked back to the countess and her maids.

Twenty-seven

The butler who had been struck by an arrow died during the night, and a shot from the darkness drew blood from the cheek of one of the teamsters.

But when the long night faded to a gray, snowy dawn, the Indians had gone, carrying their dead with them.

The reason for their hasty retreat became apparent an hour later when a troop of Buffalo Soldiers led by a middle-aged white captain trotted up to the wagon circle.

The officer sent half his troop to pursue the hostiles, and the remaining soldiers dismounted and formed a perimeter around the wagons, carbines at the ready.

A fire was lit and soon the odors of coffee and frying bacon hung in the air as the surviving muleskinners hitched up their teams and hauled the wagons into column, this time the lead wagon pointing north.

The cavalry captain, a man named Ward, was taking no chances. He would escort the president back to Fort Hays.

Fletcher stepped to the fire and spread his cold hands to the flames. The cook who'd been stung by the bullet, looking ruffled and unhappy, handed him a cup of coffee, and Fletcher accepted it gratefully.

Falcon Stark was standing with Grant, Ward, the other senator, and Count Vorishilov. Stark still held his .44.40 Winchester, and Fletcher noted that the hammer of the piece was eared back, ready to go.

"I'm sorry our trip ended so badly, Count," Grant was saying. "Perhaps our next hunt will provide better sport."

The Russian smiled. "Mr. President, I believe I've had all the sport I need for some time to come. In fact, I must admit I'm quite looking forward to getting back to the safer environs of St. Petersburg, where there are no Indians."

The men around the count laughed, and Fletcher was struck by the contrast between the tall, elegant aristocrat in his tailored uniform and Grant. The president wore a shabby army greatcoat in Confederate gray, and a battered old campaign hat. His boots were scuffed and down at heel and a long, green muffler looped carelessly around his neck. Fletcher reckoned you could buy Grant's entire wardrobe for two dollars and get fifty cents' change back.

Now Grant was staring hard at him, his smile vanished, and when Fletcher returned his look, the president inclined his head, nodding to a spot near the lead wagon where there was no one around.

Grant made a polite apology to the others and walked over to the wagon, and Fletcher followed, aware that Falcon Stark's hostile eyes were burning into him every step of the way.

The president took the cigar from between his teeth and studied Fletcher for a few long moments. Finally he shook his head slowly and said, keeping his voice low, "Major Fletcher, I've been hearing some very distressing reports about you and, quite frankly, I'm appalled."

"From Stark?"

"Yes, from the senator and others. And I do read the newspapers, Major."

"I believe I know what you've heard, Mr. President," Fletcher replied. He smiled, his face grim. "And it's all a pack of damn lies."

"I'm sure that is the case," Grant said, "but nonetheless,

two cold-blooded murders, one committed during a jail-break, are serious charges indeed." He fixed Fletcher with a cold stare, his blue eyes suddenly hard. "Major, I wish you to accompany me to Fort Hays, and there you will turn yourself over to the civilian authorities. I swear I will do everything in my power to help you." He waved a hand toward the remounted Buffalo Soldiers, who were now deploying on each side of the wagon column. "Now, I'd rather not resort to force. But be assured, if need be I will."

"I'll go along with you," Fletcher said, the utter hopelessness of his situation dawning on him. "I don't see that I have much choice."

Grant nodded. "You haven't." He extended his hands. "Now, your pistols, if you please."

Fletcher moved his hands slowly to his guns, but Estelle's shrill, angry voice froze him in midmovement. Grant's head snapped around in time to see the girl walking purposefully toward Falcon Stark.

In Tennessee, the hill folk called what was about to happen a shiriking—the moment when an angry woman, in front of witnesses, confronts a man she believes has wronged her.

Fletcher had heard of the shiriking, but now he was seeing and hearing it for the first time.

"I'm alive, Father," Estelle called out. "Your hired gunmen tried to kill me but they failed." She turned, seeking Fletcher, and pointed at him. "And the only reason they failed was because of him, the man you wanted to blame for my death."

The blood slowly drained from Stark's face and the man's eyes were wild. "Estelle, what nonsense is this? Against my wishes you fled to Arizona with a dangerous lunatic and he's poisoned your mind against me."

"The Chosen One is dead, Father, just like my child is

dead. It was your hired gunmen who killed my baby, but the real murderer was you!"

Stark took a step toward his daughter. "You poor, demented creature, what has the man standing over there, the convicted killer Buck Fletcher, done to you? You don't know what you're saying anymore."

Estelle stood her ground, her eyes blazing. "You sent that animal Wes Slaughter into the Tonto Basin after me. You wanted me dead so the disgrace of my marriage to the Chosen One and my pregnancy would not jeopardize your bid for the presidency."

The girl moved closer to Stark, her face a stiff, angry mask. "I was heavy with child when Slaughter made me ride a horse over some of the roughest country on God's earth. I pleaded with him. I told him I could lose my child. And do you know what he did, Father? He laughed. He laughed in my face and told me that Senator Stark wanted the bastard in my belly dead anyway."

"This is an outrage!" Stark screamed. He looked around the circle of faces surrounding him, seeking support, but found none. He pointed a trembling finger at Fletcher. "You put her up to this, you damned outlaw and killer."

The others had crowded closer, their faces a mix of shock, disbelief, and horror, and Countess Vorishilov was clutching her throat, her eyes wide, unable to comprehend what she was hearing.

Then Grant did something that stunned Fletcher, something so remarkable and unexpected he would remember it for the rest of his life.

"Major Fletcher," the president snapped, his eyes on Stark, hostile and calculating, "is all this true?"

Fletcher had never considered even the remote possibility that Grant, though a soldier's soldier, would still consider him an officer and gentleman despite everything he'd been told. But it did not seem to enter Grant's thinking that

a former major in the United States Army, a man who had
served his country honorably and well, would lie.

"What Estelle says is true, sir," Fletcher said. "Every
word of it—and more."

"Then tell it to me, man," Grant said. "Make your report, sir."

Fletcher knew Grant, and he was aware that the general
had never cared for long-winded dispatches. In as few
words as possible, he described what had transpired between his being sent to prison for a crime he did not commit, his visit to Stark's home in Lexington, and the present.

He left nothing out, including his imprisonment by
General Crook and his killing of Wes Slaughter, the man
who had set him up for the murder of the Wyoming sheriff. And when it was over he summed it up by saying, "I
believe Falcon Stark is a murderer, a man corrupted by
power, greed, and ambition, and such a man should never
be allowed to become president of this nation."

Stark had listened to all this, his face growing paler
with every word. Now, ashen, his half-mad eyes blazing,
he took a couple of steps toward Grant.

"He talks about me being a murderer! Look at her!
Look at Estelle! She murdered my wife, the only woman I
ever loved. She killed her! She took her from me. My dar-
ling died from the terrible disease she gave her, and where
was the justice? Where was the justice there, Mr. President? Better Estelle had died." He swung on the girl. "No,
better by far if you'd never been born."

Stark walked toward Estelle, his rifle clutched in white-
knuckled fists. "You killed my wife and I killed your child.
An eye for an eye, a tooth for a tooth. That almost evens
the score. But now there's this!"

Falcon Stark began to raise his rifle, finally stepping
over the fine line between sanity and madness. Estelle
reached in the pocket of her mackinaw and came up with

a .41-caliber derringer, the one Fletcher had seen in the sutler's store at Fort Apache.

Now he knew what had happened to his missing twenty dollars.

The girl fired as Stark's rifle swung level with his waist, and when the bullet hit, the man stumbled a single step backward. "Bitch!" he shrieked. He raised the rifle to his shoulder, and Fletcher heard Estelle's gun click on a dud round.

Fletcher drew and fired just as Stark pulled the trigger. The man's bullet went wild, but he swung the Winchester back on Estelle, and Fletcher hammered three fast shots into him. Stark, snarling, his mouth twisted with hate, went down on his knees, then fell flat on his face.

Where the hell was Hickok?

Fletcher felt the hairs rise on the back of his neck. He let out a wild, despairing cry: "Bill!"

He turned, trying to locate the gunfighter. But Hickok was not making a play. He stood with his hands spread wide, away from his guns. "It's over, Buck!" Hickok yelled, his voice urgent. "Listen to me, it's over."

It took Fletcher a few moments for the hammering of his heart to subside. Then his shoulders slumped and he holstered his Colt.

Estelle ran into Fletcher's arms and he held her close, hearing a thud as the derringer slipped from her hand and hit the hard, frozen ground.

"It is over, isn't it, Buck?" she asked, her tearstained face lifted to his own.

Fletcher nodded, glancing over at the dead man. "It's over. Falcon Stark was a tormented creature, and in the end his own hate and ambition drove him to madness."

"I can't stop hating him, Buck," Estelle said. "He was my father and he gave me life, but I'll never stop hating him."

"That you can't do, Estelle," Fletcher said, his voice gentle. "Hate will eat you up from the inside like a cancer." He kissed the girl on her forehead. "Let it go. Just try to let it go."

"I'm letting you go, Major Fletcher," Grant said, one foot in the stirrup as he prepared to mount and follow the retreating wagons. "I promise you, I plan to order a full investigation of your case, including the actions of the prison warden and the circumstances leading to the death of that young lieutenant."

"His name was 2nd Lt. Elisha Simpson," Fletcher said, a small elegy for a man he barely knew.

Grant nodded. "I will clear your name, Major. That you may depend on."

Fletcher smiled. "Mr. President, I'm no longer a major. I'm just plain old Buck Fletcher."

Grant swung into the saddle and touched his hat brim. "Till we meet again . . . Major."

He followed the wagons and didn't look back.

Fletcher turned to Estelle, who was standing at her horse's head, the reins in her hands.

"Better get going," he said. "The snow's getting thicker and you could lose the wagons."

"Come with me, Buck," Estelle said, her eyes urgent and pleading. "Once I've talked to my father's lawyers and settled the estate, you can return with me to Arizona. I want you riding at my side when I continue the Chosen One's work among the Apaches. Buck, you'll help me spread the word. You'll be my Doomsday Rider."

Fletcher grinned and shook his head. "Estelle, I'm not cut out to be a preacher. I've got places to go, a lot of places I've never seen before, and I've got things to do."

"Change your mind, Buck. Please come with me." Estelle took Fletcher's big, callused hand and raised it to her lips. "I think, given time, I could love you, Buck. I know I could."

Gently, Fletcher removed his hand from the girl's grasp. He walked to the stirrup of Estelle's horse and held it for her. "Time to go, Estelle. You can't let those wagons get too far ahead of you."

The girl put her foot in the stirrup then swung into the saddle. She looked down at Fletcher. "If you change your mind, will you come after me?"

"Maybe. Just don't count on it too much."

"I'll be looking for you, Buck. I'll be watching my back trail every hour of every day. I owe you so much, I want to spend my lifetime repaying it." She smiled. "One day I'll turn my head and you'll be there."

"*Hasta luego*, Estelle," Fletcher said. He slapped the rump of the girl's horse and stood there as she rode away.

He kept his eyes on Estelle until she was swallowed up by distance and the falling curtain of the silent snow . . . and even after that, he continued to watch a long time longer.

Twenty-eight

Two weeks later, a long wind blowing at his back, Buck Fletcher crossed into the Colorado Territory and rode into the foothills of the Rockies.

He crossed Chico Creek, and directly ahead of him soared the snow-covered bulk of Pike's Peak. Fletcher stopped in the shelter of a stand of mixed aspen and Douglas fir and built himself a smoke.

He had no clear idea where he was headed, but the supplies he'd gotten from President Grant were fast running out, and he'd soon have to make a decision.

To the north was Denver, and as he smoked he figured that was as good a choice as any, though he did not much care for cities and their crowds and less for sleeping under a hotel roof.

But Denver it would be.

Fletcher tossed the butt of his cigarette into the snow, then left the trees and swung north, keeping Cherry Creek to his right. The peaks of the mountains to the west were covered in snow, and a few flakes drifted in the wind. It was bitter cold and he huddled in his mackinaw, his breath smoking in the frigid air.

That night he camped in a stand of cottonwood on a bend of the creek, ate a hasty supper washed down with twice-boiled coffee, and was glad to seek the warmth of his blankets.

Around him the land lay empty and silent, but for the calling of the coyotes and the wind whispering through the branches of the cottonwoods. There was no moon because the sky was covered in cloud and the air smelled of pine and of dark-shadowed ravines and of loneliness.

Fletcher rose before daybreak, drank the last of his coffee, and saddled up. He figured he was fifty miles from Denver, and behind the rocky escarpment to his west must lie the South Platte, and beyond the river, Bison Peak and the majestic, pine covered Tarryall Mountains.

The night was being washed out by a gray dawn as he rode through a valley between two shallow hills and emerged once again onto the flat, the creek shining in the distance under a watery sun.

Fletcher swung his horse to the west, closer to the mountains and the tree line. The snow was deeper there, and drifting some, but the slopes would provide more shelter from the wind.

He rode across a patch of sandy, barren ground, studded here and there by shrubs of mountain mahogany, the place shielded from the worst of the snow by a rocky overhang, and headed once again into open country.

The snow here was deeper, up to his horse's knees, and the going was slower.

Fletcher glanced to his left and saw a jutting outcropping of gray rock, surrounded by a jumble of massive boulders that must have tumbled down the slope in some cataclysm in ancient times. A few stunted spruce grew in the spaces between the rocks and here and there a tangle of blackberry bushes that would fruit in the early summer.

He had chosen this route unwisely. The going was too heavy and it was tiring his horse. He swung the stud to the east, planning to ride back toward the creek where the wind would blow harder but the snow would be less deep. Above him, the clouds were building into towering ramparts, broken down in places like the colossal walls of a besieged city, and the snow was falling thicker.

The wind tugged at Fletcher's mackinaw, blowing the mane of his horse, and the only sound was the jangle of the bit and the soft footfalls of his mount in the snow.

Ahead lay the creek, cottonwoods growing at intervals along its bank, their companion willows shivering in the cold and rising wind. . . .

Fletcher never heard the shot that blasted him from the saddle.

He slammed into the ground, knowing at once that he'd been hit hard. The alarmed stud galloped away from him, stirrups flying, then stopped a couple of hundred yards away to graze on a patch of grass thrusting up from the snow.

For a few moments he lay there, stunned. Another bullet kicked up an angry vee of snow at his side; then a second burned across the top of his right thigh.

Rising to his feet, Fletcher turned and ran back toward the rock overhang he'd seen earlier. He angled in the direction of a vast snowdrift that would screen him, at least temporarily, from the view of the hidden rifleman.

Fletcher had seen a puff of smoke rise from the outcropping among the boulders where the man was hidden, but there was no way to get at him from here. Besides, his rifle was with his horse, and right now he was badly outgunned.

He reached the drift, a sheer parapet of snow rising twenty feet above his head, and stepped warily along its base, fearing that a bullet could send the whole thing crashing down on him.

Once past the drift, Fletcher ran toward the overhang, limping on his wounded leg, and at last reached the shelter of the rock.

But there was no cover here.

Fletcher explored the side of the overhang farthest from the hidden rifleman. The shelf of rock ran almost straight for about thirty yards, then curved back into the mountainside. It jutted out a good twenty-five feet, and, as far as Fletcher could tell, its top was flat, covered in scrub and maybe stunted pine.

Wounded or no, bad leg or no, he had to get up there. If he stayed out here in the open much longer he'd be a dead man.

A wide, scarlet fan rose above his belt on Fletcher's left side, and his shirt was drenched in blood. Was the bullet still in there—or had it gone right through him?

He reached inside his mackinaw to the small of his back and his hand came out wet and red. He had his answer.

Fletcher stepped to the slope where the rock shelf merged back into the mountainside and began to climb.

He was losing blood and weakening fast, and the slope was steep and covered with a tumulus of loose rocks, ice, and shingle. The higher he climbed, the more his boots slipped on the tumulus and he'd slide back down again, a shattering shower of shingle clattering over him.

Even now the bushwhacker could be coming this way, and Fletcher knew his time was running out fast.

Gritting his teeth against the hammering pain in his side, he climbed higher, slipping, sliding, the bloodstain on his shirt spreading wider. Finally the top of the rock ledge came into view. But he'd been wrong. The top was not flat, but dome-shaped, and it was mostly open, just a few sparse shrubs growing along its weathered edges, providing no cover.

Better to climb farther, then come at the rifleman from higher up the slope. Could he make it that far? He was dizzy, gasping for breath in the thin, cold air, and the pain in his side was a living thing, devouring him.

Fletcher climbed higher, beyond the overhang, and reached a band of aspen, their slender trunks crowded close together. He sat with his back against a tree, breathing hard, and after a few minutes was wishful for a smoke. But if the rifleman was alert—and why shouldn't he be?—the smell of tobacco would give his position away.

A few flakes of snow drifted lazily through the branches of the aspen, and from somewhere close by Fletcher heard the faint murmur of running water.

He rose slowly to his feet and followed the sound. After a few yards he found a small mountain stream, no more than a foot across and a few inches deep, tumbling over some rocks. Fletcher knelt and dipped a cupped hand into the stream and drank. The water was clear and ice cold and it refreshed him. He opened his mackinaw and pulled up his shirt, examining his wound. The flesh around the bullet hole was angry and inflamed, but the bleeding appeared to have stopped for now. He could not see the exit wound on his back, but he guessed it looked even worse than this one.

Fletcher dipped into the stream again and poured water into the wound. He didn't know if it was doing any good, but the icy coldness helped numb the pain a little, and perhaps the water would help keep it clean.

He looked at his shirt with unhappy eyes. "Ruined," he whispered. He didn't have another.

Painfully, Fletcher rose to his feet and made his way through the trees. There was no sign of the bushwhacker, and around him stretched only the gathering gloom of the gray day and silence.

It took him ten minutes to reach the spot on the slope he calculated was above the rock where the bushwhacker had lain in wait for him. Drawing his guns, he made his way down the steep incline.

Fletcher cleared the tree line and stepped warily. Ahead

of him lay thirty yards of slanting, open ground, covered in snow, and beyond that the bushwhacker's outcropping of rock. But of the rifleman there was no sign.

Fighting back a wave of weakness, Fletcher made his way down the slope. All his senses were clamoring, his skin crawling as, moment by moment, he expected to feel the sledgehammer blow of a bullet.

But he reached the outcropping without incident and, tense and wary, made his way among the scattered boulders along its northern edge.

At the base of the outcrop was a stretch of level ground where a saddled buckskin stood, its reins looped around a patch of brush. The animal lifted its head as Fletcher stepped toward it, ears pricked, then relaxed as it recognized a human and not a predator.

Fletcher looked around him but saw nothing but mountains and trees, the creek almost hidden in the distance by the falling snow.

He saw tracks where the bushwhacker had left his horse then climbed onto the rock. Stepping carefully, Fletcher walked to the other edge of the outcropping and came upon another set of tracks. The snow had not yet blanketed them, and they led off in the direction of the rock shelf where he'd first thought to seek cover.

Fletcher walked back to the buckskin and for the first time noticed two ornate silver letters on the skirt of the saddle—*H.C.*

Hank Crane!

Like a relentless bloodhound, the bounty hunter had tracked him here, all the way from Hays.

Fletcher shook his head, stunned. No wonder they said the man was good, maybe the best there ever was. Somehow Crane had looped around and gotten ahead of him. From there he'd watched and waited for his chance, and when Fletcher had decided to ride higher up the slope, away from the creek, Crane had taken up a position here.

Knowing his strength was giving out fast, Fletcher thought his situation through, then decided on a desperate, dangerous plan. It had to be now. If he waited any longer he'd be too weak to do what had to be done.

He stepped to the buckskin and swung into the saddle, gasping against the sudden, agonizing pain in his side.

Fletcher let the reins drop and kneed the horse around the rock, both his guns drawn. He rode around the base of the outcropping and followed Hank Crane's tracks.

When the rock shelf came in view through the tumbling snow, he reined up, squinting his eyes as he scanned the land around him for the bounty hunter.

At first he saw nothing; then he caught a quick gleam of metal on top of the shelf. Fletcher rode closer. He was still about fifty yards from the shelf when he made out Hank Crane, rifle in hand, looking up at the slope above him.

The time had come and it was now or never.

Fletcher let out with a wild rebel yell and raked the buckskin with his spurs. The big horse sprang forward as Crane turned, his rifle coming up fast. The man fired. Too fast. The bullet clipped the brim of Fletcher's hat.

Closer now. The buckskin was floundering, its head pecking into the snow, but the horse was game and fountains of white scattered up from its flying hooves.

Crane stepped to the edge of the rock shelf, sighting carefully. Fletcher fired with both guns, again and again, a hammering drumroll of sound echoing among the surrounding ravines and canyons.

Fletcher was aware that the concussion of his guns had collapsed the high snowdrift and a massive wall of white was tumbling down the slope behind him.

But right now all his attention was on Hank Crane.

The bounty hunter had been hit, and his left arm hung useless at his side. He threw down his rifle and grabbed for his holstered Colt.

Fletcher was much closer now. He fired at Crane, fired again, and the man rose on his toes and fell from the shelf, thudding onto the hard ground below.

Crane was lying on his back, looking up at him as Fletcher rode up and swung out of the saddle.

The bounty hunter's face was gray as life slowly ebbed out of him.

"Well, if this don't beat all, Buck," Crane said. "I thought I'd done for you fer sure."

Fletcher swayed on his feet, teetering on the edge of exhaustion. "You came close," he said.

Crane nodded. "You're good, Buck. Real good."

"Damn right."

"I trailed you all the way from Hays. But this was the first time I got a shot."

Blood stained Crane's mouth and the bottom of his mustache and his gray eyes were fading fast. "I wanted the thousand in gold. A man will ride a long way for that kind of money."

Fletcher wanted to tell Crane that the reward was probably no longer in effect and that he was dying for nothing. But he didn't. Instead he softened his voice as much as he was able and said, "You lie quiet now, Hank, and make your peace with your maker. Your time is short."

But Hank Crane didn't hear. He was dead.

Later Buck Fletcher walked back down the slope and found his horse.

The wound on his side had opened up again and he was bleeding heavily, the pain now a dull, all-consuming ache.

He looked around him. At the trees, the mountains, and the vast arch of the broken sky, the smell of pine and falling snow in the air.

He had thought to go to Denver, but now he would not.

Fletcher swung his horse to the west.

He would go into the mountains and there he would heal his body.

And his soul.

Historical Note

Doomsday Rider is, for the most part, set against the tumultuous backdrop of Gen. George Crook's 1872 winter campaign to encircle and destroy Apache and Yavapai marauders in Arizona's Tonto Basin and the Sierra Ancha and Superstition Mountains that bordered it.

Crook dispensed with the usual supply wagons, instead deploying flying columns of nine troops of the First and the Fifth Cavalry, riding out of Fort Apache and forts Verde, McDowell, and Grant.

Paiute scouts led each column, and Crook ordered his commanders to "stick to the trail and never lose it."

He added: "The Indians should be induced to surrender whenever possible. But if they choose to fight, give them all the fighting they want."

This strategy had a devastating effect on the Indians. Kept on the run and always short of food in the harsh winter months, they were cornered and attacked twenty times during the campaign and at least two hundred of their number killed.

The Apaches and Yavapais never recovered from these defeats, leaving the Tonto Basin to the white man, his towns, ranches, and cattle herds.

While I've tried to stay as close as possible to Ralph Compton's outline for *Doomsday Rider*, I've taken a little poetic license with its history.

The song about General Crook sung by the famous scout Al Sieber was not composed during the Tonto Basin campaign but three years later in 1875, when the general was transferred to the northern plains to take command of the Department of the Platte and the war against Dull Knife, the great Cheyenne war chief.

Similarly, the song "The Czar and Grant and Friends" was written by the good people of Topeka, Kansas, to commemorate the 1872 visit of the son of Czar Alexander II and Empress Maria Aleksandrovna, and not, as I have it, Count and Countess Vorishilov.

Among the notables who accompanied the Russian prince on the inevitable buffalo hunt were Gen. George Armstrong Custer and Gen. Phil Sheridan. Little Phil, no enthusiastic hunter, posed for the photo ops, then "made an escape on a fast train back to Chicago."

Finally, the Salado ruins near Globe, Arizona, are still there, and they're a sight to see. From about A.D. 1300 to 1450, a small group of the last of this prehistoric people lived in the now-weathered cliff dwellings, built of stone and mud mortar.

Today these cliff homes are preserved as the Tonto National Monument.

Also available

The Evil Men Do:
A Ralph Compton Novel

by David Robbins

If things are quiet in the little town of Sweetwater,
Marshal Fred Hitch sees no reason to make waves.
But when Tyree Johnson shows up, Fred's relaxed
nature is put to the test. At fifteen years old, Tyree is a
tough-as-nails bounty hunter with no patience for
anyone calling him "boy." He's come to apprehend a
killer who escaped from Cheyenne and has been
hiding in plain sight in Sweetwater.

To save face and his town's good name, Fred must ride
with Tyree and his prisoner all the way to Cheyenne.
The unlikely pair has a rough trail ahead of them, and
as tough as Tyree is, he has some lessons to learn about
the evil men do—and how to survive it.

**Available wherever books are sold or at
penguin.com**

S0575

National bestselling author
RALPH COMPTON

"A writer in the tradition of Louis L'Amour and Zane Grey!" —*Huntsville Times*

Available wherever books are sold or at
penguin.com